CW00921990

THE P*SSY NEXT DOOR

COCKY KINGMANS

BOOK THREE

AMY AWARD

Cover Design: Leni Kaufmann

THE P*SSY NEXT DOOR

He's an athlete all about focus, discipline, and achieving goals. She's the free spirited girl next door who won't be tied down to anything but her emotional support Kindle. But when the cat distribution system brings these two together, opposites attract.

Life has always been family, football, and school.

Focusing on my goals didn't leave much room for girls. But I'm not in school anymore. I'm the hottest rookie running back the league has ever seen, and I know how to score a touchdown. I don't have a clue how to score with a girl.

But I'm going to learn. Because the girl next door with all the thick curves is my new goal. And I'm going to win her heart.

She knows nothing about football, but she does like my tight end.

So does her cat.

Her older brother (by two whole minutes) does not and he'll do anything to keep us apart.

The next book in the Cocky Kingmans series will have you swooning and wishing you were a part of the Kingman family all over again.

CONTENT NOTE

This is a book of fluff. (Fluff that I worked really hard on and am extremely proud of.)

And it's a book about finding joy. Because that's what I always want to bring into the world.

This story is meant for escapism and laughs. We need fluff; it's the insulation from the harsh world around us.

However, that doesn't mean there won't be any conflict or angst.

I think it's important to have fat representation in the media, and I do that by showing fat women getting happy ever afters without ever having to lose weight.

While it was really important to me to write a story with a confident plus-size - fat - curvy heroine whose inner strength and love for herself doesn't waver, I will always put pieces of myself into every one of my curvy girl FMCs, and I'm still working on my own journey of self love - aren't we all?

That means that the heroine does face some fatphobia in this book. It's not the main storyline, because we also need to be able to read books about fat women who just exist in the world. We all don't only think about our weight every second of every day, and to me, that's true representation.

There is also talk about loss of a parent and a spouse, in the past. Our Cocky Kingmans were raised by a single father.

What I can promise you though is that my books will always hold a space that is free of violence against women including sexual assault. That just doesn't exist in the world I create in my mind.

And finally, I love to write about funny animals and pets. No pets will ever be harmed or die in any of my books.

I like to cry at touching Super Bowl commercials and Broadway musicals about witches who defy gravity, not in my romances.

wink

I wrote this so you can swoon, and giggle, and kick your feet, and find some joy. Have fun.

For all the women in the world who give up a part of themselves
trying to make other people happy.
Don't let their expectations of who they think you're meant to
be take away that joyful, authentic part of yourself.
Be you.
And anyone who doesn't love you for it, can fuck off.
Tell them I said so.

“A woman who feared being a cat lady had obviously never owned a cat.”

— JACQUELINE FROST

"Cat lady" has been aimed for decades at any woman who believes there's more to life than snagging a wedding band. Do you want a career? An education? A little fun in your youth? Your "punishment": To live alone with cats.

Taylor Swift's answer to the "cat lady" insult? Don't threaten me with a good time.

— AMANDA MARCOTTE

““you’re going to become a cat lady living all alone in a book-filled apartment” is such a weird insult, like when a witch tries to curse you and accidentally gives you the life of your dreams. oh nooo not the cats and the books, however will I manage”

— BOZE HERRINGTON

THE CAT DISTRIBUTION SYSTEM STRIKES

HAYES

I don't own a cat.

I've never even had one as a pet in my life. I've always thought of myself as more of a dog kinda guy. We had big old bear-sized dogs growing up and I loved each of them.

But being a single guy with a lot on my plate, rocking my rookie year on the Mustangs, gaming live streams with my brothers, and living on my own for the first time in this way-too-big-for-one-man house, I didn't think it was right to get a dog that I wouldn't have time to give all the love he deserves.

Someone should tell the cat, who was currently snuggled up between my knees, all of that. This snoring or purring fluffball was the only warm body I'd had in my bed, so I wasn't complaining. Simply confused AF.

I was awake at stupid o'clock in the morning partly

because I had practice and mostly because of the neighborhood alarm rooster known as Luke Skycocker. His crowing didn't seem to faze the cat.

No wait. It was Saturday. The running team's meeting wasn't until this afternoon. Dammit. I could have slept in.

Maybe I was still asleep, because how did a cat even get in my house, much less upstairs to my bedroom, not to mention on my bed and curled up between my legs?

And if I was dreaming, I might as well dream up a warm, fluffy, purring woman between my legs. I stared down at the fluffball and squinted my eyes, trying with all my might to transform it into the girl of my dreams.

It rolled over and yawned, stretched out its paws, and stuck me right in the thigh with nails sharper than ninja stars.

"Yowch. Watch where you put those things." I yanked my leg away and the cat went flying off the bed like a speed racer.

"Wait, where are you going, cat?" Shit. I didn't mean to yell at the thing. And now it was probably cowering somewhere in my house. I threw the covers off, noting three bright red puncture wounds way too close to the family jewels, and padded out into the hallway and down the stairs. "Here, kitty, kitty, kitty. Sorry I scared you."

"Dude. I don't know what kind of weird sex games you and whatever girl you've got up there are playing, but I can already see your junk."

I stopped dead in my tracks at the foot of the stairs for two reasons. One, my older brother Flynn was standing in my kitchen and I was bare ass naked, and two, the cat was perched right above his head on top of the refrigerator and it looked like it was about to pounce.

"Don't move," I said very quietly so as not to scare it into action.

"Come on, it's fine. I'll just close my eyes so you can get your girl back up to your room in private. I swear, I haven't seen anything." Flynn closed his eyes, but also shoved a spoonful of Peanut Butter Cap'n Crunch into his mouth without missing a beat.

"There's no girl." There was never a girl. "But there is a scared cat who looks like it's about to launch itself at your head. Which is why I said don't move."

Flynn did, in fact, move. He dropped to a crouch, cupping the cereal bowl against his chest, which is the only reason the cat landed on his back instead of his head. "Ow, ow, holy shit, get it off, get it off."

"Hold still, dumbass, and I'll grab it." I reached for the animal, and I swear it smiled before digging its hind leg claws in deeper and launching itself off Flynn's back and straight for my face.

But if there was one thing I knew how to do, it was catch a compact package when it was thrown at my head. I zigged to the left, snagged the cat in mid-air, tucked it under my arm like a furry little football, and rolled across Flynn's back, right to the open sliding glass doors that led to my backyard.

That must be how both the cat and Flynn got in. The lot of us Kingmans were in and out of each other's houses all the time, since we lived on the same street. I honestly liked having them around, had even converted my living room into a state-of-the-art gaming and streaming center for the four youngest of us brothers.

But I was just getting used to living on my own. I'd even taken to sleeping naked, since there weren't usually family or cats... or women in my house at the butt crack of dawn. Better go haul my PJ pants back out of the bottom of the dresser.

I planned to release the demon cat back into the wild. I darted through the door and into the backyard thinking I'd just plop the cat come football on the lawn so it could be on its merry way.

But for the second time that morning, I stopped dead in my tracks.

"Hiya, Hayes. Have you seen—" A messy bed head of dark brown hair poked up on the other side of the fence, and then those pretty blue eyes, that cute button of a nose, and the sweet round cheeks of Willa Rosemount popped up too.

"Oh my god, oh my god." She slapped her hand over her eyes and turned her face into the sun. "Why are you naked?"

If I was Everett, or even Flynn or Gryffen, I'd have something cool to say in answer to her question and freak out. But I was the one Kingman with no rizz and stood there like a lump on a log. Or rather a lump with a log.

What can I say, I was fresh out of bed and I'd already had a shot of adrenaline. The combo meant I was sporting some serious morning wood, and I absolutely refused to use this cat to cover it up. I'd already felt the razor slice of its claws a bit too close for comfort.

Flynn, somehow still munching away on his bowl of

my cereal, stepped onto the grass beside me. "Hey, Willa. I didn't know you were back in town. Where in the world were you this time? Istanbul? No, that was last year."

With me still frozen and her hand firmly covering her eyes, she answered in an adorable squeak that did nothing to temper my hard-on. "Ho Chi Minh City, also known as Saigon, this year."

My brother looked between me and Willa and that's when I knew I was dead meat. I recognized the how-much-fun-can-I-have-torturing-my-little-brother glint in his eyes. As if we'd just run into her at the fucking mall or something, he said, all nonchalant, "That's cool. Just get in?"

Willa pressed her lips together and if her hand hadn't been covering her eyes, I'd bet she was doing that one-eyebrow raise of annoyance. I wasn't the only one with an older brother who knew how to be a D-bag. But with her well-honed give-no-shits attitude, which I found sexy as hell, she replied, "No. A couple of days ago. Could you, uh, grab that cat and hand him over the fence to me? I need to give him his medication."

Flynn glanced at the cat, looked at me, and winked. "No can do, Willabean. I don't think it likes me. Hayes? You got this?"

"Don't call her that. She hates it." I'd seen her punch a lesser man, a.k.a. her brother Xander, for a similar offense. And when a woman set a boundary, it should be respected. I'd never once called her Willabean, even if I thought it was cute as shit. She was cute as… no she was freaking beautiful.

Flynn smiled and took another bite of cereal and

crunched it a whole lot louder than necessary. If I didn't do something immediately, she and I were both going to be subjected to Fun Time with Flynn for a whole lot longer.

I willed my erection to go down, which it did not, and trucked over to the fence. I lifted the furball, who had legit started purring, up to her face to block her view. "Here's your cat, sorry about the show and Flynn being a dick."

"Thanks, for catching Seven... and, you know, the show." She kept her eyes closed as she took the cat, but I definitely noticed a grin and her cheeks got all pink. Was she flirting with me? "And that's what older brothers are for. I think they get paid extra for being asshats."

"We do," Flynn shouted, but he was already walking back into the house. "You're welcome."

Her cat was called Seven? Kind of a weird name. But we weren't ones to talk. Every dog we'd ever had was named Bear. All of them. I think my dad thought we wouldn't notice when one went over the rainbow bridge if he replaced it with a close look-alike and started calling it by the same name.

Willa stepped down off whatever she was standing on to get her head above the top of the fence. I was tall enough to see into her backyard, but she was a shorty-short pants. I don't think she'd grown an inch since she'd been the tallest girl in the sixth grade. By seventh, she was just average, and I'd shot well past her by eighth. Not, you know, that I'd kept close track of that or anything. She'd been the sister of one of my high school teammates, so no flirting, dating, or even thinking about her allowed.

Even though I should be hightailing it back inside my house, I wasn't ready. But how exactly did one flirt with the previously off-limits girl next door while naked? "I'll murder him later so he won't bother you again."

Right. Yep. Nothing said flirty banter like death and dismemberment.

"Nah, that's okay. We'd be weak little baby birds if we hadn't grown thick skins because of them. But thanks anyway." She paused for a moment and I should have said something else.

A thousand ideas flipped through my mind, none of which made it out of my mouth. Girls didn't usually want to talk about Everett's total rushing yards, Chris's average yards per pass attempt, or Declan's sack record. I could tell her about the humorous science book about cadavers I'd read on the plane home from our last game and ask her what she'd read lately. But that would mean more talk about dead people.

What the hell was wrong with me? This was why I never had a girlfriend. Shit.

"See ya around, Hayes."

Would she? I definitely wanted to see her.

I hadn't seen much of her since we graduated, and now I couldn't look away. Back then, I was off to DSU to play football and she went to locations far and wide. She'd only come home to Colorado a few times since then. And, in fact, it was usually in the summer for her and Xander's birthday. This was October.

Willa Rosemount had always been my type, with thick thighs and an ass that didn't quit. But in the past few years, she'd grown even curvier. When had she gotten so damn hot? This hard-on wasn't going anywhere if I kept thinking about her like that.

Say something else to her, dumbass. "You home for a while?"

At least that time I didn't sound like an idiot. Nary a mention of death. The question even implied I was hoping to see her again. Shit. Did that even sound flirty? Ten seconds trying to talk to the cute and curvy girl next door and every brain cell I'd ever had melted away into the ether. Or maybe they'd all gone south.

My erection wasn't any closer to going down, and I was well beyond the excuse of morning wood. The longer I stared at her, the harder I got. Yeah, this was all fucking for her and those luscious curves that were going to be starring in all my fantasies.

I was going to have to take care of business in the shower this morning just so I could walk around like a normal person all day. Until I saw her again.

"Not sure. I'm just on a short break from my teaching gig. Gonna hang with the Guncles at the coffee shop for a bit." Didn't sound like she was entirely happy about that. I wondered if there was more to the story than I was getting in a chat over the fence.

"I'll be sure to stop by for a coffee." The right words came out, but I didn't know whether to smile or look serious.

Willa turned back to her house, the cat in her arms, looking over her shoulder at me and our eyes held for one breath, two, three. She licked her perfect lips, pulling my gaze from her eyes, and I so wanted to know what her mouth would feel like against mine. My eyes traced down and over her body, greedily taking in every thick bit of her to commit to memory… for later. My dick was very much in favor of that line of fantasies and hardened even more if that was even possible.

"You should probably put some clothes on first." She gave me a suggestive little eyebrow waggle that sent electricity down my chest and stomach. "Unless you became a nudist or something. Stranger things have happened."

She went into the house, and I stood there staring like a weird, naked stalker for far too long. Willa Rosemount was the last person I thought I'd be showing my junk to this morning. Man, she looked good. Still cute as pie, but there was something more to her now. Had her hips always swayed like that?

Or was I just horny as hell and as likely to fantasize about video game characters as I was about the girl next door? Both, both were happening at the same time. I could definitely imagine Willa in some trooper armor wielding a set of katanas.

And didn't that thought have my cock insisting I jump over the fence and... and nothing. My cock and I were acting like I was a teenager who couldn't control his hormones. I was a grown-ass man with a job and responsibilities.

I marched back into the house and smacked Flynn on the side of the head as I walked past him sitting on the couch. "You're evil."

"Did you ask her out?" He bobbed his chin at me. "At least tell me you got her number."

I ignored him, walked into the laundry room off the kitchen to grab some boxers out of the dryer, and then returned to pour my own bowl of cereal. What was left of it anyway. Dammit. I was going to have to go grocery shopping. Again. This had to be how Dad felt whenever we inhaled all the food in the house.

"What are you doing here anyway?" I plopped down onto the other end of the couch. "Don't you have a game today?"

"Yeah. Why do you think I'm carb-loading?" He gave me a shit-eating grin. "You should bring your new girlfriend."

I knew this game just as well as any other Fun Times with Flynn. He wanted me to say she wasn't my girlfriend so he could tease me mercilessly. But this wasn't high school and I was smarter than he was. "Sorry, no can do. We're having coffee later."

That wasn't exactly a lie.

"Hells to the yeah, bro. I knew I set you up to score. You can thank me later." He gulped the last of his cereal and milk and left his bowl and spoon perched precariously on the arm of the couch. "Be sure to leave a sock on the door so we know not to come barging in later tonight."

"I'm locking all my doors and you're no longer welcome in my house." Which was a lie. We had a live stream on our gaming channel later tonight with Gryffen and Isak. Besides, he had set me up so I had to talk to her. He might be an asshole, but he really did use his powers for good.

The question now was how I was going to capitalize on the one time I had successfully flirted with a girl. I guess I really should go over to the café her family owned for that cup of coffee. Not that I was a big coffee drinker or anything. And she hadn't said she was working there today.

Shit. I was already fucking this up and I hadn't even properly asked her out yet. Lord, help me.

No. Wait. Love Guru help me. This was Everett's area of expertise, and if anyone could coach me through how to romance a woman like Willa, it was him.

I finished my cereal, did the damn dishes myself, got ready, and jogged on over to Everett's, which was just a few doors down from me. For once there wasn't some little sports car in his driveway which was his personal version of a sock on the door. Interesting. It wasn't like Ev not to have a lady over on a Friday night.

He'd better not be sick or something. We needed him for the game on Sunday.

I jumped over the gate to his backyard, planning to slip in through his house's sliding glass door, just like Flynn had done to me. Although I planned to knock and announce myself. But I found Ev sitting on his lawn furniture, in a robe, drinking coffee, staring out at the clear autumn sky, listening to a Kelsey Best break up song on his phone.

Uh-oh.

"What're you doing, Ev?" I used a cautious and quiet voice because I wasn't sure I'd ever seen my brother like this. He was downright melancholy and I was worried I knew why.

He grabbed for the phone, spilling half his coffee in the process, and turned the song off too quickly. "Sup, Hayes?"

I sat across from him, leaned in, and folded my hands. "I was here to ask you for advice, but you look like you could use some yourself. Look, if you've got a crush on Kels, none of us would blame you. I mean, Dec might pulverize you, but—"

"Geez, no, kid. I don't have a crush on my brother's fiancée. I just like her music, okay? Everybody does, it's no big deal." He took a sip of the remaining coffee, made a face at it like he just realized it was cold piss-water, and set it down on the wooden side table. "Now tell me what kind of advice you're here for."

His smile was a little too forced, but Ev and I had gotten a lot closer since I joined the Mustangs this year. We spent a lot of time together, and I knew when he wasn't ready to talk about whatever was bothering him. I'd get it out of him eventually.

"So... there's this girl."

"It's about fucking time, my man." This time his smile was genuine. "I thought you were going to be a virgin forever."

Oh shit. He knew? Did everyone in the family know? Probably. That's the kind of family we had. That explained why Flynn had been so excited when I said I had a coffee date. "Yeah, well, you weren't the only one."

Not that I was thinking about having sex with Willa. I hadn't even asked her out yet.

Who was I kidding? I was definitely thinking about all the things I wanted to do with Willa. And next time, I hoped I wouldn't be the only one who was naked.

NINE LIVES

WILLA

Holy Cheez-its, Hayes Kingman had certainly filled out. Not that he was ever small in the first place, but he had muscles where I didn't even know muscles existed. Not to mention the absolute monstrosity between his legs.

I wondered if he would have even been able to cover it up with my pussy... cat. Not that I'd wanted him to, and not that he'd tried. He'd definitely given me a show.

My cat squirmed, wanting to be put down. Probably just so he could go off on another adventure through the neighborhood.

"Seven of Nine Lives," he knew he was in trouble when I used his full name, "you poop. I just got home, and you can't even let me have a snuggle?"

I was up at this ungodly hour, still feeling the jet lag from my last-minute, twenty-four hour series of flights to get from Vietnam back to Denver with a good mix of wackadoo time changes. I could use a snuggle.

But when the Guncles called to say I needed to come home right away and here's first-class plane tickets, I made the arrangements with my school to take a little bit of time off. Time changes and jet lag be damned.

I loved my parents, I did, and they loved me. But they always had expectations for me and my life that I just never felt like I could fulfill. Liam and George weren't like that. They were the ones who encouraged, and initially bankrolled, me and my backpack when I headed to Europe to see the world instead of going to college.

So, if they needed me home to give us all The Big News, I'd put my job on hold. I'd put my life on hold for them, honestly. I just wish they'd indicated whether this was good news or potentially devastating. Like, was I coming home for a party, or should I have packed a black dress and all the tissues I could fit in my suitcase?

The two of them loved a secret and a reveal, but this was Liam's life we were talking about. Would a hint have killed them?

It was killing me.

And I was apparently killing Seven, because he gave me a desperate "mrrow" and wiggled. "Sorry I was squishing you, bubby."

I propped him up on my shoulder like a baby and gave his butt some pats. He resigned himself to accepting my attentions and even deigned to give me some purrs.

"See, you missed me." I'd just been home a few months ago, and he couldn't leave me alone then. Now I was home under a lot more stress and he would barely give me the time of day. Unless, of course, I was giving him treats.

"Come on, let's get your ear drops and I'll give you a treat." His tail swished at the offer of a snack. Same, buddy, same.

"Willabean, you here?" Xander called for me from inside the house.

Ah, the bane that was my older brother. "Don't make me murder you, Xan."

"You can try, Beanie."

If I didn't have a cat in my arms, I would find something to throw at his head. Willabean had been cute when we were six. At sixteen he'd used it as a weapon of mass embarrassment, and at twenty-one, I still hated it. Which, of course, he found hilarious to no end.

If he wasn't a six-three wall of muscle and headed for a career in professional football next year, I would take him down and sit on him like I did when were younger. Except I was the one who got in trouble and he always got off scot-free.

Butthead.

Unfortunately, he was also the one who sweetly threatened to beat up any boy who broke my heart, used his golden-child persuasion to convince my mom to allow me to get a cat, and was the one who flew all the way to Ho Chi Minh City to teach me how to ride a motorcycle when I first got the job teaching English, just so I wouldn't crack my head open.

He popped into the backyard and waved for me to come back inside. "Let's go hit the coffee shop and force the Guncles to tell us what's going on now. I've got a game this afternoon, and I need to know if I'm gonna be playing like a badass or if I need to call Coach and take some time off."

Xander loved Liam and George just as much as I did, and he might be a big, tough guy, but I heard the fear in his words. He didn't even have to say anything. I knew. "Unless, of course, you got it out of them last night?"

I was staying at their house instead of with Mom and Dad, because... reasons. "No go. They were tight-lipped and insistent that we all had to go to bed the minute we got home. And of course were up and at Cool Beans at the butt crack of dawn. I think I've actually seen them for all of about thirty minutes since I landed."

I'd seen more of Hayes Kingman than—oh, nope. No, don't go there. And dammit. Now I was thinking about naked Hayes again.

Ever since the draft, we don't talk about Kingman, no, no, no. We don't talk about Kingman.

"I doubt we'll get it out of them, but I could definitely use some caffeine. It's eight o'clock at night for me and I didn't get a whole lot of sleep on the plane or last night." I would just get adjusted to Denver time when I had to go back to Saigon. My body was going to be all kinds of pissed.

I hauled Seven up to my room, gave him his eardrops, which he hated and immediately bolted from, and then got dressed. But what I had in my suitcase was not suitable for a cool Colorado autumn day. I had mostly the lightweight dresses I wore to teach in. That was dumb. I hadn't really been thinking when I was tossing things into my bag to hurry and catch the flight.

This wasn't going to work. I popped into Liam and George's room and raided their closet. George was a Mustangs fan through and through, and most of his comfy clothes were jerseys and logoed t-shirts. That would work fine with the singular pair of leggings I'd had the foresight to bring.

Xander made a face at me when I came back downstairs. Shizz. I wasn't thinking. He used to love the Mustangs, had always hoped he'd get drafted by them. Not anymore. He was still mad. I got that.

I'd planned to hit Lane Bryant or Torrid while I was here anyway. I even had orders from a few other teachers who also weren't Vietnamese sized. We could get clothes made by the plethora of tailors easily enough, since clothes big enough to fit even the average-sized American, Brit, Aussie, or Kiwi simply weren't available. But the one thing we all still needed to get from home were bras and underwear. No one was making me a forty-two double D over the shoulder boulder holder.

I'd grab a couple pairs of jeans and some plain sweaters for the rest of the time I was home, because I hated to see that hurt look in my brother's eyes that he thought he hid so well. Can't hide much from twin telepathy though.

"All right, I'm as ready as I'll ever be." Was anyone really ready to find out their favorite human on the planet might not have long to live? "Just let me grab my Kindle and my bag and we can go."

I had a feeling I was going to need my emotional support Kindle for some escapism later.

Even though it wasn't that far, we drove over in the

new car my parents bought for Xander last spring. I did not need a car. My cute motorbike was third hand from a teacher who'd been leaving and wanted to pass it along. It was yellow and I'd named it Captain Kirk. I missed the Captain right now.

There usually wasn't any parking this time of day, but Cool Beans was not what I'd call hopping this morning. Wasn't this supposed to be their busy time? Xander pulled into a spot right in front. My mom waved to us through the window, and I didn't see any other customers inside even though the glowing neon sign said the place was open.

A yucky niggle in my gut had me worried that Liam and George had shooed the customers away because nobody needed to see a grieving family cry. I sent a quick prayer out to the universe, hoping that wasn't true. Please let this be good news. We could all use that.

Xander pulled the door open, and the moment I walked inside, the aroma of coffee wrapped me up in its warmth. I loved the smell of toasty, roasted coffee beans. It reminded me of everything childhood. I just wish a cup of brew tasted like what it smelled like. I'd never admitted to a soul that I didn't actually like coffee. I was in it exclusively for the cream and sugar.

George saw me first and there was nothing I wanted more than one of his big, squishy bear hugs. Which is exactly what I got. After a longer than normal embrace, which worried me, he gave me a twirl. "Willa, don't you look cute as shit in that jersey. It's the newest addition to the collection."

I let him give me an extra twirl just like when I was little. "I raided your closet, hope you don't mind."

"Not a bit. Everything has been such a flurry the past few days, or I would have pulled my head out of my butt and grabbed you some warmer clothes for the fall. You keep that one. I'm happy to get another later on. As if I need a reason to buy more Mustangs' paraphernalia."

He gave Xander a wink. "Or DSU Dragons."

He'd said *later on*.

If he was planning for the future, that was good, right? I wanted to ask him to tell me what was going on, but I held my tongue. They brought us all together as a family to do this. Either we'd all be crying together or cheering together.

Liam gave me a smile from behind the counter. "You two want a drink while we wait for your dad?"

Did he look paler than when I'd seen him over the summer? No? Maybe? He sure didn't look like he was dying. But that might be my wishful thinking. He certainly wasn't giving me even a clue, and he knew it. "Sure. Surprise me, but make it something sweet and extra—"

"Extra whip. I got you, boo." He handed me a mug already covered in whipped cream and caramel drizzle. He also pulled out a super disgusting plain black coffee for Xander. How did I have a twin brother that was so boring and staid? The world may never know.

Xander took his gross cup of joe and leaned against the counter. "Give us just a little hint about your news, Li."

"You two can wait a couple more minutes." He nodded toward the window. "Your dad is pulling up now."

Probably straight from the golf course, if his super goofy plaid pants and polo were any indication. But knowing Dad, it might just be what he chose to wear today. Fifty-fifty chances on that one. He pushed in through the door. "I'm here, so you can get the party started now. And it had better be a party, little brother, because if you're still dying, I'm going to kill you."

Dad crossed the room and went right over the counter to wrap Liam in a huge hug. I swore I caught a grin on Liam's face, but it might have just been because Dad was squashing the air out of him.

George waved us all over to the table where Mom was sitting, and I took the seat next to her. "Hello, Willabean. What in the world are you wearing?"

"Hi, Mom." I didn't answer her question, because... why? She didn't listen to me anyway. Sigh. That wasn't fair of me. Mom just had selective hearing when it came to what I wanted, in my wardrobe and my life. At least she hadn't mentioned anything about my weight. I had steeled myself for that and was happy not to have to bring out that particular piece of armor.

She smiled at my brother. "Alexander, how was your math test?"

"Flying colors, Mom."

"Good boy. And you're on the starting lineup this afternoon?" Welcome to the mom-ish inquisition. I'd be lucky if I wasn't next.

I felt Xander's mental eyeroll. I had to bite the inside of my cheek not to roll my own. As if Xander hadn't started in every game since halfway through his freshmen year of high school. Along with Hayes Kingman, of course.

"As always." He took another swig of his coffee and turned in his seat to face the Guncles, who, it seemed, were finally ready to give us the news. Lucky break. Or maybe unlucky. We were about to find out.

I couldn't help it, I grabbed my mom's hand under the table. While she and I very rarely saw eye to eye on anything, she gave my fingers the squeeze I needed.

Liam and George gathered everyone's attention, and a hush fell over the table, the clinking of coffee mugs fading into the background. My heart quickened, nerves prickling at the edges of my skin. This was it, the moment we had all been dreading or hoping for.

Liam cleared his throat, exchanging a glance with George before speaking. "Well, I want to thank all of you for being here. It means the world to us." He looked right at me and his voice, though steady, carried a weight that hung heavy in the air.

George reached out, his hand finding Liam's, a silent show of support.

"We've had some news from the doctor," Liam continued, his gaze sweeping over each of us, lingering for a moment on my face. "And it's good. Really, really good."

Just like that, I could breathe again. The muscles in my chest and shoulders released, and I pulled my hand from my mother's, needing to shake all that tension away. Good news. The words echoed in my brain like a mantra. Thank the fucking universe. I owed it a cupcake, or a dozen.

Xander let out a whoop and fist bumped the air like he'd just scored another touchdown. Dad gave him a high five and me a smiling wink. Mom's eyes glistened, which was as close as I'd ever seen her to crying. I saw that flicker of vulnerability in her expression, a crack in the facade she wore so effortlessly.

"What exactly did they say?" Dad's voice was gruff with the same emotions we were all feeling.

Liam smiled, a genuine, heartfelt, toothy grin that should have been in a toothpaste commercial. "The doctor gave me a clean bill of health. It seems I'm going to be around for a while longer, much to our customer's dismay," he added, a hint of humor coloring his words.

Scattered laughs and the rustle of shifting chairs were the only sounds in the coffee shop. The weight that had been pressing down on us lifted, leaving behind a sense of buoyancy that I hadn't felt in far too long.

"Thank the heavens," George murmured, his voice thick with emotion.

Xander grinned, the tension draining from his features as if it had never been there. "Looks like I won't have to take over the coffee shop after all."

Liam chuckled, the sound a melody of joy that filled the room. "That's ninety percent of the reason I worked so hard to get better. Nobody wants a bunch of football players serving their coffee."

George raised his hand. "Excuse me. I would absolutely like that, thank you very much."

I let out a shaky breath. Had Xan really thought he'd take over the shop? In what spare time? Although, knowing Golden Boy, he probably already had a business plan and was ready to sink his future signing bonus into our little home away from home.

Because it wasn't like anyone was going to ask me to take over Cool Beans. I didn't even want to. I had a whole life, a burgeoning career, and the world to see. I didn't want to be tied down, especially not in Denver.

But I did have a whole week off work, and I was going to celebrate in style. Which was starting with some really long Guncle hugs. Which were the best kind.

"Hey, Wills," Liam said after I held him tight for about a thousand years, "if you're not too jet lagged, I was hoping you might stick around and work with me this afternoon while everyone else goes to the game. I doubt we'll be terribly busy and it will give us a chance to hang out."

Party, work at the coffee shop... same, same but different. "If it gets me out of going to the game, I'm definitely down to clown."

And Liam was exactly the right person to relay the morning, ahem, glory story to. I whispered so Xander didn't overhear. "You won't believe who I saw this morning."

GOAL SETTER

HAYES

I had time for exactly three things in my life if I was going to dedicate my all to them. Family, football, and school.

But I wasn't in school anymore.

Sure, gaming with the boys, keeping up with the social media for our streaming channel, and what my agent scheduled for me to do for sponsorships added some to my schedule, but nothing like school. Especially my last semester when I took as many classes as I could knowing I was going into the draft. Not graduating just because I'd been drafted was never in the plan.

For the first time in my life, I had room in my schedule for a love life. Not just getting laid, although, that was high on the priority list, but a real relationship. I'd seen plenty of guys in college let their game take a dive when a girl got up in their head. It was part of the reason I didn't date.

I knew full well I'd missed out on some very specific experiences when I swore off dating to concentrate on other more important things. That strategy had paid off. Not only had I gotten drafted as a junior, but I was having one hell of a rookie year on the Mustangs.

I made a goal, I went after it, and I accomplished that goal.

Everett told me I was being a punk by thinking I could do the same with Willa Rosemount. I didn't really see why. I just needed to put the same study and effort into learning how to get her to date me as I did football and graduating.

His advice was decidedly different. Normally, I'd listen to the love guru of the family as he was the learned expert. He certainly had the experience with women to back it up, and his advice had helped Chris and Dec get the loves of their lives to fall for them. But this time, he was wrong.

Just being myself with Willa and getting to know her wouldn't get her to go out with me. We already knew each other, although not very well, and she wasn't all goo-goo ga-ga for me. If that worked, she would've fallen for me back in high school. Not that I had given her the chance. She'd been off-limits then. Friends don't date their friend's little sisters.

But Xan hadn't spoken to me since the draft. And I'd tried. But according to him, we weren't friends anymore. Which meant I wasn't breaking any guy code rules by asking her out. *If* I could fucking figure out how to do that and not look like a total fool.

I highly doubted a conversation about what she did and didn't like would get me into her bed. Nope. I needed a better plan than that. Especially after how damn awkward I'd been this morning.

What I had to do was turn myself into a love guru, and fast. Which meant I didn't have time to go out and get the amount of practice in this area that Everett had. But if I knew one thing, besides football, it was how to study. I already had a reading list a mile long on everything from flirting to the female orgasm. I'd skimmed three books this morning, and on my phone, I had a mile-long list of bookmarks for dating advice sites.

Practice today couldn't end soon enough. I'd already reviewed all the tapes the offensive coordinator wanted me to earlier in the week. I was ready for the game against the Rebels because I was always prepared. One more walkthrough of the plays wasn't going to make me a better player tomorrow. But I had enough discipline and focus to pay attention until Coach dismissed us.

After a shower and a shave, because stinky ballplayer was not the scent to make a good impression with, I snagged my bag, ignored the chatter around me, and headed straight for Willa's family's coffee shop.

I rehearsed the conversation in my head, discarding every attempt at a smooth pickup line as soon as they formed.

"Hey, beautiful, got any coffee for a tired athlete?" Not enough pickup. Flirt level one.

"Can I get a shot of espresso and a shot at dinner with you?" Too forward. But much higher on the flirtablilty scale.

I parked and then pulled up the list of pickup lines

from some dating coach. One popped out at me immediately. *"If I were a cat, I'd spend all nine of my lives with you."*

That had distinct possibilities given the way we'd met this morning. Except it was entirely too cheesy. I unbookmarked the site on my phone and made a mental note to find some better resources later.

By the time the bell announcing my arrival jingled above the coffee shop door, I had settled on nothing more than a simple hello.

Willa was behind the counter, her hair pulled back in a casual ponytail, wearing an adorable frilly apron that emphasized the curve of her hips, and her smile lit up the room as she chatted with the person in line ahead of me. I cleared my throat, trying to appear casual as I approached the counter.

"Hey, Willa."

Okay, good start, good start.

She looked up at me and grinned, and I swear her cheeks got a little pinker. Was she thinking about this morning? I wasn't sure if that was good or bad. "Hayes. What can I get for you?"

I fumbled with my wallet, pulling it out as if it held the script to this encounter. "Uh, just a coffee. Black." Great, Hayes, real smooth.

She raised an eyebrow but turned to make my coffee. "Thought you were more fun than boring-old, plain black coffee. That's what Xa... uh... don't you want something more exciting? I pegged you as a caramel macchiato kind of guy."

Crap. Boring was bad, and she'd definitely almost compared me to her brother. Which was the last thing I wanted. "Yeah, sure. The caramel whats-ee-ah-toe sounds... fun. Gimme that."

"Fun is good," she said with a nod, her voice playful. "Fun can be really good."

I leaned on the counter, trying to muster the Kingman charm I knew was buried somewhere deep inside me. "So, I was thinking, maybe, you know, we could..."

Willa handed me my frou-frou drink with whipped cream and then gave it another squirt of caramel on top in the shape of a smiley face, her eyes twinkling very distractingly. "We could...?"

Oh, yes, we could indeed. I stared into those gorgeous eyes and forgot that anything else in the world existed for a moment. But her eyes got wider and she tilted her head like a puppy that's wondering what the hell you're doing.

Shit.

"Hang out? Sometime?" I blurted out, immediately wincing at how juvenile that sounded. Real fucking smooth. We weren't in junior high.

Her eyes went from are-you-okay to are-you-serious real fast. Good god. I'd better just turn and walk away to drown my dumb ass in my fancy-ass cup of coffee. Somehow my feet did not get the message my embarrassed as shit brain was sending.

A smile slowly spread across Willa's face. "Hayes Kingman, are you asking me out?"

Lifeline, lifeline. Catch it you fool. This message brought to you from your dick who'd like to get wet some fucking day and your ass who is feeling really fucking lucky to be saved by the pretty girl who threw us said lifeline.

"Yes?" It came out as more of a question than I

intended. I took a deep breath, straightening up. "I mean, yes. I am."

Willa leaned in a bit, her voice lowering to a conspiratorial whisper. "You know, for a big, tough football player, you're pretty cute when you're nervous."

My heart thumped hard trying to jump up and out my throat, but I managed a chuckle to push it back down. "Is that a yes?"

"It's a maybe." She winked at me.

She.

Winked.

At me.

And I was going to have wet dreams about her doing that.

"I want to know more about this 'fun' Hayes," she waggled her fingers in front of my chest like she was performing a spell on me, "before I make any decisions."

"Fair enough." I could be fun. Or I could just pretend I was Flynn or Gryff for a night. "How about I show you how fun I can be tomorrow night?"

She scowled at me, and I had no idea what made her give me the face of doom. "If you're inviting me to watch you play football, pass."

Shit. The how-to-get-a-girl guide I'd read this morning said it made girls all hot and bothered to see a man dominating in sports. I thought for sure I could impress her with tickets to the Kingman VIP suite at the stadium. But Willa looked more like she'd rather give her cat a bath. Scratch that book off the list too. Maybe feed it to said cat. "No, of course not. I meant after the game. I promise, no football talk."

She considered it, her finger tapping against her chin thoughtfully. "Okay, Kingman, you've got yourself a date. But I'm choosing the place. I have a feeling you're as good at picking restaurants as you are at picking coffee."

I grinned and had to keep myself from giving a fist pump in the air. "It's a deal. But I do know a fairly good restaurant that just opened up this summer."

Manniway's Steakhouse was an excellent choice. I was sure of it. But I'd let her choose anywhere she wanted, because I didn't care where we went as long as I got to be near her.

"Wills," a man with Willa's same dark blue eyes popped out from a backroom door. "Sure you can't stay another week or so?"

Wow. Was this her uncle Liam? He didn't look like the same man I remembered. His face was almost gaunt, and he had much shorter hair than the messy mop he'd always had before. He must have been ill. What was that he said about staying another week?

"Oh look, a Kingman. George is gonna die that he wasn't here. Willa, get a pic with our celebrity guest for him." He gave her an eyebrow waggle that was not as discreet as he thought it was.

"Liam, you remember Hayes. He went to school with Xander and me." She turned to me with a smirk, trying to communicate that her uncle was being a weirdo.

"I do remember." Liam extended his hand to me and shook it, grinning at Willa the whole time. "That doesn't mean he's not a celebrity and that George won't pee his pants when he finds out he was here while they were all at the Dragons' game."

Willa's forehead wrinkled along with her nose in the cutest WTF face. She whispered to me, "Is this because you got drafted? George is a nutter for all things Mustangs."

I shrugged. It was hard to feel like anything but just another guy on the team when your three older brothers were not just at the top of their games but recognized as the best players in the League for several years running. Not to mention their car commercials, big-brand shoe sponsorships, and a particularly famous underwear ad in Times Square.

I kind of liked that she wasn't wowed by the notoriety. I didn't give a shit about being a celebrity. I just wanted to be a good ballplayer.

Her uncle shook his head and patted Willa on the shoulder. "Willa, Willa, Willa. Your boy Hayes here is the hottest rookie to hit the League in a half century. Or so George and most of the talking head sports bros say. You're wearing his jersey for goodness' sake, and it's already going for three times what I bought it for at the start of the season."

Willa spun, looking over her shoulder as if she could read the name. I saw it well before she could.

H. Kingman.

She was wearing my jersey.

Every bit of blood I had rushed out of my extremities and straight to my cock. The couple of brain cells I had left in my head growled like a cocaine bear inhabited by a very possessive demon.

Mine.

Whoa. Slow down there lizard brain. I was raised

better than to think I could lay claim to a woman or her body like that. I may not have needed to ask for it as of yet, but I full well knew the name of the game was enthusiastic consent.

But fuck me, I wanted to see Willa wearing my name and number and absolutely nothing else while I enthusiastically consented the shit out of her. That didn't even make sense. But my lizard brain was high fiving the demon bear that wanted to... nope, stop it. We hadn't even been on a date yet.

But the sooner we went on that date, the sooner I could kiss her, the sooner I could get her to fall for me, and the sooner I could get her into bed.

I had some more homework to do.

MISADVENTURES IN SITTING

WILLA

I'd honestly so much rather be taking a nap than watching the Mustangs game. But here I sat, with Seven in my lap and bowl of popcorn by my side, keeping a running tally in my head of the best football butts. I'd be reading, but when I pulled out my Kindle, my mom gave me the look, and I put it away.

"Yeah, take that 'Stangs, you pussies," Xander shouted at the television and the rest of us pretended that was normal.

Football games were long and slow and... shh... boring to me. They just did the same thing, over and over. Then the other team did the same thing over and over going the other way. I knew the rules of the game. How could I not, living among the footballiest family next to the Kingmans? I just didn't care.

When your twin brother plays football in junior high, high school, and college, a supportive and discerning sister must find something to occupy her time at all those damn games. At least I'd been spared most of the college games since I was always very, very out of town.

To make sure my mind didn't melt into a pile of bored goo at a thousand and one football games, I ranked the butts of football players. In my head of course. Couldn't let a list like that get out. In school, Hayes hadn't ranked high or low on that list. He'd just sort of been in the middle.

Until yesterday.

Apparently, I'd been paying attention to the wrong side of the uniform, which became very obvious when he'd gotten a huge bulge in the front of his pants. And it wasn't like he'd been wearing gray sweatpants or something either. He'd had on jeans, and I could still see the outline of his dick. Poor guy probably had an imprint of his zipper in his flesh.

I snort-laughed and then had to shove a mouthful of popcorn in my mouth when everyone in the living room looked over at me like I was cuckoo for cocaine puffs. Even Seven made an irritated, be-quiet-human, squeaking meow and tried his best to poke me in the leg disguising it as a stretch.

I'd spent way too much time thinking about Hayes and his dick. But he started it by prancing around naked in his backyard.

There had always been girl talk back when we were in high school, saying that the Kingman boys were well hung, but how did that monster between his legs even fit into his football uniform pants? His cup had to be a size eleventy-billion.

"Woo-hoo," George, sporting his new autographed H. Kingman jersey that he swore he'd never wash, jumped up and did a little dance. "Touchdown Mustangs!"

Uh-oh. Xan scowled and grabbed his empty beer bottle. He didn't even say anything, just skulked away toward the kitchen. We all tolerated the way he cheered for any team playing the Mustangs. Except George, who refused to dampen his pure love for the team.

Of course, George was the one who gave me the head nod to go after Xan and make sure he wasn't crying in the kitchen. Not that I'd ever seen my brother cry. Even when he maybe should have.

I waved at the cat on my lap. It was against the rules to move a sleeping feline. The universe might implode or something.

Liam shook his head at me, but with a smile. "Anyone need any refills?"

The second Liam moved toward the one room in the house that Seven was allowed to have treats, my traitorous cat jumped off my lap like I was made of dog slobber. Fine. I'd accept the sign from the universe that I, too, was needed in the kitchen.

Xan was leaning against the kitchen island nursing a new bottle of Fat Tire. He'd never been a big drinker, since he was forever in training, so it niggled at my brain that this was his fourth, and the game wasn't even at half-time yet.

I glanced at Liam, who just shrugged and grabbed the bag of treats from above the fridge. Seven curled around his leg until he tossed a few crunchy snacks on the floor. Then the rest of us no longer existed to him.

I worked on filling up a tray with more of Liam's famous fall caramel apple cider. Then I snagged one off the tray and propped myself against the fridge, across from Xan. "How was your game yesterday?"

I already knew it had gone well and that he'd scored the game-winning touchdown. But nothing put Xan in a good mood like getting to relay his accomplishments. To me.

Instead of answering my question, he pointed his beer bottle at me and then Liam with a glare. "You two were awfully cozy with Kingman yesterday."

"He just stopped in to get a cup of coffee, and you know Liam couldn't resist doing something for George." Regardless of his mad-on for Hayes and all things Mustangs, I knew Xan could never hold a grudge when it came to George and Liam. Me, on the other hand, well, let's just say twin telepathy made it too hard to keep very many secrets from each other, and that made it hard to hold grudges.

I had a secret, and I was afraid Xan would go off the rails when he found out I was going on a date with Hayes. I should have just said no. But he was so stinking cute trying to ask me out that I couldn't resist. Besides, it wasn't like anything could come of it, I was only here for a few more days.

It wasn't even enough time for a fling, really. Did it

count as a one-night stand if it was a few nights in a row and you were likely to run into your one-night stand every summer?

Ooh. Could we be one of those couples that only saw each other once a year and fucked like bunny rabbits for those few days, trying to get as much of each other as possible to hold us over until the next year?

Or... uh, had I been reading too many romance novels and was creating a ridiculous rom-com scenario in my head? Probably. Because never once in my life had I even considered a one-night stand or had a fuck-like-bunnies boy toy. I had the bare minimum of sexual experience, and most of that had been with a French guy who didn't speak a lick of English.

It might be nice to kiss, and touch, and suck, and be sucked by someone who could actually understand when I said, "No, no, not that hole."

"Well, he'd better not become a regular." Xan took another swig. "There are a hundred other places he could get a cup of coffee. He doesn't need to take up space at my spot."

I curled my toes and gritted my teeth not to roll my eyes. Xan was allowed to have feelings. But I think we were now on the fifty-seventh stage of grief that he didn't get drafted. Fifty of those steps had been anger directed at Hayes, who did.

Liam picked up his tray and headed back to the living room. "I think I hear your mother actively dying of thirst. I'd better get these drinks out there."

Before he got past the little hallway between the two

rooms, George whispered to Liam, just loud enough to hear. "Did you ask her?"

"No." Liam whispered back. "And I told you, I'm not going to. She's got a whole-ass life and I love that for her. I'm not interfering with that."

"But you have a whole-ass life too, Li." George's whisper got a bit gruffier and cracked a little. "When we didn't think you would. It doesn't hurt to ask, does it? Maybe she wants a new adventure."

I glanced at Xan and pointed to my chest, mouthing the word "me?"

He mouthed back, "duh."

I strained to listen to more of their conversation, but they moved away and I didn't catch anything else. "What was that all about? Liam already asked me if I wanted to stay a little longer, but I really have to get back to work."

"I'm not supposed to interfere." Xan shrugged.

"Tell me, or I'll sit on you when you least expect it." He had a good ten inches on me, but I had a good hundred pounds on him.

"You're going to make them more mad at me than they already are."

"Wait, why are they mad at you? You're the golden child, the one who will bring fame and football upon us all."

He ignored my jab and went and actually answered my real question. Dammit. "They want to go on a cruise."

"Okay." And what? That was no biggie. Did they want to do one in Asia, like out of Singapore, and come visit? I probably couldn't take a whole lot more time off, but I had enough free time during the weekdays to show them around. When I was working evenings and weekends, they could surely entertain themselves. "They should."

"They can't." The way he said it made it sound like a prompt I'd give to one of my students to get them to fill in the blanks and figure out the answer to the problem.

"Why? I though Liam had a clean bill of health." They'd said he was well. He had to be better. "He really is okay, right?"

It was a good thing I was the teacher and Xan wasn't because he sucked at the whole helping me figure out what was going on thing. "They don't want to do a three-day Caribbean cruise or some shit. When Li wasn't doing great, George bought them tickets for an around-the-world cruise so they'd have something to look forward to, something to live for."

Whoa. "That's badass. So, why can't they?" I was done guessing and made a motion for him to continue.

"Liam won't close Cool Beans to do it."

"Oh." The coffee shop meant everything to the two of them. Not because it was their income. George had a gazillion dollars from an inheritance and some smart investing, and then there was that app he designed and sold to some big online betting conglomerate. They were rolling in it. The coffee shop was more of a hobby.

But it was the place they'd met. And then George had bought it for Liam as a wedding present. The coffee shop was a symbol of their love, and so, yeah, they'd never close it. Not even to go on an around-the-world cruise to celebrate life in a bangarang way.

"Yeah, oh."

Oh. Oh shit. They wanted to ask me to run it for them,

didn't they? Come back to Denver. Live here. Be stuck here.

"Uh, I gotta go." I turned from the kitchen and bolted right upstairs to hide far, far away from family obligations.

Seven raced up the stairs ahead of me and made it to my room before I did. When I flopped down on the bed and covered my eyes with my arms, he crawled onto my chest and made himself into a purring loaf of bread.

George and Liam had granted me my freedom from life in Denver under the disappointed eyes of my parents and brother. They knew how much that meant to me. No way they'd force me to come back.

I laid there for a long time, my mind just racing around and around like the Indy 500 worrying about when and how they might ask, and what I'd say, and if I should say yes, or no, or what alternatives there could possibly be. I might have sunk into the pits of despair all night letting Seven snuggle me into sleep if my phone didn't buzz.

I'm on my way. Can't wait to see where you picked.

Shit. The date.

I definitely needed to get out of this house for a little while. Immediately if not sooner. I sent a quick reply message to Hayes.

Stay where you are. I'll meet you at your house.

He replied with the big eyes scared emoji and I

laughed. I imagined he was now running around his house picking up beer cans, throwing out pizza boxes, hiding the porn mags, and spraying air freshener everywhere.

I'd give him a minute while I brushed my teeth and ran a brush through my ponytail. I still hadn't told him where we were going, and I hoped he was at least slightly food adventurous. I'd known him most of my life, but honestly didn't really know him at all. I was rarely allowed to hang out with my brother and his friends, especially once we hit puberty.

Xan was always warning his teammates and buddies that I was off-limits. Whatever. I hadn't really cared that much because, besides their butts, I wasn't into athletes. I liked someone who could talk books, or had traveled or wanted to, or other things that according to my brother were nerdy.

So I'd dated the drama nerds, or the band geeks, or the AV club guys, which turned out to be code for gamer boys. Gamer boy plus book girlie was a great combo because I could read while he gamed, and that counted as spending quality time together. Although, not real romantic.

I couldn't imagine Hayes sitting around on his couch for hours on end. Xan could never sit still for more than a few minutes. They'd never know the joy of curling up with a cat and a good book for a long weekend afternoon.

Wait, where had Seven gone? I wanted to give him another snuggle before I headed out. Poop face.

I put on a layer of mascara, some light lip gloss, and dotted some vanilla behind my ears, on my wrists, and just for good measure, a touch of it right between my boobs. Might as well manifest some making out in my future. And then I put a fingerful of vanilla down my pants.

Now I really hoped Hayes was an adventurous eater.

MISADVENTURES IN EATING

HAYES

This was my first ever real date. With an actual woman. I was going to rock it, just like I did everything else I put my mind to.

The doorbell rang and my heart leapt into my throat. Game time. I dragged in a deep breath and headed to open it, plastering on what I hoped was a casual smile.

"Hey," I greeted Willa, unable to stop my eyes from roving over her form-fitting jeans and the pretty pink sweater she was wearing. I swear I was just admiring the color and not staring at the way her boobs were so soft looking and round, just begging for me to press my face between them.

She looked incredible with those stray loose curls that weren't pulled up into her ponytail framing her face. Willa was a beautiful, curvy woman who made my brain short-circuit just thinking about her.

Bad brain, bad, bad brain. Get on track.

"So, uhh, where are we headed?" I asked, rubbing my sweaty palms against my jeans.

"This little hole-in-the-wall Vietnamese place over on 120th. I'll show you where to go."

"Okay, cool." I tried not to let my nerves show. This was already so far out of my experience zone. Shouldn't I be taking her somewhere fancy for a first date?

As we headed out to my car, she looped her arm through mine, and I couldn't breathe for a second. The sweet vanilla scent of her hair wafted around me and her body was pressed against my side. Was she trying to kill me?

Don't screw this up, Kingman. This might be your only chance.

By the time we arrived at the run-down little shopping plaza, my palms were straight up drenched. The first date checklist I'd downloaded was basically already thrown out the window. I didn't even know whether I was supposed to open her car door or not.

Luckily, Willa didn't seem to notice my internal panic and grabbed my hand to tug me along as we approached a run-down looking restaurant with a strange name on the weathered sign.

"Pho seventeen," I said, reading the name out loud. "Is this a restaurant?"

"It's not faux, like fake. It's pronounced fuh, as in fuh-cking incredible. I hope you like it." She beamed up at me. "Supposed to be the best phở in Denver, or so the internet reports."

Inside, it was just a small room crammed with tables

and chairs, decorated with enormous photos of green tree'd islands on a lake, and a picture menu on the opposite wall. At least I'd have a clue what I was ordering, even though none of it looked even vaguely familiar. The aroma of spices did smell good though.

A tiny man around a hundred and seventy with a drawn face and glasses emerged through swinging kitchen doors. He pointed for us to choose from any one of the four top tables and went to grab us some menus.

I pulled out a chair for Willa and her eyes crinkled smiling up at me. Check one off for the first date etiquette list. I really fucking wanted to show her I could be more than an athlete. I was also a gentleman who would treat her right.

Once she was seated, I slid in next to her instead of across. Side by side was more intimate, and I stretched my arm along the back of her chair as if it was no big deal, then wrapped my arm around her shoulder. Nailed it.

Willa laughed and shook her head at me. That was not the reaction I'd been hoping for. Before I could analyze what I'd done wrong, our waiter handed over the menus. Thank god for those pictures. I'd definitely be pointing, even though there were words in English too. None of them were anything I'd ever heard of outside of the noodles and rice.

Our waiter looked bored until Willa opened her mouth. *"Xin chào. Tôi muốn đặt hai tô phở tái."*

At first the waiter looked at her like she was on crack, but quickly broke into a smile and replied. *"Ô! Bạn nói tiếng Việt rất tốt! Tôi rất ấn tượng."*

I watched, awed by Willa's expressive face and the way

she talked with her hands, marveling at how at ease she seemed speaking in a whole other language.

They said a couple more things to each other, and then the waiter headed toward the kitchen, hollering something to whoever was working in the back. If I had to guess, it was something about the crazy-hot white chick in their dining room who spoke Vietnamese.

She turned to me with a grin. "I hope you don't mind that I just ordered for us. They totally speak English, but it's fun for me to surprise them with my mediocre-at-best Vietnamese. They never expect a chubby white girl to know a word of their language, even when I'm in Saigon."

I couldn't resist reaching out to tuck an errant chestnut curl behind her ear. "You'll have to teach me how to order too."

The first date guide suggested that I teach her how to do something on our date, but I doubt she wanted to know how to read a defense or memorize the play book. I'd been trained to make snap decisions on the field, so I was using that skill now to call an audible on this play and flip the script on the dating playbook just like she had on the waiter.

Before I could pull out any of the other smooth lines I'd planned to try out on her, the waiter reappeared with a tray holding a pile of leaves and sprouts, and two steaming bowls of broth with noodles and pink slices of beef. He set them down and I stared at the food I was sure was from Mars or Venus. "Isn't this what Klingons eat?"

"This is phở tái, a pretty classic version, not generally found on Kronos," Willa teasingly explained and grabbed a handful of the leaves, which she tore up and sprinkled across the soup.

The fact that she got my Star Trek reference made her ten times hotter.

Next, she grabbed some bright red but tiny peppers, broke them in half and added those to the broth too. "But I'm impressed that you thought of *gagh*, and I'm about ninety percent more attracted to you now."

Huh. I was not expecting Willa to be a Trekkie. But if that's what she was attracted to, I was going to let my Trek flag fly. "Star Trek is my jam, *Imzadi.*"

Willa paused, her hand mid-air, and gave me a look that I absolutely couldn't interpret. "I'm way more Lwaxana than Deanna."

Ah, she was testing me to see if I was really a Trekkie or not. "If I remember correctly, they both had a thing for Riker, and I'm the man when it comes to throwing my leg over a chair and sitting in it backward."

She gave me the tiniest of nods, licked her lips but didn't reply, and went back to preparing her bowl of *gagh*. I was both planning our next date where we watched whichever Star Trek episode or movie she deemed was the best in full surround sound in my living room, hopefully while making out, while also watching in stunned fascination as she built up the concoction in front of her.

She added bean sprouts, some deep brown sauce out of a squeeze bottle, and then bright red Sriracha in thick swirls, topping the whole thing off with a squeeze of lime.

So weird. But it did smell great and not at all like hot worms.

"We'll have to Star Trek and chill sometime, huh? Now

you try," she urged, pushing a plate of garnishes across to me. "I'll walk you through it."

My brain was stuck on the "and chill" part of her offer and I thoroughly mangled several sprigs of herbs and added way too much Sriracha, until I had a questionable-looking mound in my bowl. "I'll provide the Star Trek and you bring the chill."

Yeah. I'd just said that. Dumb. I'm a football player not a Casanova, Jim.

Luckily, there was a fork and one of those big Chinese-style spoons, so I didn't have to embarrass myself too badly trying to eat with the chopsticks. I'd made enough of a fool out of myself tonight.

Willa did use her chopsticks, and I watched her loosen the pile of noodles and mix all the garnishes and goop we'd piled on top into the broth. I did the same but with my fork.

"Bon appétit," she said and deftly lifted a pile of noodles from the bowl into her mouth, slurping them right up. I maybe stared at her mouth for a minute too long before I ducked my head and did my best to twirl some noodles onto my fork. One bite, and I nearly moaned out loud. "Oh man, this is fuh-cking delicious."

Willa grinned around a mouthful of noodles. "Told ya. Denver has quite the Vietnamese community, and that means great Vietnamese food right here in the Rocky Mountains. Who knew?"

I nodded vigorously, slurping up another big bite of the savory soup. Drops of the broth dribbled down the noodles hanging from my mouth, off my chin, and onto my shirt. So much for dating manners. I slurped those noodles right up and licked my lips.

"Hey, Hayes?" Willa's voice had dropped to a low, sultry register that made my body lock up. I glanced over to find her watching me intently, that full bottom lip caught between her teeth.

"Yeah?"

Leaning in close, her eyes danced with mischief. "If you're that enthusiastic about slurping noodles, I can only imagine how good you'll be at other things you can do with your mouth."

Oh, ho. My dick went nuclear at her brazen innuendo, arousal zinging straight through my heart and down my spine. So, we were onto the sexually charged flirting phase of the date, were we? We'd skipped a few steps on my checklist, but I was down for the changeup if it meant she was thinking about all the things my mouth could do to hers and her body.

Not that I knew what I was doing, but once again, I'd learn, and I was always a straight A student.

I went to lean in and whisper in her ear that I was particularly good at using my mouth for entertaining purposes, but instead, I upended the tray with the bottles of sauce and the full jar of chili oil.

"Fuck a duck." I cut the litany of swear words I wanted to say and blinked down at the hot mess that was now my crotch.

Willa burst into peals of laughter, drawing looks from the other patrons. I couldn't even be mad, not with how light and free her humor was. She reached over to dab at the spots on my jeans with her napkin, still giggling.

I grabbed her wrist and held her hand in place about two centimeters from my dick, both wanting her to touch me and knowing better than that. "Willa."

The words I wanted to say, that she shouldn't touch me there right now, wouldn't come out. It was only her name, and that was a strained whisper.

"Hayes." She was still smiling, but there was a sultry twinkle in her eyes and her voice was just a whisper too. "Maybe we should get you home and out of those pants."

"Yeah, that's an excellent idea." I pulled out my wallet and threw a hundred dollar bill on the table. That should cover the food and the mess.

Willa grabbed my hand and pulled me back out to the car so fast, you'd think she was on fire. I certainly was. Thank goodness it was a super short ride back to my place. Not that I had a game plan for this. The stuff I'd been studying must have been old-fashioned as shit, because it implied there wouldn't be any action until date three at the earliest.

I hadn't even read up on the first kiss yet. Damn it. I called upon my ancestors to bestow upon me natural skill and ability to kiss the daylights out of a girl.

I'd planned to romance her, woo her, court her, so she could fall... well, maybe not in love with me, but at least in lust. Whatever it was we were doing now was a whole hell of a lot more fun. She made my head spin, and I didn't know whether I loved it or wanted to throw up from being on her roller coaster ride.

No one in my life was like Willa.

I pulled into the driveway in front of my house, and before I even turned off the car, she twisted, rolled across the bench seat, and straddled my lap. I was too stunned to warn her about getting her pants messy on the leftover condiments on my crotch.

"Good thing you have such long legs, or I'd have a steering wheel up my ass." She wiggled said ass and honked the horn, which had her laughing again. I loved how much she smiled and laughed when she was with me.

I'd tell her so, but I was apparently having an out-of-body experience, because I couldn't move or talk or breathe or think with her on my lap.

Willa cupped my face between her palms and leaned in, brushing her lips across one of my cheekbones, which ignited my face to the temperature of lava, then glanced at me and smiled like the Cheshire Cat before she pressed her lips to the other side. "I like you, Hayes Kingman."

"I like you too, a hell of a lot."

"I can tell." She ran her teeth over her bottom lip. "Unless that's a football you've got in your pants."

It was not.

"Have you ever done this before?" I don't know why I blurted that out, and I knew it was a mistake the second it hit my lips.

"Had sex in the front seat of a car?" She grinned and shook her head. "No. Have you?"

"I've..." Shit, was I supposed to admit I'd never had sex in a car or anywhere else? This was the one instance in my life I was not the head of the class. I wasn't ready for this. I hadn't studied how to please a woman in bed yet. I thought I'd have more time.

But if this was what Willa wanted, I was ready to learn

on the job. So I didn't say anything and simply shook my head.

She stared deep into my eyes, all the way to my soul, and then blinked a few times. "Oh. You, sweet, sweet man."

Fuck.

Everything in Willa's body language and face changed. She moved off my lap and opened the car door on her side.

Fucking fuck fuckity fuck fuck.

I got out too, my mind racing through scenarios to assure her I was not some inexperienced simp who wouldn't be able to get her off. Willa tipped her head to the side and frowned, jerking her head toward the living room windows. "My cat's here again."

I was buying cat treats for that cat, because this was my way back in, or rather how to get her to come inside where I could redouble my efforts, but on my turf. I shrugged and tried hard to keep the smile off my face. "Oh no. How does he keep getting in?"

"I swear that cat is part ninja." Willa wrinkled her nose and waited for me to open the door.

"Be careful, he's..." I watched Willa take in the line of gaming chairs, multiple monitors, and stacks of consoles carefully placed in position for our weekly live streams. My not so grownup side was on full display for her. Maybe this whole idea of having her on my turf wasn't so smart after all.

"You guys have a pretty intense setup. You and your brothers play a lot?" Willa said, giving me a sidelong glance.

I rubbed the back of my neck. "Uhh yeah. The twins, Isak, and I live stream games together sometimes."

"That's... interesting." She turned back to the shelf, hands on her hips. "So how are we extracting the furry fugitive?"

The gray and white furball was perched atop one of the entertainment center shelves, grooming himself with a smug look. I tried reaching up and snagging the cat from the shelf, but he crammed himself so far back that I'd have to take the whole unit apart to get to him.

After staring at the layout a long moment, Willa grabbed one of the gaming remotes and unplugged it. "Oh, Seven. I've got a snakey snake for you to chase."

She got down on her hands and knees and started moving the cord back and forth, swishing it across the floor.

I forgot how to talk as she crawled across the floor away from me with her thick thighs and ass wiggling in time to the way she moved the cord.

"Quit ogling my butt and make yourself useful." She looked up at me from the floor with a grin that was insanely suggestive. "Any second now, Seven is going to try to jump down here and capture the cord snake. You gotta grab him and hold him tight."

I wanted to hold something tight alright, and it wasn't her cat.

The cat stuck his head out and did his own butt wiggle. He jumped just like she said he would, and with a deft snatch, I plucked Seven out of the air. The moment I had him tucked under my arm like a football, once again, he started purring. I had a feeling this was going to become a routine for us, and I wouldn't mind one bit.

Willa got up, unfortunately for me and my fantasy, and put her hands on her hips. "Seven, if I didn't know better, I'd think you were doing this on purpose."

She took her cat from me and went straight for the front door. I wanted so badly for her to stay, but this date was over, and we both knew it. "I'll walk you home."

I thought she was going to refuse, but then she nodded and gave me a soft smile that gave me fucking hope. It was only fifty yards around the corner from my house to hers, and she said a quick goodnight and disappeared.

God dammit. I was not used to blowing it, and that's exactly what I'd just done. Instead of heading back to my house, I jogged over to Everett's, hoping he was alone. Even though he rarely was on a game day. But there weren't any other cars in the driveway, which I took as a good sign.

I found him in the backyard, sipping a Fat Tire and listening to some Kelsey Best. Again. Unusual, but I was simply happy he was here for the consult I needed.

"What's the best porn?" I was enrolling myself in the advanced level courses from here on out. I didn't ever want to feel unprepared when it came to Willa again.

"That's a bit personal, kid." He took a sip of his beer and turned the music off. "Just go search the categories on CornHob if you're bored or looking for a new kink."

"No, I mean the best porn to learn how to please a woman."

JUST A FLING

WILLA

If I knew one thing, it was that Hayes Kingman was not a fling kind of a guy. He was even saving it for the right girl. Which shocked the shit out of me, and somehow at the same time made me like him even more. To be honest, I wasn't actually a fling kind of girl. But I'd almost become one by jumping into bed with him.

He probably thought I'd been turned off by his lack of experience, but it was just the opposite. Which scared the sweet bejeesus out of me. He was a commitment guy. I was not that girl.

I saved us both a whole hell of a lot of heartbreak and walked away.

But I couldn't stop smiling, even as Seven squirmed in my arms. The date with Hayes had been... unexpected. In all the best possible ways. And when he'd admitted to being a Trekkie? Be still my geeky heart.

Sure, he was a bit of straight arrow, just like Xander, which was a total turn off for me, but on him it was so endearing. He was trying so hard to impress me, and damn if it wasn't working. The way I knew the whole night was out of his comfort zone, but he'd tried hard to take it all in as if every scenario I put him in was all the most fascinating thing he'd ever experienced. It was nice to feel so, seen and, honestly, pursued.

It wasn't that I didn't want a committed relationship. But I was not staying in Thornminster the rest of my life. Blech, blurgh, hurl. Colorado was fine and all, but forever? No thank you. There was so much more out there to see. And I needed a guy that wanted to see it with me.

Hayes hadn't even left the neighborhood we grew up in. Except, of course, for away games. His new house was literally down the street from his dad's. I couldn't even stay at my parents' a second after I graduated. But then again, the Rosemounts weren't the Kingmans. Unwavering support of each other was not on our list of strengths.

I deposited a disgruntled Seven inside and flopped onto the couch in the now empty living room, grinning up at the ceiling like a loon. I hadn't felt this giddy about a guy in... ever. Too bad, because it wasn't like I'd get him to up and leave Denver and the Mustangs to go galivanting around the world with me.

The muffled sound of my uncles' voices coming from the kitchen popped my happy bubble. Curious, I tiptoed closer to the door, Seven trailing behind me. Probably because he wanted treats.

"I won't leave Cool Beans unattended for that long, George." Uncle Liam's voice was strained, and this was the last thing I expected after his new healthy prognosis. He should be happy-go-lucky right now. "It means too much to me."

"Sweetheart, I know. But if we were ever going to celebrate our life and love, it's now, when I'm so fucking grateful I get more years with you." Uncle George sounded uncharacteristically subdued. Normally he was the positive gregarious one, always ready to make the rest of us feel like a million bucks, even though he was the one with literally millions of bucks.

A swell of guilt tumbled over me. This was the trip Xander had told me about.

"It was the perfect thing to keep us both going in those dark days, babe," Liam sighed. "But we don't have to run away to get that same feeling. I get it every day when I open up the shop because it always makes me think of the day you gave it to me."

"Couldn't we at least ask Willa? She could..." George's hopeful voice trailed off.

"No, absolutely not. We can't ask her to give up her job, her life. You know how much it means to her."

Tears pricked the backs of my eyes at Liam's fierce protectiveness. He'd always been my rock with his quiet understanding and unconditional support.

My stomach twisted into a pretzel. One of those hard crunchy ones—not the soft, delicious kind. These two men had done so much for me—taking me in when I'd wanted to escape my parents' endless parade of college applications, supporting my wanderlust. And now I was the one person who could make it so they could go on this much-deserved trip of their own.

"You're right, of course," George acquiesced, a tinge of disappointment coloring his tone. "We'll figure something out. Maybe Javier can take on more shifts, or we can hire a temporary manager..."

Their voices faded as they moved deeper into the kitchen, but I remained rooted to the spot, my mind whirling.

They were willing to sacrifice their dream trip... for me. To protect the life I'd chosen, even if they didn't quite understand it.

A wave of shame crashed over me, stealing my breath. Here I was, bouncing around the world trying to "find myself," while all they wanted was a chance to celebrate the fact that Liam didn't fucking die. And I was scared to death of offering to help.

Seven weaved between my ankles, jolting me out of my spiraling thoughts. I scooped him up and buried my face in his fur, my throat tight.

I knew what I had to do. But it made me want to puke.

Well, suck it up, buttercup. I could do this for them. I squared my shoulders and marched into the kitchen, ready to face the music.

Uncle Liam startled as I burst through the swinging door, nearly dropping the mug he was drying. "Willa, you scared me half to death."

"Oh god. Too soon, Uncle Li, too soon. You're not allowed to talk about dying for at least another fifty-seven years." I swallowed hard, my grand speech deserting me. "I couldn't help overhearing about the cruise. And the café."

They exchanged a loaded glance, an entire conversation passing between them in the space of a heartbeat.

"Oh, sweet wild child," George said softly and pulled me into his best kind of bear hug. "Don't you worry about all that."

"But I do worry. You two have done so much for me, and now you're willing to give up your trip because of me, and I just..." I blinked back the sudden sting of tears, my fingers curling into George's jersey.

"Enough of that nonsense." Liam set down his mug and crossed the room and joined us in a big group hug. "Seeing you happy and unburdened, out living your best life in the world, makes us happy. We wouldn't trade that, not for all the cruises around the world."

"He's right," George chimed in, enveloping us both in his big burly embrace. "You're worth a thousand trips around the globe."

For a moment, I let myself sink into the comfort of their love, the unwavering faith they'd always had in me. Even when I didn't have it in myself. "We aren't done talking about this. I'll step up if I need to."

"You don't need to," Liam said. "You need to live your wild child life, Willa. That's what we want for you. I can't tell you how often I lived vicariously through you and your adventures."

Oh man. Now I was gonna cry again.

A change of subject was in order. "You wanna live two minutes of vicariousness right now?"

In unison, they said, "Absolutely."

I took a step back and simply could not hide my smile from them. "Guess who I went out with tonight."

Liam made waggly eyebrows at me, and George clasped his hands together, looked up to the sky and moved his mouth as if in prayer, then crossed himself and looked right at me. "Who?"

"Hayes Kingman."

George dropped to his knees and wrapped his arms around my waist. "Please, Willa, please tell me you're going to marry that boy, and then adopt me and make me a Kingman."

Seven jumped up on George's shoulder and I swear he looked up at me in the exact same way as George. I wagged my fingers at both of them. "You two are very strange."

Liam laughed and rolled his eyes. "You have no idea."

After a flurry of begging on George's part with promises of an exotic destination wedding and an unusual number of meows from Seven, I escaped to my room.

If there was anyone in the world I'd play shopkeeper for the better part of a year, it would be Liam and George. What I needed was someone else to talk me into it, and I knew just who would. But instead of calling my mother, I messaged Xan.

Should I really stay and run Cool Beans?

Duh.

But I'd have to quit my job.

I'd be putting my whole life on hold. But it wasn't like it would be hard to get it all back. There were always a million schools that needed enthusiastic teachers. With the credentials I'd gotten over the last three years, I had my choice of jobs and locations.

Willa, your life is wherever you are. This is something you need to do. It's only temporary.

I sighed. He had a point. It wasn't like I was signing away my future. Just taking a little detour.

A pair of earnest blue eyes popped into my head, and I bit back a smile. A detour with some appealing scenery.

I definitely wasn't ready to tell my brother about my... whatever-it-was with Hayes. He'd flip out at me dating his arch nemesis. Not that he would have approved of me dating Hayes when they'd been friends either.

I went to bed with thoughts of Hayes in my mind, which did not help me go to sleep. I opted for a little one-handed reading to help me get my mind off him, but all I did was picture him in place of the dragon-shifter hero in the book I was reading. The combination had me moaning Hayes's name with my unicorn tongue vibrator between my legs.

Since I'd volunteered for the afternoon shift at the coffee shop, I got to sleep in and was surprised that I was adjusting back to Denver time so easily. That was going to be murder when I got back to Asia.

If I went back. Ugh.

The afternoon shift was super slow, and I was glad I'd shoved my Kindle into my bag to pass the time. I was just getting to a good part, by which I mean sexy times, in the story when the bell above the door jingled. I glanced up from the story and got some butterflies in my stomach for my trouble. I'd know that broad-shouldered silhouette anywhere.

Hayes stepped inside, a pretty brunette trailing behind him. Her bright blue eyes, so like his, darted around the cozy interior of the café with undisguised curiosity.

"Hey, you," I called out, shoving my Kindle into the apron pocket. "I was hoping I'd get to see you again today."

Hayes's eyebrows went up and surprise flashed across his face, but he shut that down real fast. He probably thought I'd ignore him after last night. "Me too."

"And you brought us a customer?" I gestured to the girl, who was now openly grinning at me.

"This is my little sister, Jules."

"The infamous Willa." Jules bounded over to the counter, thrusting out a hand for me to shake. "I'm sure you don't remember me. I was three years behind you guys in school and thoroughly ignored by my older brothers back then. But I've heard so much about you."

I raised an eyebrow at Hayes as I took her hand. "Oh, have you now?"

He coughed, suddenly fascinated by the chalkboard menu. "Just, you know... that we had a nice time last night."

Jules snorted. "Please. He hasn't shut up about you all afternoon. It's been Willa this, Willa that. I finally told him to put up or shut up and bring me to meet this goddess among women."

I bit back a laugh at Hayes's mortified expression. "Well, I don't know about goddess, but it's nice to see you again, Jules."

"You too. I've been dying for Hayes to find a girl who can keep him on his toes. Lord knows he needs it. With all those awards and accolades and touchdowns, he's getting a big head."

"Jules," Hayes groaned, but I could tell he was fighting a smile.

She elbowed him in the ribs and stage whispered out of the side of her mouth. "Shut up. I'm making you look good."

Then she smiled back at me again. "But also, it's all true. He's a literal genius and always gets whatever it is he puts his mind to. Like beating the Rebels yesterday, and if he's real lucky, getting you to go out on another date with him."

I pressed my lips together trying not to burst out laughing because Hayes was about to combust on the spot.

Hayes might be dying, but I was charmed by their easy sibling rapport. It reminded me of Xander and I when we were younger, before life and expectations had sent us on very different paths.

"Alright, alright," Hayes interjected after a particularly detailed account of how he'd bamboozled the entire Rebels defense and scored before they were even facing the right way. "I think Willa's heard enough of my exploits for one day."

"Aw, but I was just getting to the good stuff." Jules pouted, but her eyes danced with laughter.

I grinned, reaching over to pat Hayes's hand where it rested on the counter. "Don't worry, I still think you're pretty cool. For a football player, that is."

He caught my fingers with his, giving them a quick squeeze. "High praise, indeed."

We smiled at each other for a long moment, lost in our own little bubble, until Jules cleared her throat pointedly.

"So, Willa," she said, propping her elbows on the counter and resting her chin in her hands. "Tell me all about yourself. I want to know everything about the girl who's got my brother all twitterpated."

I laughed, even as a pang of guilt twisted my stomach. I'd already told myself I wasn't going to get involved with Hayes. I wasn't his kind of girl, and he was the opposite of the kind of guy I thought I'd ever be with. But here I was, flirting and not only leading him on but leading his little sister on. "Oh, I don't know about that. I'm really not that interesting."

"Doubtful," Hayes murmured, his gaze warm on my face.

I fiddled with the strings of my apron. "I've got a wonderful job teaching English. I just started a new contract in Vietnam a few months ago."

Jules's eyes widened. "That's so interesting. I bet you have some cool-ass stories."

"A few," I admitted with a wry smile. "Getting to experience new cultures, connect with people from all walks of life, I love it."

Hayes was watching me intently, something unreadable flickering in his eyes. "Sounds like quite the adventure."

I nodded, a wistful sigh escaping me. "It has been. I am, was, looking forward to going back next week."

I trailed off, biting my lip. I hadn't meant to bring that up. I didn't know whether I was staying or coming or going.

"You're leaving next week?" Jules prompted, leaning forward.

I hesitated, glancing at Hayes. This wasn't how I'd wanted to tell him, but I couldn't lie. "My uncles, Liam and George... they've got this big round-the-world cruise planned. To celebrate Liam's clean bill of health after his scare."

Understanding dawned on Hayes's face, followed by a flash of something that looked almost like... disappointment? "And you're going with them?"

"No, I..." I took a deep breath. "I'm thinking about staying and running the café for them while they're gone."

Good god, had I actually said that out loud?

Silence hung between us for a long moment, heavy with unspoken questions. Jules glanced back and forth between Hayes and I, her brow furrowed.

"How long will they be gone?" Hayes asked finally, his voice carefully neutral.

I swallowed hard. "Nine months, give or take."

He blinked, clearly taken aback. "That's... wow. That's a big commitment."

"I know." My heart was hammering against my ribs, feeling like a bird in cage. "I just... they've done so much for me, you know? I can't let them give up this trip. Not when I can do something to help."

Hayes nodded slowly, a strange mix of emotions

playing across his face, surprise, respect, and something softer I couldn't quite name. "That's really amazing of you, Willa. Truly."

Tingles pricked along my scalp at the quiet sincerity in his voice. "I'm trying to be. I don't know if I'm cut out for this whole responsibility thing, but... I have to try. For them."

"You'll be great," he said firmly, holding my gaze. "I know you will."

Jules, who had been uncharacteristically silent through our exchange, suddenly clapped her hands together. "Wait, so this means you're sticking around? In Thornminster?"

I nodded, tearing my eyes away from Hayes's intense stare. "Looks like it. At least for the foreseeable future."

A slow, sly smile spread across her face as she glanced between us again. "Well, well. Isn't that interesting."

Hayes shot her a warning look. "Jules..."

She held up her hands in mock surrender. "What? I'm just saying it's awfully convenient timing." Her eyes sparkled with barely contained glee. "It's like fate or something."

I barked out a laugh, even as my cheeks heated. Did she somehow know that my favorite romance trope was fated mates? Partly because it was so unreal. Total escapism. "I don't know about that."

"Well I do," she declared with all the confidence of a seventeen-year-old who thought she had the world figured out. Maybe she did. "You and Hayes, thrown together by circumstance, falling madly in love as you navigate the perils of small-town life..." She sighed dreamily. "It's like a romance novel come to life."

"Okay, first of all, we don't live in a small town. Thornminster is an enormous suburb of a major metropolitan area. Not New York or LA, but we're big enough to have a bunch of pro sports teams." Hayes stood abruptly, the tips of his ears flaming red. "We should let Willa get back to work."

I bit my lip to hide my smile. He was even cuter when he was flustered. I added, "Because the coffee shop has so many customers right now."

Jules winked at me as Hayes ushered her toward the door, grumbling under his breath. She twisted out of his grip to call over her shoulder, "I'll be seeing you around, Willa. Don't be a stranger."

"Not if I see you first," I returned with a grin.

Hayes came back and leaned against the counter, giving me such an adorably sincere look I maybe fell in love with him a teensy tiny bit. "I'm really happy you're staying, Willa."

My fluttery bird heart stuttered in my chest. "Me too."

Maybe I was.

It was madness. It was impulsive. And that was what made me kind of like the whole idea. And just to prove it to myself and Hayes, I jumped up on the counter and kissed him.

TWATWAFFLES

HAYES

Willa's kiss hit me like a linebacker, stealing my breath and making my head spin. For a moment, I forgot where I was, forgot my own name. There was only her. Her soft lips moving against mine, her fingers tangling in my hair, the sweet vanilla scent of her invading my senses.

Fireworks exploded behind my eyelids, a kaleidoscope of color and light that rivaled any touchdown celebration. I'd never been kissed before, and if anyone had told me this was what I was missing, I might have fucking figured out a way to fit girls into my rigid schedule.

This intensity, this bone-deep rightness made me feel like I'd finally found a missing piece of myself. No book or article by a dating coach or even a dating dude's Flip-Flop could have prepared me for this.

My hands found her waist, tugging her closer as I

angled my head to taste more of her. She made a soft noise in the back of her throat that set my blood on fire. I could have happily drowned in her, let the rest of the world fade away until it was just us, just this perfect moment stretching into eternity.

"What the fuck?"

The angry shout jolted us apart, Willa nearly tumbling off the counter in her haste. I steadied her automatically, my gaze snapping to the seething figure in the doorway.

Xander Rosemount glared at us, his fists clenched at his sides, jaw tight with barely suppressed fury. "Someone want to tell me what the hell is going on here?"

Willa slid off the counter, putting herself between her twin and me. "Xan, calm down. We were just—"

"Just what? Playing tonsil hockey in the middle of the café?" Xander took an aggressive step forward, his eyes never leaving my face. "Real classy, Kingman."

I bristled at his tone, my own temper sparking to life. "Watch it, man. You don't know what you're talking about."

"I know you've got your hands all over my sister," he snarled, trying to shoulder past Willa.

She held her ground, planting a hand on his chest. "I'm not a child, Xander. I can kiss whoever I want."

He barked out a harsh laugh. "Oh, so you want this lying sack of shit? The same guy who ditched me—ditched our team—without a second thought?"

I frowned, a trickle of unease winding through my anger. "What are you talking about? I didn't ditch anyone."

Xander sneered at me over Willa's head. "Right. Because getting drafted as a junior and running off to play pro, leaving the rest of us high and dry, that's totally not ditching us."

My stomach sank as understanding dawned. I'd always known Xander was angry with me for going pro early, but I'd thought it was about the competition, about him wanting to be the first picked. I never considered that he might have felt... betrayed.

"Xan, that's not... I didn't mean to hurt you or the team."

"Bullshit," he spat, shrugging off Willa's restraining hand. "You never even looked back, did you? Too busy bathing in glory and chasing your next headline. Well, guess what, buddy boy? You don't get to have it all. You don't get my sister."

Willa whirled on him, her expression thunderous. "Excuse me? I'm not a trophy for you two to fight over. I make my own damn choices."

A muscle ticked in Xander's jaw, but he kept his glare trained on me. "I mean it, Kingman. Stay the hell away from her."

I opened my mouth to argue, to tell him that I cared about Willa, that I would never hurt her the way I apparently hurt him. But the words lodged in my throat as I caught sight of Willa's face.

Beneath the anger, there was a glimmer of raw pain in her eyes that cut me to the quick. The last thing I wanted was to come between her and Xander, to make her feel like she had to choose sides.

Every cell in my body told me to knock Xander the fuck out, throw Willa over my shoulder, and haul her off to my bed, to claim her as mine and only mine. But I wasn't some wolf man, and Willa deserved better than that.

So I swallowed my protests and took a step back, my hands held up in surrender. "I don't want to fight with you, man. Not about this."

Xander blinked, clearly taken aback by my easy capitulation. He'd been spoiling for a fight, and I'd just yanked the rug out from under him.

Willa turned to me, her brow furrowed. "Hayes, you don't have to—"

"It's okay," I said softly, trying to inject some reassurance into my tone. "I get it. You two need to talk. I'm gonna go, but I will see you later."

No way I was walking away without letting her know this wasn't over just because her brother was mad.

I hated leaving her to deal with his misplaced anger, but I didn't see any other way to defuse the situation. Pushing back against Xander now would only make things worse.

I held Willa's gaze for a long moment, trying to silently communicate everything I couldn't say. That this wasn't over, that I wasn't going anywhere, that she was worth fighting for.

Something softened in her expression, a hint of understanding mingled with gratitude. She gave me a tiny nod, so subtle, if I hadn't been entirely focused on her, I'd have missed it.

With a final pointed look at Xander, I turned and walked out of the café, my hands shoved deep in my pockets to hide the fists I couldn't help. It took every ounce of willpower not to look back, to stride away with my head held high like the bigger man Willa deserved.

But I needed to answer another question and messaged Gryff and Flynn promising to pay for dinner if they'd meet me. Food was always the best bribe with those two.

An hour later I slid into the booth at Gino's Diner, just across from campus. I nodded gratefully as the waitress set a steaming mug of coffee in front of me. I needed the caffeine boost after the emotional rollercoaster of the day. But one sip and I made a face. This needed a whole hell of a lot more cream and sugar. How the hell had I ever drunk it black?

Across from me, my brothers Flynn and Gryff exchanged a curious look before turning their attention to me.

"So, what's with the cryptic summons, bro?" Flynn asked, snagging a menu from the holder. "Not that we mind an excuse to grab a bite, but you never offer to pay."

"I never had money before, you twatwaffles." I wrapped my hands around the mug, letting the warmth seep into my skin. "I need to ask you guys something. About the team, about... Xander."

Gryff's eyebrows shot up. "Rosemount? Aren't you guys friends? What about him?"

"We used to be. I ran into him today, and he said some things..." I hesitated, trying to find the right words. "He basically accused me of ditching the team, of betraying you guys by going pro early."

Kingmans were ultra-competitive, but we were raised to adamantly support the hell out of each other. Even though I was ten months younger than they were, they'd never indicated that they'd been anything but happy to have another brother in their classes or on the team with them when I'd skipped a year in school. But maybe I was the one who was a dick, and it hurt them when I jumped ahead of the pack.

Flynn and Gryff stared at me for a long moment before bursting into laughter.

"Is he serious?" Flynn managed between guffaws. "That's the stupidest thing I've ever heard."

Gryff nodded, wiping tears of mirth from his eyes. "Bro, no one was mad about you getting drafted. We're stoked for you. Hell, we're still fucking bragging about it."

A knot of tension unwound in my chest. "Really? You guys weren't... I don't know, resentful?"

"Not even a little," Flynn assured me, clapping me on the shoulder. "You're living the dream, man. We're proud as hell of you."

"Even though I'm your little brother?"

"You're the best of us all, man. Anyone who is resentful of that needs to take a long look at themselves. And I, for one, like it way better when other people are looking at me." He pointed his fork at a girl at another table and winked at her. She rolled her eyes but smiled at him. "And when I say other people, I mean the ladies."

Gryff shook his head. "We know, dude. Everyone knows. You just let me know when you can get the shes, theys, and gays sliding into your DMs."

"Just because you're bi and I'm not, doesn't mean you get more action than I do." Flynn stuck his fork into his pie with way more force than was necessary. Even in matters of love—or bed—they were competitive, but supportive.

"Xander's always been a bit... intense." Gryff looked at me and ignored Flynn's pout. "We knew he had a bug up his ass about something, but we never guessed it was about you."

I sighed, running a hand through my hair. "I fucking hate the thought that I might have hurt you guys, even unintentionally."

Flynn leaned forward, his expression uncharacteristically serious. "Hayes, listen to me. You did nothing wrong. You earned that spot in the draft honestly. Anyone who says otherwise is jealous or delusional or both."

"Especially Xander," Gryff chimed in. "I love the guy when he's scoring a ridiculous number of points, but he's got a real problem with always wanting to be top dog. Your success probably just rankled him."

Right. Xan always pushed the edges of extreme, which I'd always assumed was the same kind of passion for the game that I had. Competitiveness could be one hell of a bitch if you let it get under your skin. My brothers' support and validation that I wasn't the bad guy here meant more than I could say.

"Okay. I needed to hear that."

Flynn grinned, signaling the waitress for another round of coffees. "Anytime, bro. Now, onto more important matters..." He waggled his eyebrows suggestively. "What's this I hear about you and a certain barista getting cozy?"

I nearly choked on my coffee. "What? How did you—"

"Please," Gryff scoffed, smirking. "You think news like

that doesn't travel faster than a wide receiver on game day? Spill, lover boy."

Flynn and Gryff peppered me with good-natured teasing and increasingly invasive questions. I remained closed-lipped, giving them nothing more than a grin. I was a hundred percent sure I knew who'd told them about Willa anyway, and Jules was eternally exempt from all repercussions of being the family gossip.

They gave up when it was clear I wasn't going to be the kind to kiss and tell, and after another piece of pie each, we headed for the parking lot.

"Uh, bro. Is there a cat in your ride?" Gryff pointed to my car, and yep, sure enough, a certain gray and white furball was sitting on my dashboard like an off-brand guard dog.

"Shit. How the hell did he get in there?" I sprinted over and carefully opened the door, hoping he wasn't going to make a run for it. I could never face Willa again if I lost her cat on the DSU campus. "Gotta go, guys. I need to see a girl about her cat."

Gryff was already laughing his ass off, and Flynn shook his head. "That had better be code for getting laid."

I wished it was. Wait, it could be. All depended on what happened when I arrived at Willa's door.

Seven, my favorite little escape artist, climbed up on my shoulder and meowed like he was either having the time of his life or hated me for taking him home. I couldn't tell which.

"You're lucky you're cute," I informed him, reaching up to scratch his chin. "And that your mom is even cuter."

I pulled up to Willa's house, a man with a plan. This

was the part where I swept her off her feet. Maybe literally if she let me. I scooped up Seven and marched to her front door, rapping my knuckles against the wood, then leaned in the doorframe as if showing up unannounced with her cat in tow was what all the cool kids were doing.

The door swung open, revealing a pajama clad Willa. And holy shit was I going to have dreams of her wearing those cat nap jammies, or rather taking them off. "Hayes? What are you—"

Her eyes landed on the furry bundle in my arms. "Seven? How did you...? You little rat, I'm going to assimilate you."

"Found this little guy lounging in my car..." I handed him toward Willa and our fingers brushed. Electricity zinged up my arm and I almost dropped the cat to pull her to me. "Wait, wait, wait. I can't believe I didn't get this before right this second, but did you name your cat Seven because of Voyager?"

Willa laughed, cuddling Seven close. "Yes. His full name is Seven of Nine Lives. He's pursuing you like a rogue Borg cube, and I'm going to have to have a serious talk with him."

Seven squirmed like he knew exactly what that talk was going to entail and he wanted nothing to do with it. He promptly scampered off to parts unknown. "I'm pretty sure resistance to him is futile."

That made Willa smile, and god did I love the sparkle in her eyes and the curve of her lips.

"Listen, about earlier," Willa began, scratching her bright blue painted toes across the doormat. "I'm sorry about Xander. He had no right to go off on you like that."

I shrugged and put my arm up on the doorframe just to be another inch closer to her. "It's not your fault. Xan's always been competitive. I get it. But that's not going to stop me from... pursuing you."

She'd been staring down at the rug, but her head snapped up and she stared up at me. "You, I mean, I, it's just—"

I reached forward and ran the back of my knuckles along her jaw line. "Did you talk to your uncles? About staying, about running the café while they're on their world tour of love?"

"Yeah. They're already packing."

We stared at each other for a long moment, the air between us crackling with tension. I wanted to pull her into my arms and pick up where we left off. But there was something in her eyes that told me not to push.

So I settled for running my thumb across her bottom lip. "I'm really glad you're staying, Willa."

She clasped my fingers and held them still. "It's just temporary. The minute they're back, I'll be out of here."

"A lot can happen in that amount of time." I leaned in closer, not able to resist her pull. Hello flame, this is the moth calling.

"Don't, Hayes. Don't fall for me. This can't be more than," she shrugged, "a few months thing. A fling."

"I'll take every minute I can get with you." Besides, it was too late. I was already falling for her.

Her cheeks flushed prettily, and I couldn't resist any longer. I bent my head and brushed a feather-light kiss across the corner of her mouth.

"I'll take every one of these I can get too," I murmured, my lips a hairsbreadth from hers.

Willa's breath hitched, and she stood up on her toes to close the space between us. "Don't make me fall in love with you either."

The enthusiastic consent mantra rang through my mind. I had more work to do, because I wasn't going to take anything she wasn't willing to give me. But I wasn't afraid of hard work.

With a groan, I forced myself to pull away, to saunter back to my car with a casual wave. "No promises. See you tomorrow, Willa."

Willa was staying. And I was going to make damn sure it was worth it. As I drove away, my lips still tingling from our almost-kiss, I couldn't wipe the goofy smile off my face.

Until my phone buzzed with a text message from a number that hadn't popped up for a long time.

Stay

The Fuck

Away

From my sister

WILLA'S BEAN

WILLA

The bell above the door jingled, announcing a new customer, but I barely glanced up from the inventory spreadsheet Uncle Liam had me poring over. "Be with you in just a sec," I called out, my brow furrowed as the numbers blurred from staring at them for so long. Was that a three or a nine?

"Take your time, kiddo." Uncle George's amused voice had my head snapping up, a grin already tugging at my lips.

"What are you two doing here? I thought you'd be knee-deep in the fifth repack by now." I saved the spreadsheet and closed the laptop, giving them my full attention. "You don't have time to be here, you leave in, like, three hours."

Uncle Liam hefted a suspiciously full tote bag onto the

counter. "Had a few last minute things to go over with you before we jet off into the sunset."

I eyed the bag warily. "Please tell me that's not more paperwork. I'm already drowning in coffee order forms and employee schedules."

He chuckled, patting my hand. "Just a few essentials we forgot to mention. Like the fact that we have a standing arrangement with the local cat shelter."

He opened the bag that was full of brand new cat toys, containers of cat nip, and one exceedingly long peacock feather. My eyebrows shot up. "Cat shelter?"

Uncle George nodded, snatched the peacock feather, and hid it behind his back. "Oops, that was supposed to go in my bag not this one."

He winked at Liam, and I pretended not to notice how freaking adorable they were.

Liam didn't pretend for one second and gave George a playful pinch. But then they remembered I was standing there and that they were leaving me in charge of the coffee shop. "Once a month, they bring a few adoptable cats to the café. We set up a little play area in the corner, let customers interact with them. It's been great for business and for finding those furry angels forever homes."

I blinked, trying to process this latest information. "Any other grand marketing schemes you've got in your back pockets?"

"Nope, that's the main one," Uncle Liam assured me. "You just need to coordinate with them on dates and logistics. I've got all the contact info in here." He tapped the tote bag.

I blew out a breath, mentally adding cat adoption facilitator to my ever-growing list of responsibilities. "Okay, got it. Anything else I should know?"

Uncle George exchanged a glance with Liam, his expression turning serious. "Willa, we just want to say... thank you. For doing this, for putting your life on hold for us. We know it's a lot to ask—"

I held up a hand, cutting him off. "Stop right there. You guys have done so much for me, been there for me through everything. This is the least I can do."

Uncle Liam's eyes misted over, and he pulled me into a bone-crushing hug. "We're so proud of you, and I promise you can go back to being the wild one soon. In the meantime, you're going to do great."

"Just remember," Uncle George added, joining in on the hug, "it doesn't really matter what you do with the place. As long as it's still standing when we get back, we'll count it as a win."

I laughed, extricating myself from their octopus embrace. "Be careful what you wish for. It might be a European nightclub when you get back."

Uncle Liam grinned, his eyes twinkling. "Fun. While you're going crazy, make it a cat café disco. You're halfway there. Just adopt all the kitties at the next cat rescue day and voilà, Discothèque Chat Noir is born."

We all burst into laughter at the absurdity of the idea. Or maybe it was nervous laughter on all our parts for being crazy enough to leave me in charge of their business. I was never labeled the reliable one. But I was going to do my best. It was only for a few months.

Still giggling, I shooed them off to finish packing, promising to give the café my all. As the door swung shut behind them, I leaned against the counter, shaking my head.

A cat café discothèque. Honestly, where did they come up with this stuff?

My phone buzzed with an incoming text, and I fished it out of my apron pocket, expecting a last-minute reminder from my uncles.

Instead, Xander's name flashed across the screen. I thought it might be a teasing message meant to tell me good luck with the shop. But it sure as shit wasn't that.

> I saw you with Kingman. What the hell, Willa? I told you to stay away from him.

I stared at the screen, my heart pounding. How did he know about my moment with Hayes on the porch? Had he been watching the house? That was over the top and unacceptable.

A flutter of unease stirred in my gut. I knew my brother could be overprotective, but this felt different. Darker.

I closed my eyes, remembering the soft brush of Hayes's lips against mine, the promise in his words. I couldn't let Xander's misplaced anger ruin this. Nope, wait, no, no, no. I wasn't even getting involved with Hayes. I'd already told him not to fall for me, and he'd taken the hint and walked away. Although without some loaded promises about no promises.

Didn't matter. Xander didn't get to tell me what to do. Jaw set, I typed out a response.

Back off, Xan. My life, my choices. I mean it.

I hit send before I could second guess myself, then shoved the phone back in my pocket. I had a café to run and future adventures to plan. With a half a year of savings in my pocket and hardly any expenses since I'd be living at the Guncles' house while they were gone, I didn't even have to find another teaching job right away. I could explore some places first and pick someplace I was willing to stay for a whole contract, without getting bored.

But even as I daydreamed about places like the ice hotel and the northern lights, or the famous mountain hot springs and bath houses in Japan, somehow Hayes was in each of those fantasies with me. Which was unlikely. He had a whole-ass family and a successful football career here in Denver.

So I don't even know why Xan was worried in the first place. It wasn't like I was marrying a Kingman. I'd more likely open a cat café first.

Stupid overprotective twin brother.

The rest of the day passed in a blur, just a few coffee orders, inventory checks, and a minor mishap with the espresso machine that left me smelling like a walking latte. I was adding more herbal teas to the menu immediately if not sooner. Thank goodness it was almost closing time. I did love having the evenings off for the first time in forever. I was more than ready to throw in the towel and call it a day. What I needed was some Netflix.

But, of course, my mind went to whether Hayes might want to come over for the chill portion of the evening.

Bad brain. No nookie with Hayes. That was a dangerous path that led to feelings. Ain't nobody got time for feelings.

But then the chime over the door dinged, I looked up, and my heart did a little flip.

Hayes stood in the doorway, looking like a big, yummy snack. He was freshly showered, his hair still damp, and I'd bet he'd come straight from practice. He had no right to look that good.

"Hey," he said, his voice sending a shiver down my spine. "How's the official first day of being a café owner?"

I bit my lip, torn between the giddy flutter in my chest and the nagging voice in my head reminding me that this couldn't go anywhere.

"You need to stop coming in here looking like that." I waved my hand up and down to indicate his utter deliciousness. "I told you not to make me fall for you."

He held up a hand, cutting me off. "No pressure, no expectations. I'm not going to take anything you don't want to give. If you just wanna be friends while you're here, we'll be friends. But might I suggest friends with benefits?"

It would be so easy to say yes, to let myself fall into the promise of his words and the warmth of his smile. What if we did just have a fling? We were young, nobody was looking to get married at twenty-two. I don't know why I was so fixated on this having to be some long-term commitment with him. We were flirting. We'd been on one whole date. He hadn't proposed or anything.

"What kind of benefits are we talking, Kingman?" I

waggled my eyebrows at him and waved a finger at him to come a little closer.

I could do this. I could have a fling with a Kingman.

Unless of course Xander threw a monkey in the wrench. Like he was about to. "Shit, my brother just pulled up out front. You've got to hide."

I didn't even give him a chance to respond before I shoved him toward the back room. But Xan could just as easily go back there as I could. My gaze shot everywhere, and I definitely considered shoving Hayes under the espresso machine. But I looked at the cubby, then up at all six foot eleventy-billion inches of muscle standing in front of me, and rethought.

The cleaning supplies closet. I shoved Hayes through the door and slammed it shut behind us, leaning against it with a shaky exhale.

Hayes raised an eyebrow, a slow grin spreading across his face. "Well, this is cozy."

I smacked his arm, fighting a smile of my own. "Shut up. I'm trying to save your ass from my brother's wrath."

His expression sobered, his hand coming up to cup my cheek. "Willa, I don't want to cause problems between you and Xander. If me being here is too much—"

I covered his hand with my own, my heart in my throat. "I want you here, Hayes. I do. But Xander... he's not going to make this easy on us."

Hayes leaned in, resting his forehead against mine. "Then we'll just have to be sneaky about it."

A laugh bubbled out of me, some of the tension easing from my shoulders. "Sneaky, huh? There is something fun about a forbidden—" I almost said romance. Eyeroll to myself. This wasn't some rom-com. This was my actual life. "—adventure."

"I like adventure." Hayes leaned forward, put both his hands on either side of my head against the door behind me, and kissed the holy bejeezus out of me.

For being the guy who was saving himself for the right girl, he sure was a good kisser. Like, my knees just about went out from under me and I had no intention of leaving this broom closet until they did, kind of kisser.

The little bell at the cash register made us jump apart, reality crashing back in. "Willa, customer, hello?"

I sighed, giving Hayes an apologetic look. "I'd better go deal with him. Wait here, okay? I'll get rid of him and then we can... talk more."

Hayes nodded, a glimmer of mischief in his eyes. "I'll be waiting."

Steeling myself, I slipped out of the supply closet, closing the door firmly behind me. Xander was pacing the length of the café, his agitation palpable.

"Xan, stop. Please."

He whirled on me, his eyes flashing. "What the hell? My life, my choices? Really? Like I'm Mom or something?"

I had said something similar, or perhaps the exact same words, to her when she tried to forbid me from going to Europe instead of college.

I crossed my arms, meeting his glare head-on. "You can't tell me who I can and cannot be friends with, or see, or date, or whatever. I'm home for a while and I'd rather not fight with you the whole time."

Some of the fight drained out of him, his shoulders

slumping. "I just... I don't want to see you get hurt, Willabean. I know you don't see it, but Kingman can be a dick. All he cares about is his career and he doesn't care who he steps on to get what he wants."

I softened, stepping closer to lay a hand on his arm. "I know you're trying to protect me, Xan. And I love you for it."

I didn't want to straight out lie because I was going to spend time with Hayes. It would be better just to keep that part of my life away from him.

Xander was quiet for a long moment, his jaw working. Finally, he blew out a breath and rubbed his eye with his thumb like he had a headache. "I don't like it. I don't like him. But... I'll try to back off. Just... be careful, okay?"

Of course I hadn't fooled him by omitting the truth. He was my twin brother after all. But it also meant I could see something going on with him too.

I hugged him, and at first, he flinched, like he'd forgotten what it felt like. "Thank you, Xan. That's all I ask."

He held me tight for a beat before releasing me, his gaze sliding to the supply closet door. "He's here, isn't he?"

I bit my lip, fighting a grin. "Maybe."

Xander rolled his eyes, but I caught a hint of a smile tugging at his mouth. "Right. Well, I'll leave you to... whatever it is you two are doing. But I'm watching him, Wills. One wrong move, and he's toast. I won't fucking let him hurt you."

With that, he strode out of the café, the bell jingling merrily in his wake. I wasn't sure exactly what had just happened. And I wondered how much of it Hayes had heard. Hopefully the mops cut off some of the sound.

The closet door creaked open, and Hayes peeked out, a hopeful expression on his face. "Is it safe to come out now?"

I laughed, feeling lighter than I had in days. "Yes, you dork. Now get out here and help me close up. I believe we have some sneaking around to do."

I'll say one thing about football players, they are hard workers with the right motivation. Those floors had never been mopped faster or been cleaner in the history of ever.

When we were done, I'd convinced myself to ask Hayes to climb over the fence into the backyard of my house to come over. Mostly because it was kind of hot to think of sneaking around with him.

He beat me to the punch. "Come over to my place?"

"I was gonna ask you the same thing."

"No way anyone in your family is going to interrupt our evening if you come to mine."

Good point. I checked up and down the street to make sure Xander wasn't parked somewhere nearby and spying on us and then got into Hayes's car with him. But when we pulled into his driveway, the lights in his living room were not only on, but flashing.

"Shit. I forgot. There's a live stream tonight." He looked at me like the last piece of pie that someone else had just ordered. "I can cut it short. I swear. Come in and I'll kick the guys out in just a few minutes."

"You're cute. Don't hurry. I've got my Kindle." I reached into my bag and pulled it out to show him. "I'm happy to read for a bit while you play. I don't want to take away time from hanging with your brothers."

He leaned in and brushed his lips across mine. "I've been hanging with them my whole life and I've only got a few months with you."

I grabbed the shoulder seams of his shirt and yanked him close. "You listen to me now, Mr. Kingman. You kiss me and tell me to enjoy my book while you play video games, and we'll get along just fine and dandy. You hear me?"

"Yes, ma'am." He grinned and did as he was told, once again kissing me till I forgot all about my book and his games and his brothers.

Until one of them knocked on the window.

"Quit making out and bring your girl inside already," one of Hayes's older brothers hollered at us and walked toward the front door with a curvy woman on his arm.

"Wait, do your brothers bring dates to games night?" Why did I have the feeling I was about to walk into a Kingman orgy or something?

PURR STATE UNIVERSITY

HAYES

Willa and I walked into my living room, and I pushed down a nervous niggle in my brain. She knew my family, the twins especially since we'd all been in the same class, but this felt like we were walking into a reception and there were going to be questions.

And that was the opposite of sneaking around. I hoped she was going to be okay with this. I could still call the live stream off if she wasn't.

"Hey, guys," I called out, greeting everyone. It was a full house tonight, and I liked that. Felt more like a home filled with family. "I brought new talent."

Five heads swiveled toward us. Flynn and Gryff gave a wave, but I could already sense the buzz of their twin telepathy rehashing our convo from last night. Fuckers had better be on their best behavior.

"Well, well, if it isn't the infamous Willa Rosemount," Everett said with a grin, standing up to greet her. "Nice to finally meet the girl who's got Hayes all twisted up."

I shot him a glare, but Willa just laughed. "Twisted up, is he? Good to know."

I rolled my eyes, gesturing to the others. "You know Flynn and Gryff. And if I'm lucky, you won't remember Everett. And that's Isak."

Isak waved from his spot on the couch, his eyes glued to the video game on the screen. He was only a freshman rookie barely getting game time for the Dragons and already had more followers than the rest of us combined, except for maybe Everett who was sort of FlipFlop famous. "Hey, Willa."

I introduced Penelope next, and I noticed how close she was sitting to Everett, their shoulders brushing. That was new. I made a mental note to grill the love guru on his own love life later. "And this is Penelope. She brings in the big numbers to our live streams when she's in town."

Willa gave her a smile and a wave. "Hi, Penelope. Nice to have another girl at this testosterone fest. Have you known these yahoos long?"

Flynn straightened up as if that raised his hackles. "Hey, who you calling yahoo?"

Willa wrinkled her nose and glared right back at him. "You."

"Right you are," Gryff interjected. "Carry on."

Pen laughed and threw some popcorn at the twins. She really was just one of the guys around us. "Just a few months. My boss is engaged to Declan."

Willa glanced over at me like I'd committed a gossip sin. "Your brother got engaged?"

"Two of them actually." The Kingmans were having a busy year when it came to the falling in love department. "Chris is finally fucking engaged to Trixie, and Declan is engaged to—" Flynn and Gryff played a drumroll on their consoles with their fingers. It was going to be fun to see Willa's reaction to this news. "—Kelsey Best."

"What?" Her head jerked back, and she looked at me like I was either on crack or a god. "Kelsey Best. As in the best songs of all time "Book Boyfriend" and "Cozy Kind of Love", and *The Choicest Voice* season three winner? That Kelsey Best?"

I shrugged. That was Kelsey, but while she was more famous than almost anyone else in the world, she was just a cool chick that was genuinely nice and almost family. "That's her."

"I maybe just peed my pants a little bit. What the hell, Kingman?" She gave me a playful punch on the shoulder. "You've been holding out on me."

I grabbed her fist and rubbed my thumb over her taut knuckles. "Everyone in the whole world seems to know, so you must have been living under a rock or something."

"Wait, you work for Kelsey?" Willa asked, her eyes wide as she jerked away from me, shoved Everett aside, and sat on the couch next to Pen.

"I'm her assistant." Pen grinned, nodding, and then did her now infamous intro to all her videos on social media, with the cute head tilt and the heart fingers. "Hey, Besties."

"These two are practically family at this point," Everett added, smirking at Willa's shocked expression.

Hmm. Family didn't look at family like that, Mr. Love Guru.

"Okay, I know I was out of the what's going on in America loop for the past three years, but damn." Willa shook her head, laughing. "I have clearly missed a lot."

"Oh, you have no idea," Gryff teased. "Stick around, and we'll catch you up on all the Kingman family drama. Can you say sex scandal?"

Willa was going to get permanent wrinkles in her forehead from how often her eyebrows were raised in surprise tonight.

The way she interacted with my brothers and Pen had a warm feeling spreading through my chest, filling in a place I hadn't realized felt empty until now. She fit in so effortlessly, trading quips with the boys and swapping travel stories with Penelope. This is what I'd been missing ever since I moved into this new house and started a big career.

Home.

Family.

Love.

Willa.

Shit.

She told me not to get too attached. Too fucking late.

"Who's ready for some football?" I pretended I hadn't just thought any of that and started the prep for our live stream. Nothing like some good, old-fashioned competition to keep me on track.

Showtime was coming up and I pulled out extra

controllers for Everett, Willa, and Pen. Pen waved it off and went and retrieved a couple of headsets, handing one to Willa too. "I like to play and whip the boys' butts on occasion, but it's more fun to talk shit. It'll be a riot if you'll join in."

Oh boy. This was going to be a wild live stream tonight. Good thing I'd upgraded my internet again.

Willa came over to me for help with her set up. "You don't think Xan watches your stream, do you?"

"It's a distinct possibility. We've got a pretty big following at DSU, and it is football." Seeing and hearing Willa on the live would definitely blow our sneaking around cover. "If you sit on that corner of the couch, you won't be on screen, and thanks to Isak, we've got a voice filter. You can sound like anything from a little kid to an old man."

I set Willa up with a generic username and showed her how to play around with the voice filters. "You don't have to be on if you don't want to. We can—"

"No, I want to. Xan never let me hang out with his friends like this." She put her headset on and looked cute as fuck wearing it. I wondered if it would be too geeky for me to ask her to wear it for me later. Only the headset.

"And we're live," Isak said and launched into our intro and naming tonight's sponsors. I walked Willa back over to the couch, blocking her body with mine until she was out of screen. Then I hopped on and introduced tonight's players.

"Tonight's matchup is guest star Everett Kingman and Isak playing as, you guessed it, the Denver Mustangs, against big time rivals, the twin terrors, Flynn and Gryff playing everyone's favorite losing team, the LA Bandits." The guys played their parts, cheering and booing like the dorks that we all were.

"We've got some special guests with us in the announcing booth tonight. Say hello to everyone's favorite Bestie, Penelope, and... super-secret sneaky guest announcer—" I glanced up at the screen name she'd chosen and snort-laughed so hard, I had to mute my mic for a second. "Please welcome... Patty Meowhomes."

Willa smacked her lips and said, "Thanks, Kingman, good to be here, looking forward to a watching you all play with your balls."

The chat on our live stream exploded. Lots of viewers asked if we actually had the KC Chefs QB in the house, because of course, Willa had chosen the voice filter that had her sounding like a twenty-something dude bro.

Pen leaned over to whisper something to Willa, and they both burst into laughter. I caught Everett's eye, and he grinned, shrugging as if to say, "Women, am I right?"

If Pen and Willa were already thick as thieves, that was one more point in my favor. It was harder to go off to lands unknown when you had lots of friends you were leaving behind.

We launched into the game, and while Willa was funny as shit with her commentary and trash talk, she actually knew the game and quickly won over the live stream with her game analysis. Of course, she also got a chuckle every time she changed her screen name. She went as Dijon Sanders, Puma Esiason, Joey Montuna, and my personal favorite of the night, Purringle McKringleberry - Purr State University.

I immediately changed my name to A.A. Ron Purrlawkay, and Pen became Stray Jay Kwelin. Even as the video game tournament heated up, I kept missing my announcements because I was stealing glances at Willa, loving how natural it felt to have her here, in my space, with my family.

I settled into the couch, Willa tucked against my side. Yeah, I could definitely get used to this. Sneaking around or not, having her here just felt... right.

Now I just had to make sure Xander didn't catch wind of our little arrangement. Because if he did, all bets were off.

But damn if it wasn't like the asshat had mental telepathy, because just as I thought that, Willa's phone buzzed. "Shit, it's Xander." She yanked off her headset and held up her phone.

On my way with pizza. My way of apologizing for being a dick

Fuck a duck. I muted my mic and noted that at least it was the fourth quarter. If the two of us bolted, we'd only be missed for a few moments. "How long do we have?"

Willa was already grabbing her shoes, her fingers flying over the screen as she typed a response. Her phone buzzed again. "Like three minutes."

"Okay, don't panic." I stood up, trying to think. "We can get you home before he arrives."

My brothers exchanged confused looks, but the twins caught on first.

"Xander?" Flynn asked, raising an eyebrow.

Willa nodded, biting her lip. "He's not exactly thrilled about me hanging out with Hayes."

"Understatement of the century," I muttered, and threw the sliding glass door to the backyard open. "Come on, this will be faster."

We raced out the door, ignoring the catcalls and whistles from my brothers. I led Willa through my backyard, our hands clasped tightly.

"There is no way I'm climbing over that fence." She ran toward it with me anyway, and she panted as we reached the fence separating our properties. "And don't you think for a minute you can just give me a boost. I'm a big girl and will not be responsible for taking out Denver's hope for the future with my ass."

I grinned, boosting her up. "You're cute if you think I can't pick you up, haul you over my shoulder, and carry you all the way up to your bedroom, Willa. These muscles are good for a lot more than just playing games."

"Why is that so hot?" She yanked on my shirt and pulled me down for a kiss.

"I'd tell you two to get a room, but I think that might be what you were trying to do." Isak jogged over with Flynn and Gryff right behind him.

"Welcome to Kingman Rescue Services." Without even needing to coordinate, Isak, Flynn, and Gryff lined themselves up in front of the fence, Isak on his hands and knees, Flynn half bent with his hands on his thighs, and Gryff with locked hands in front of his chest, like a set of Kingman man-made steps for Willa to crawl up and over.

"I feel like these guys have done this before," Willa said.

She scrambled up the guys and then stared over the

top and looked back at me. "I... I don't think I can jump from here. I'm gonna break my leg and then Xan will know for sure that we've been sneaking around."

I took a couple of steps back, took a running start, and launched myself off Isak, who grunted and swore at me. But in one big leap, I landed superhero style in Willa's backyard. Then I reached up and steadied her, my hands gripping her waist and she crawled-rolled-climbed over the fence.

"Easy there, sweetheart." I helped her down, reluctant to let go. "You good?"

Willa nodded, her face flushed and her hair mussed. "Yeah, I think so."

We stared at each other for a long moment, the tension crackling between us. I wanted nothing more than to pull her into my arms and pick up where we'd left off in the car.

But the flash of headlights and the sound of an engine had us springing apart, reality crashing back in.

"That's Xander's car," Willa hissed, her eyes wide. "You need to go, now."

I hesitated, hating the thought of leaving her to face her brother alone. "Are you sure you're okay?"

She softened, reaching up to cup my cheek. "I'm fine, Hayes. I promise. I've got years of practice handling Xander."

I leaned into her touch for a fleeting second before stepping back. "Text me later?"

"You know I will." With a wink and a blow of a kiss, she turned and raced toward her back door.

I watched until she disappeared inside, my heart

hammering in my chest. That had been close. Too close. This whole secret relationship thing was going to be a lot harder than I'd thought.

But the memory of Willa's smile, the feel of her hand in mine, the way she fit so seamlessly into my life... it was all worth it.

We just had to be careful. More than careful. And I couldn't lose Willa. Not now, not when I was just starting to realize how much fun we were having together.

I jumped back over the fence, right into the knowing looks from my brothers.

"Sneaking around?" Isak asked, his tone disapproving. Great. My one and only little brother thought I was a dumbass. Maybe I was.

I nodded, slinking back toward the house. "For now. But I have a feeling things are about to get a lot more complicated."

Gryff clapped me on the shoulder, but he had none of his usual smirky grins for me. "Take it from someone with experience being a twin. It is fucking hard to keep a secret from the other half. Almost impossible."

He and Flynn shared a wise nod with each other. Isak frowned and didn't say anything more.

"I know, I know." It was hard to keep a secret in this family too. "It wasn't my idea. But I'm still trying to woo her, so I'll take whatever I can get."

"Woo her?" Everett joined us in the yard. "You've been reading those dating books again, haven't you?"

"Shut up. Your be-yourself advice wasn't useful. I needed a plan with actionable steps." Now that plan needed some serious revision. I didn't remember seeing anything on secret relationships in anything I'd studied. I'd have to dig deeper though, because there were always resources available to learn anything if you knew where to look for them.

"Wait, what about the live stream? Where's Pen?" The TV still flashed in the living room, but I sure as shit hoped none of them were mic'd up for the events and subsequent conversation we'd just had.

Everett did not answer that question.

Isak waved it off. "I've got an ad running from one of our new sponsors and more in the queue if we need them. It's fine."

How many sponsors did we have? Because I needed time to think through this problem and figure out a better solution.

And I'd start tomorrow morning. I was hitting the hardware store to buy some gate hinges and a magnetic latch to build an invisible gate between our two backyards. If we had to sneak around behind Xander's back, we were going to do it right.

COFFEE, TEA, OR ME?

WILLA

I was just finishing up another chapter of the book I was reading, because, well, there certainly weren't any customers. Which was starting to worry me. How was I supposed to keep Cool Beans afloat without people coming to buy coffee? That marketing thing Liam had set up with the cat shelter was starting to sound better and better. But the next one wasn't for a few more weeks.

Until then, I'd cut back on most everyone's hours to at least try to save on labor. I had help in the mornings to open, but after that first morning rush, we were pretty much dead. Until Hayes showed up.

Right now, the only time I got to see him was when he came to the café. Xan had taken to showing up at the house most nights, pretending he simply wanted to spend time with me while I was home. I saw right through him but hadn't yet figured out how in the world to tell him to back off. And he knew it.

Right on time, I spotted Hayes walking into the café, a grin on his face. My heart did a little flip, and I chastised the fickle organ for trying so hard to talk me into falling for him. It wasn't going to work. This was just a fling. It was fun and short term, so no one got hurt.

"Hey, you," I said as he approached the counter. "The usual?"

He leaned in, his eyes sparkling with mischief. "If the usual includes a daily dose of caffeine and a kiss from the cute barista."

I rolled my eyes, fighting a blush. Falling into the easy banter had become second nature over the past few days. "Flattery will get you everywhere, Kingman."

We chatted as I made his usual-unusual order. He always got a latte, but he let me make a blend of flavors to surprise him and he had to guess what it was. I'd been concocting today's drink in my mind all afternoon. No way he'd guess this one.

The espresso machine made a funny sputter and spit the last few drops into the little shot glasses. It was throwing a fit and I did not know how to placate it. A few squirts of this and a few squirts of that, and I had today's special ready to go.

I handed it over and watched carefully as he took a few tentative sips. "You're never going to guess this one."

"I guessed Snickers, Girl Scout Samoa cookie, and Peeps, so I think I'm winning." He took another sip and winked.

I hated when he did that because it made my tummy

do the same funny flips as my heart. The two were in cahoots.

"Huh." He took a longer sip this time and narrowed his eyes at me. "You cheated. This isn't a latte with some flavors in it at all, is it?"

"Expand your horizons, Kingman. The entire world doesn't drink coffee." I certainly didn't. Blech.

"This tastes like Christmas flavored coffee. I'm getting strong cinnamon, nutmeg, and something else." He smacked his tongue against the roof of his mouth. "Is that... cardamom?"

"How do you know that?"

"This is a chai latte with an espresso shot in it. Fuck yeah." He gave himself a fist pump and I wrinkled my nose at him.

"It's called a dirty chai, just so you know, and I was sure I had you on that one."

"Kelsey makes the most amazing chai cookies. Otherwise you would have stumped me. I swear." He leaned over the counter. "Now pay up."

"Fine." I gave him the kiss he was owed, and he cupped the back of my head, taking this a whole lot deeper than was appropriate for a public place. Or maybe that was just what my imagination was doing fantasizing about what else he could do with his tongue.

I was just about to count his teeth with my own tongue as a guide when I spotted Xander's stupid car pulling up. Again.

"Shoot, it's Xander," I sighed. This was getting to be a damn routine. "Off you go to hide."

Hayes didn't need to be told twice. He ducked behind

the counter just as my brother walked in, another guy in tow.

"Hey, Willabean," Xander said, his grin a little too wide. "I want you to meet someone."

I plastered on a smile, my stomach sinking. I had a feeling I knew exactly where this was going.

"Willa, this is Cai," Xander continued, gesturing to the tall, athletic-looking guy beside him, who coincidentally was also wearing a DSU Dragons hoodie. "He's on the team with me."

Surprise, surprise.

Cai stepped forward, offering his hand. "Nice to meet you, Willa. Xander's told me a lot about you."

I shook his hand, shooting my brother a subtle glare. "Has he now? All good things, I hope."

Xander clapped Cai on the shoulder, his smile turning sly. "Oh, definitely. In fact, I thought maybe you two might like to grab dinner sometime. You know, get to know each other better."

Cai glanced over at Xander with more than a little surprise. Great, even he didn't know this was a set up. How embarrassing.

I gritted my teeth. I was going to murder my brother. Possibly with this espresso machine, because it was the handiest weapon I could find. "That's really sweet of you, Xan, but I'm not really looking to date right now. Running the coffee shop is keeping me pretty busy."

Cai's shoulders relaxed, and he nodded. "No worries, I get it. Maybe I'll just come hang out at your coffee shop sometime."

"Sure, that'd be great," I said, trying to sound enthusiastic. The last thing I needed was another complication in my already messy love life. Hanging out with any of Xander's friends or teammates was definitely a complication. And he knew it.

Xander frowned, clearly not happy with my response. "Come on, Willa. You can't work all the time. Live a little. Cai's family is Hmong. You guys could swap stories of Vietnam."

Cai looked at Xan like he was on crack, and I felt bad for the guy.

"Right, I was teaching there earlier this year. But I'm stuck in good old Thornminster for the time being."

"Oh, right. Well, that's cool. I've never actually been, but my grandmother sure wants me to go." Poor Cai looked like he wanted to flee the country right now.

I opened my mouth to say something about how much I liked living in Ho Chi Minh City but hadn't yet made it the north were the Hmong people traditionally lived, when I was cut off by a sudden hissing and sputtering from the espresso machine. I whirled around, my eyes widening in horror as steam billowed out from the top.

"No, no, no," I muttered, frantically pressing buttons, and turning knobs. "Not now, please not now."

I glanced down at Hayes whose eyes were as wide as mine. Not that he could do anything. It was too late anyway. With a final, pathetic wheeze, the machine went dead, leaving me staring at it in dismay.

"What the hell was that?" Xander asked, peering across the counter.

I forced a laugh, hoping it didn't sound as hysterical as I felt. "Just a little technical difficulty."

"I'd better get going," Cai said, glancing between me and the defunct espresso machine. "But it was really nice meeting you, Willa. Maybe I'll see you around."

"Yep, super, come in for... a drink anytime," I said distractedly, already wondering how much a repair was going to cost. Or worse, a whole new machine. "Thanks for stopping by."

Once Cai was out the door, Xan hissed at me with the same vehemence as the espresso machine. "You could have been friendlier. I'm trying to help you out."

"No you aren't, you're being a dick, and you told me you were going to knock that shit off." I swirled my hand in a circle. "Remember, you swore on your pizza?"

"You're a brat." The espresso machine rattled again, and Xan stepped away. "Good luck with that. See you later, beanie."

I'd yell at him for not offering to help, but I still had Hayes at my feet.

As soon as Xander was gone, Hayes popped up from his hiding spot, his brow furrowed. "You okay?"

I sighed, running a hand through my hair. "Not really. This is a disaster. I can't run a coffee shop without an espresso machine, and I have no idea if there's room in the budget for repairs. In fact, I don't even know if there is a budget at all. Accounting is not my strongest suit, and I don't want to bother the Guncles. They're on their way to the Drake Passage to see the penguins."

Damn, I wish I was on my way to see penguins.

"I can help you with the books." He pushed the now sweaty strands of hair from my face. "Numbers come easy to me. I even do half my family's taxes for them."

"I can't ask you to do that."

He stepped closer and pulled me into a hug. I melted into his embrace, some of the tension draining out of me.

"You can, and I will help," he murmured, rubbing soothing circles over my shoulder blades, right where all my tension was building up.

I don't know how he did it, always making me feel like he had my back. But I think it was a fundamental difference in his family and mine. I'd seen it even just playing games with him and his brothers. They were all there for each other in every little way.

That was the opposite of the Rosemounts. Our family motto might as well be winner takes all, loser gets the shaft. They didn't mean it, I knew that. But it was how they made me feel.

Somewhere deep inside where I wasn't ready to look, I wished I was a Kingman. And not as a sister.

With a heavy sigh, I flipped the sign on the café door to "Closed" and locked up. The broken espresso machine had effectively killed any chance of staying open for the rest of the day.

Hayes followed me back to the small office, his presence a comforting warmth at my back. I collapsed into the chair in front of the laptop, rubbing my temples.

"I guess we should take a look at the books," I said, my mind laced with exhaustion before we even started. I did not enjoy digging into the details like this. I was a whole lot better with people than I was data. "Let's see how much I can afford to spend on repairs."

I doubted it was much based on the first weeks' worth of business.

Hayes perched on the edge of the desk, his hand coming to rest on my shoulder. "Okay, let's boot it up and see what we're working with."

I opened up the financial spreadsheet, but the rows of numbers swam before my eyes. I couldn't focus, and the only thing that kept me staring at it for as long as I did was the way Hayes's thumb traced soft circles on my skin. After I entered today's sales and the row calculated this week's running total, I groaned and slammed the laptop shut. We were in the red. Literally. That stupid little box turned bright red, taunting me with its negativity.

Crappity crap. I hated feeling so absolutely inept. I always did whenever I was home surrounded by my family's expectations. Which I never lived up to.

"I shouldn't have said I could do this." I sank into my chair. I also shouldn't have said that out loud. What I didn't need was Hayes thinking I was a whiny, weak bitch who didn't care about anyone but myself.

Hayes cupped my head and gave my temple a soft kiss, then slowly opened the laptop back up. "I think it's my turn."

He pulled me out of the chair and took over, typing away, making the spreadsheet move in ways I didn't even know were possible. He even made some pretty graphs that, while colorful, didn't mean a damn thing to me.

"Huh. Umm, I think we're going to be here a while, babe." He stared back at the screen and honestly, his face looked a bit horrified. "These books are a mess. Make us some tea? I'm gonna need some caffeine."

Tea? Since when did he drink tea? "Don't you mean coffee?"

He glanced up at me and gave one of those small don't-be-ridiculous headshakes. "You don't like coffee."

Exqueeze me? I put my hand over my heart, mightily offended. "Of course I do. I'm working in my family's coffee shop. I'm a barista for goodness' sake."

Hayes spun the chair around, yanked me into his lap, and gave me a long, lingering, extra tongue-filled kiss. "You taste like some kind of tea that I don't know the name of. Never once have you tasted like coffee."

"Maybe I just don't want coffee breath." I gave him a so-there smirk. Besides, coffee breath wasn't conducive to getting kissed.

"The first day I was in here, you told me I was boring for wanting a cup of black coffee."

"Black coffee is boring. Who drinks hot bean water plain?"

"See, just the fact that you refer to coffee as hot bean water is disdainful. You come up with all kinds of crazy flavor combinations that taste more like ice cream than java, the cups with your name on them always have the strings with the little paper flags hanging off the side, and," he poked me in the chest, right over my heart, "you broke the espresso machine."

I had no response to that. He was on a roll now, and it was scary correct.

"Not only do you not like coffee, I think you've got a bit of a mad-on for it. I'd go so far as to say you hate coffee."

"I... don't..." He'd noticed all of that in the ten-ish days I'd been here and figured out what no one else in my family ever had? "I don't know whether to be weirded out that you've been coffee stalking me, or relieved that you've figured out my deepest darkest secret."

I wrapped my arms around his neck and leaned in for another kiss. He whispered against my lips, "I want to know all your secrets, Willa."

He was the first person I ever wanted to share the real me with, and that was bad, because I was already ignoring my own advice and getting way too attached to Hayes Kingman.

WELCOME TO THE KINGMAN LIFE

HAYES

It took some long hours to work through the mess Willa's uncles had left the books in. By the time I had them sorted out, it was real damn clear that George had been floating the business for years. It wasn't even close to profitable.

At least he'd left plenty of money in the business bank account so that Willa didn't have to worry about actually paying the bills, but she was not fucking happy when I showed her how much money the place was bleeding.

"The good news is that you can afford to hire the maintenance guy to fix the espresso machine." I showed her the details I'd found. "And you don't have to worry about paying him, because it seems George has him on retainer."

Willa nodded and sagged a little. "I don't know if that's

good or bad. Good for the moment, but how often does that piece of crap break down?"

"According to the books, a lot. And if you look here, the shop had no income on the days following, so I think Liam had the same idea as you and shut the place up for those days."

"I think maybe I'd better cook up some new fancy tea drinks and marketing to go with, because if I'm going to stay open, we have to sell more than our currently out of stock lattes." She yawned and stretched, putting her hands on her back, and looking up at the ceiling.

I followed her in that yawn. Practice was going to be rough in the morning.

"Holy crap, Hayes, it's getting light out, the sun is coming up." She pointed out the door to the front of the coffee shop. There was only a crack in the door between the two spaces, but a thin ray of light shined through. "We were here all night. I'm so sorry. I didn't mean to keep you here fixing this mess with me that long."

Well, shit. Wouldn't be the first time I'd pulled an all-nighter studying and then had to hit the field. I stood and stretched and then wrapped my arms around Willa, resting my head on the top of hers. "Don't worry about me. I got this, sweetheart. Sleep is for suckers."

It wasn't. I full well knew the importance of rest, but I also knew how to push my body to its limits. For Willa, I would push to the end.

"At least let me make you a strong cup of coffee. I might think it's gross, but I have a feeling it's all I'll be selling this morning." She made a stink face. "Unless I can convert more people to the goodness that is Earl Grey tea - hot."

"Make it so, Number One." I did the Captain Picard voice and two-fingered point, which was one of the dorkier things I'd ever done in my life. But it made Willa smile, and I swear I'd dress up in a full Star Trek uniform if it would make her happy.

"Get out of here with that impression. That was the worst." She shoved me toward the door, and I let her because I really did have to go home and grab my gear for practice.

An hour later, I was on the field, lining up for the next play. The familiar rush of adrenaline coursed through my veins, better than any cup of coffee.

The ball snapped, and I sprinted down the field, dodging defenders left and right. Chris's pass spiraled through the air, a perfect arc heading straight for me. I leaped, snagging the ball out of the air, and tucking it securely against my chest as I landed in the end zone.

"Nice catch, Kingman," Coach called out, clapping his hands. "That's the kind of move we need to win this weekend. Keep it up, kid."

I grinned, tossing the ball back to Chris. "Just doing my job, sir."

We were all going to need to bring our A-game if we wanted to take down the Miami Sharks this weekend. That meant running those pass plays again and again. Practice continued, with each of us pushing ourselves to the limit. By the time Coach blew the final whistle, I was drenched in sweat but feeling good about the way we were playing.

I also needed a nap. But what I was going to do was finally get that cup of coffee and hopefully bring a few more patrons along with me.

In the locker room, as we changed out of our gear, I brought up the idea that had been brewing in my mind to my brothers. "Hey, guys, Willa's been having a tough time getting a steady flow of customers into the coffee shop. Would you come by with me this afternoon and post something on your socials? I figure if people think it's a Mustangs hangout, they'll come by. Give her a little boost, you know?"

Everett looked up from tying his shoes, a grin spreading across his face. "Count me in. I've been meaning to try out her crazy latte concoctions."

Shit. I'd forgotten about the fact she couldn't make lattes. Maybe this wasn't a good idea. "Uh, her espresso machine is down, but she makes a mean Earl Grey latte."

Everett made a face at that. But Dec and Chris didn't seem bothered by it.

"I'll call Trix," Chris chimed in and pulled out his phone. A couple of texts later and he gave me the thumbs up.

"She's been itching to find a new coffee shop to write at when the words aren't flowing for her. And I do love it when her words flow." He wiggled his eyebrows suggestively, and I threw a towel at his head. His fiancée was writing a romance novel, and according to him, it was all sex scenes so far.

Declan shook his head at Chris, then clapped me on the shoulder. "I'm down too. But unless she's staffed and prepared to have the Besties descend on her shop, I'd better not ask Kels to join us."

An hour later, we all strolled into the coffee shop, bell jingling merrily above the door. Willa looked up from the counter, her eyes widening as she took in the sight of four burly football players crowding into her tiny café.

"Whoa." She gave me a wave and did this cute WTF head tilt. "What are you all doing here?"

I leaned over the counter, giving her a quick peck on the cheek. "We're here to support our favorite barista, of course. And maybe bring in some new business while we're at it." I showed her the posts we'd each done on InstaSnap, and Everett was already filming a FlipFlop with his feet up on one of the tables near the window.

She laughed, shaking her head. "Oh my god. Thank you. Okay, boys, what'll it be? Just don't order too fast, because the only espresso I've got at the moment is from my shiny new Nespresso from Wally World. But I promise I've got all kinds of other tasty beverages to caffeinate your afternoon."

Willa pointed to a chalkboard sign that she'd clearly spent quite a bit of time on. It had drawings of flags and bits of maps and indicated an around-the-world tour of hot beverages including Mexican hot chocolate, Earl Grey tea lattes, and something called café sua da from Vietnam.

"You came up with all of those ideas today?" God, I loved how creative she was, and under pressure at that. It was hot.

"Yep, and I think you boys had better become really familiar with making them, fast, because I'm about to recruit you as baristas." She pointed to the front of the café where the street parking was quickly filling up and more people were walking up the street, most wearing Mustangs jerseys and other paraphernalia.

What followed was a serious rendition of The Barista Bull in the China Tea Shop, a four act comedy where my brothers and I attempted to help Willa handle the unexpected rush.

Declan managed to burn himself on the Nespresso, while Chris slid glass mugs of coffee down the counter to waiting customers who were not as skilled at catching them as he was at passing. Everett, bless him, just ignored the actual orders Willa threw at him and started mixing up teas and syrups and other strange concoctions that I could tell by some patrons' faces were truly vile flavor combinations. But none of the chaos fazed anyone since they were also getting to interact with their hometown favorite Mustangs and get lots and lots of photo ops.

Through it all, Willa remained a beacon of calm, guiding us through it all with a smile on her face. She thrived in this chaos, and it was the sexiest thing to watch her in her element. She was so good with people and had them all charmed the second she took their orders. Even Everett couldn't hold a candle to the way Willa made people feel welcome.

I felt a swell of pride and something deeper, something I wasn't quite ready to name.

As the rush finally died down and the last customer left with their latte-ish drink in hand, Willa turned to us, her hands on her hips. "Well, that was... an experience."

"We killed it, didn't we?" Everett asked, grinning broadly despite the smear of chocolate sauce on his cheek.

Willa laughed, tossing him a towel. "Let's just say it's a good thing you boys have football to fall back on. I don't think the barista life is for you."

I flipped her open sign to closed. My brothers and Trixie, who I hadn't even seen come in, said their goodbyes, and headed out. I lingered behind, needing to be near her and all that energetic charm a little longer.

"Thank you for today," she murmured, resting her head against my chest. "I know it wasn't exactly smooth sailing, but it meant a lot that you all tried so hard to help the coffee shop out."

I kissed the top of her head, breathing in the sweet scent of sugar and tea. "It was fun. But I won't be able to do it tomorrow or Sunday, we've got a game in Florida."

"Oh my god, I wish I was going to Florida." She fake pouted and her shoulders dropped. "I cannot tell you how much I miss the humidity. Why didn't anyone remind me I was going to need a gallon of lotion a day in this damn three-hundred-days-of-sunshine hell hole of a mountain desert?"

I tingle ran up my spine and ended in me blurting out, "Then why don't you come with me?"

"Yeah, right." She didn't think my offer was legitimate. I was more serious than a roughing the receiver flag on the play.

"For real, flower." This was the perfect chance for me to show her that I could give her the freedom and adventure she craved. "Liam closed when the espresso machine was down anyway, so the regulars won't even blink an eye if you're not open. And we've got room on the jet for you with us. Come with me. It will be fun."

"You say 'on the jet' like that's no big deal." She gave me a sideways look and she still wasn't convinced. "You know it isn't, right? Not everyone has a family jet."

"The Kingmans aren't any family." And if anyone could help me show Willa life in Denver was interesting, it would be my family. Today, more than ever, showed me I should have been relying on my brothers to help me win Willa's favor. She had fun with us today.

"That's the understatement of the year." She bit her lip and smiled up at me from under her lashes. "I really would like to come along though. If you're sure it's okay if I invade your man jet."

Yes. I got her. "Jules and the girls were already planning to come along too, so it will be perfectly boy-girl, boy-girl. I was going to be the odd man out, so see, you have to come to even the numbers out."

"By girls, you mean some friends of Jules?"

Oh, I was definitely waiting until tomorrow to let her find out she'd be riding in the jet with Kelsey Best. To the rest of us, she was just one of the girls, and she and Jules were definitely friends, so this wasn't a lie. Just a fun secret. "Yeah."

As we boarded the Kingman private jet, I couldn't help but grin at the look of awe on Willa's face. "This is really how you travel to every game?" she asked, running her hand along the plush leather seats.

"Perks of being a Kingman," I said with a wink, guiding her to a seat at the plane's table next to Jules and across from Penelope. "Stick with me, kid, and you'll go places."

She laughed, settling in as my dad and Everett followed us onto the plane. I watched with more than a little giddiness as she easily fell into conversation with Jules and Penelope, their chatter filling the cabin.

A few minutes later, Chris and Trixie boarded. Upon seeing the table of girls, Trixie shoved Chris into the seat next to me and sat with the other ladies. Then Declan and Kelsey joined us. Willa's eyes widened as Kelsey greeted her warmly and sat across from her.

"I'll have to stop by your coffee shop when we get back," Kelsey said, her megawatt smile genuine. "Declan's been raving about your interesting drink offerings."

Willa just nodded until Kelsey's dachshund poked its head up out of her bag and made everyone laugh. "Is this the infamous Wiener the Pooh? I follow her on InstaSnap."

Pooh wiggled and barked until Kelsey handed her over to Willa. "She sure seems to like you."

"I think she probably smells my cat, Seven of Nine Lives."

Trixie snort-laughed and pulled out her phone. "You named your cat after a Star Trek character? I have a feeling we're going to be BFFs, because this is my pet rooster named Luke Skycocker."

She showed her screen to Willa and that was all it took for my girl to relax. After the flight got underway, Willa showed even more how she fit in with my family so fucking easily. She already had the girls in the palm of her hand when she recommended some kind of romance novels about wolf shifters who played college football. She instantly won my brothers over even more than she had yesterday at the coffee shop when she started talking stats with them.

My dad watched on with a quiet smile, and during a lull in the conversation, he leaned over to me, his voice low. "She's a keeper, son. Don't let that one get away."

I swallowed hard, my heart swelling at his approval. "I don't plan on it, Pops. Trust me."

When we arrived at the hotel, I walked Willa to the room she'd be sharing with Jules, trying to ignore the pang of disappointment that I couldn't have her all to myself.

"Sorry about the separate rooms," I said, rubbing the back of my neck. "Coach's rules."

She smiled up at me, her eyes sparkling with mischief. "It's okay. I'm sure Jules and I will find some way to entertain ourselves."

As if on cue, Jules held up her phone with Kelsey's face on the screen. "Ladies, pre-game pajama party in my room. Presidential suite, five minutes. Be there or be square."

Willa laughed, pressing a quick kiss to my cheek. "Duty calls. See you in the morning, superstar."

She took a few steps away, but I snagged her hand and pulled her back to me, giving her a quick kiss. Then I pressed my lips to her ear. "I've already proven I'm pretty good at sneaking around, so don't be surprised if you find yourself kidnapped to my room after bed check tonight."

"Why, Mr. Kingman, aren't you the naughty little rule breaker?" She laughed and wagged her finger at me. Then she broke away and jogged after Jules, giving me one last wink before she got into the elevator.

"Flower, there is nothing little about me." And tonight, I was going to prove that to her.

SNEAKING AROUND IS SEXY

WILLA

There was something a little too hilarious about Hayes sneaking me into his hotel room. We were hundreds of miles away from Xander's disapproving brotherdom, and we were still playing the forbidden lovers.

And this time... I kind of hoped we were actually going to get to the lovers part. Even if I was a tiny bit nervous about it. I'm sure I'd get over it when the time came.

Hayes popped his head out of the stairwell door two floors below Kelsey's suite, looked left, looked right, and said, "Come on, the coast is clear."

I seriously had to hold in my giggle when he dragged me along the wall, then ducked into the little bay with the ice machine. "Shh... someone's coming."

He pressed his body against mine, using it to block any prying eyes from seeing me. "You'd better kiss me so they think we're just some ordinary horny couple who can't make it to our room and not an escaped running back and his ball bunny breaking the rules."

"Good thinking." He crushed his lips down on mine and I shoved my hands into his hair, not wanting this kiss to end.

The ice machine dropped a load of cubes in a crash, and I jerked away with a gasp. Hayes chuckled and I smacked him on the arm. "That scared the bejeesus out of me. You've got me all worked up about getting caught."

"Then we'd better get to safety fast." He stuck his head out of the ice machine cubby, looked around, then turned to me with a finger to his lips. We crept down the hall toward his room, hand in hand, sliding along the walls past any number of doors that could be concealing his teammates or coaches. He made out as if we were hiding from the guards in some spy thriller, and I'd never had more fun.

We stopped, and he tapped his key card against a door, but the light went red instead of green. He tapped it again, and then looked up at the number. "Shit, this isn't my room."

A voice came from inside. "Just a minute."

"Run, Willa, run." He shoved me in front of him and covered the door like he was protecting me from the bad guy squad hot on our heels. "That's Coach."

Sprinting was not my usual mode of transportation, but I ran like there was a pack of zombies after us. Hayes burst past me, grabbed my hand, and hauled me around the corner, through the elevator area, and down the opposite hallway. Another three doors down, and he swiped his card over the lock on another door, and it popped right open.

We dashed inside and shut the door tight. I leaned against it breathing fast and hard. Hayes came over and caged me against the door with his arms on either side of my head.

"You," pant, "did," pant, "that," pant, "on purpose." No way I believed he'd gotten the location of his hotel room that wrong.

"Now why would I do that?" He shook his head and narrowed his eyes. "Do you know the consequences of having a woman in our room the night before a game?"

I'd heard about the tens of thousands of dollars in fines that pro football players had to pay for infractions of some of the silliest rules you've ever heard. "Worth it for the adrenaline rush?"

"That did get my heart racing and my blood pumping." He ran the back of his knuckles down my cheek and over the pulse point in my throat. "And made you pink-cheeked and out of breath."

"I can think of way better ways for you to get me hot and bothered, Kingman." God, I loved kissing him. I stood on my tiptoes, but I wasn't tall enough to reach his mouth with mine if he didn't meet me part way, so I grabbed the collar of his shirt and tugged him to right where I wanted him. "For example, like this."

We came together so fervently that our mouths mashed, our teeth clacked, and our tongues slipped and slid over each other. Hayes groaned into my mouth and pressed me harder against the door, grabbing one of my thighs and lifting it so he could press his body that much closer to mine.

If ever I wished for a magical power, it was right now. It would be really great if I could just wiggle my nose to turn out the lights, make our clothes disappear, and be under the covers with him. Attachments be damned, I wanted Hayes Kingman so badly I ached from the inside out. But he wasn't a fuck-up-against-the-door kind of guy.

I needed to be more careful about what this would mean to him. If this truly was his first time, it ought to be a little more special than a door banger. The least we could do is make it to a bed.

He stroked his hand up the back of my thigh and I'd never been happier that I'd pulled out my sundresses from Vietnam for this trip to Florida. Bed, schmed, maybe we'd find it later.

I reached for the hem of his shirt and lifted it to pull it up over his head. He snagged it with his free hand and yanked on it so hard the buttons went flying. He tossed the whole thing over his shoulder, fast enough that I took only one breath before our mouths were seeking and searching for each other again.

His bare chest under my hands was more magical than any damn superpowers anyway, and I wanted more of him. I grabbed for his belt, and there was something about hearing a buckle slide free and a zipper go down that made me weak in the knees.

I'd been denying myself the touch, feel, and everything else about this man for so long that now I was practically in a frenzy to finally get to be with him. It was going to be really hard to slow down if he wasn't actually ready to have sex with me. I should check in with him on that... and I would... in a minute.

With his pants slug low across his hips, I arched my back into him, and couldn't help the little whimper that escaped as my lower belly rubbed across his boxer-covered erection. Hayes paused and broke the frantic kiss. "Willa, we don't have to do anything more than this. We don't have to do something you're not absolutely sure you want to do."

I pressed my lips together to keep from snort-laughing. "I was just going to... I think I'm the one who is supposed to be saying that to you."

"If you're worried I won't be able to," he bit one side of his lip, "please you in bed, I assure you, I have been studying."

First of all, I was dying at how cute he was talking about pleasing me in bed. Who talks like that? Hayes Kingman is who. And also... he'd been studying? Had he been born with all these green flags or was he simply raised this way? "By studying, do you mean watching porn?"

He grinned and shrugged. "Some. There are some very educational things on the internet."

"You adorable horndog." I was looking forward to him showing me what he'd learned. "But you know I meant because you, you're, you..." How did I put this so I didn't embarrass him? I knew full well that a man's sexual prowess was a point of pride, and I didn't want to wound his right before he got to show me all that prowess.

"Because I haven't done this before?" He nibbled his way from a sensitive spot on my throat up to my ear.

"Aren't you, like, saving yourself for the right girl or something?" I didn't want to admit it, even to myself, but I did not feel like the right girl for him at all. In fact, I was quite sure I was the wrong one.

Hayes laughed at me this time. "Virginity is a social construct, babe. I don't give a damn about that."

He didn't? "You don't?"

But...

He pulled me down the hall toward the main part of the room, where there was a desk, a couch, a TV, and the bed. "No. That is not why I haven't had sex."

Huh. Why did I think he'd said that? Had I made it up in my mind? Because there had to be a good reason why a hottie like Hayes wasn't getting laid left and right. "It's not for religious reasons, is it?"

"Not even close." He turned us so the back of my knees bumped against the bed.

"Old-fashioned values?" I doubted we'd be in this situation if he was a fan of Victorian or even Old West morays. "Because you should know this doesn't mean we're getting married in the morning."

He laughed again. "Nope. That's not it either. Willa? Are you stalling? Because I meant it when I said we don't have to do anything. We can lay here and watch a movie if you want. I might need a cold shower first, but sweetheart, I only want to do whatever you're comfortable with. I mean it."

I made the mistake of glancing at the enormous king-sized bed, and with that one look, I knew I was going to look like a huge dork even trying to climb up on this thing. The mattress was almost up to my waist. This hotel definitely catered to giant football players and not short teacher-barista-cat ladies.

Wait, was I stalling? Nooo. Yes? Maybe.

"If it's not any of those..."

Before I even had a chance to either finish my sentence or look like a roly-poly princess trying to avoid a pea, Hayes grabbed me by the hips and literally tossed me onto the center of the mattress. I squealed like a little girl until he and all those naked, rippling muscles climbed up with me and crawled over me. Then I squealed on the inside like a full-grown woman about to get laid by one of the hottest men on the planet.

"Willa?" He looked down into my eyes, and if I wasn't already on the bed, I'd have fallen down. Or fallen in love.

"Yes?" That came out more of a squeak than the sex kitten whisper I'd meant it to be. I couldn't be in love with this man. It wasn't fair to either of us.

He licked his lips and all I could do was stare. "Can we save the questions for later?"

"Uh-huh." I'd never ask him another question again if he'd just kiss me and not stop.

He blinked really slowly and let out a soft sigh. And... oh my heart, he was nervous. "Good."

His nerves were sweet and lovable, and somehow had my own rearing their ugly head. I knew I was the more experienced one here, but I'd only been with two other guys before him. I didn't want him to have some unrealistic expectations about what he was about to see and what would happen. "But you know how you said you've been watching porn to, you know, get ready for this?"

"Yeah." A dash of pink flashed under each of his cheekbones. I hadn't meant to make him feel abashed about that. This was about my hang-ups. No, that wasn't quite right. I wasn't ashamed of what I looked like, of my body. But I also knew that the world was a judgy place, and I might as well set the right expectations from the start. Because the sooner I did, the sooner I could get over it and... get under Hayes.

And I really, really wanted to be with him. Here goes.

"Under this dress is not the body of a porn star. I've got stretch marks and a squishy belly and my boobs haven't been perky since I was twelve." I didn't mean for that to sound like a warning label about what I looked like. It's not like I wanted to warn him off.

We were so opposite, and I didn't know if I actually believed in the whole opposites attract thing. There was this tiny part inside of me that wasn't ready to believe that the sexy, over-achieving, celebrity, sports star was attracted to the flighty, chubby, bookworm with only a semi-permanent job.

That mean girl's voice inside my head asked what he was doing with a girl like me.

I didn't want to think that way. But I had to admit, after years of feeling like a failure at school, with my family, even friends, I did not fulfill society's expectations on most things. My body just being one. So far Hayes hadn't seemed to care about any of my shortcomings. But would this be the thing that put that disappointed look in his eyes?

I'd seen it before. My whole life. I never met anyone's expectations. Maybe this would set the right one so no one was disappointed.

"I don't want a porn star, Willa. I want you." I looked anywhere but at him. He pushed a hand into my hair and didn't let me turn my face away. Hayes the one challenging my presumptions now. "Porn and the bodies in it are nothing more than a fantasy. I'm much more interested in reality, especially the reality of you, in my bed, right here, right now."

I closed my eyes. "You haven't seen the real me yet."

"Haven't I?" He said that unlike a question, and it made my eyes pop open and stare up and him. There was this sparkle in his eyes like firecrackers on New Year's Eve. And that was the opposite of disappointment.

He didn't mean he'd seen my body. When no one else paid attention, he did. Hayes Kingman saw... me. And he still wanted me.

I didn't always like what I saw in the mirror, I don't think any woman did. But being a big girl living in an Ozempic world, the expectations were that I needed to change because my body wasn't worthy of love the way it was. That was almost unbearable and a reality I rejected.

The absolute lust for me in Hayes's eyes made those particular insecurities flee the scene. If he could look at me this way, I could rethink how I looked at myself.

My chest contracted and I forgot how to breathe.

So I didn't. Instead I kissed him and wrapped my legs around his waist. Who needed to breathe anyway?

MAKE ME BEG

HAYES

A willing Willa wasn't good enough. I wanted, needed, craved a Willa who didn't keep a part of herself back. She was still seeing the roadblocks between us when all I saw was how incredible we were going to be together.

But if she wasn't ready to let go with me, I'd just have to work harder to get her there. It was enthusiastic consent or nothing.

Well, maybe not absolutely nothing.

She had practically stripped me, after all. And I might die if I didn't get to see every inch of her body immediately if not sooner. Nobody wanted me to die right before the game against Florida. So I'd better do my damnedest to figure out what was holding her back.

"Tell me what you like, Willa." I kissed my way down her throat, shoving the straps of her dress aside, loving every bit of the taste of her skin. "Show me what will make you feel good."

She ran her fingers through my hair, and her voice was so soft and breathy it made me ache with needing her. "Anything you do will be great, I'm sure."

"No, no." I lifted my head and stared right into her eyes so she could see how serious I was. "This is all about you, making you comfortable enough to relax and have some fun with me."

"First of all, I am having fun." That soft tone was gone, and there was an edge to her voice now. Either I was in trouble, or I was doing exactly the right thing. God, I hoped I didn't fuck this up.

I glanced down at the way her hands were alternating between balling up into a fist and stretching her fingers out. She shoved them under her back and smirked at me like I'd caught her doing something she shouldn't. "And what do you mean this is all about me? You're the one about to lose your virginity."

"Hmm." Was that really what this was all about? I didn't think so. "I told you that wasn't important to me, but if it is to you, then we can talk about that."

"I don't want to talk, I want you to..." She waved her hand around in a let's get a move on motion.

Not sure what I'd done to make her think this was a wham-bam-thank-you-ma'am situation. If it was because of the dudes in her past, I'd find them all and... I'd love to beat the shit out of them, but it would be better for the whole world if I subjected them to sex advice from Trixie's mom, the porn star turned sex positivity guru.

I mirrored Willa's hand motion, trying to get her to actually say what she wanted. "Yes?"

"You know." She narrowed her eyes at me, and color rose up her throat. I was making her mad, and damn, it was so fucking hot on her. I would never truly try to make her angry, but getting a little fighting spirit in her, hell to the yeah. I was going to do that all the time. Besides, it was helping her step away from whatever was all up in her head, holding her back.

"Make you feel good?" I knew I was pushing some buttons here. If I was right, then they would get her riled up enough to blurt out whatever it was she couldn't say. "Then show me what you like."

She frowned at me again. "This is not all about me. I want you to feel good too."

"Willa." I traced my fingers along those frowny wrinkles she was making next to her mouth and then ran my thumb along her lip. "Anytime I fuck you, and I am going to fuck you, or when I make love to you, or even if we're just fooling around, it will always be about you."

She blinked at me like I'd grown three heads and two of them were snakes, but there was a vulnerability that flashed through her eyes. "That's not how this works."

"Sure it is." What I was about to say would either pull her out of this little battle of wills or she'd tell me off for being a jackass. I was going to risk it because she was worth it. "If it wasn't, I could continue getting my rocks off in the shower fantasizing that my own damn hand was yours, or your mouth, or your wet, warm pussy."

Her eyes flared, going wide and so dark I could practically see the arousal I'd just ignited in her, blazing in her mind. "You... you masturbate... thinking about me?"

Got her. "You're my whole reason to masturbate."

She licked her lips and took two shallow breaths. "Show me."

This was my in. This was how I could get her out of her head and quite literally show her how much I wanted her, wanted to please her.

I sat up on my knees, one leg on either side of her thigh, and shoved my trousers, belt, and boxers down. She'd seen my cock, she'd even seen it hard. But it felt bigger and harder in my hand right now than it had ever been. More sensitive too. If she wanted to see me come for her, it wasn't going to take fucking long.

The way she was looking at me, it was only going to take a few strokes before I shot my load right on her thighs. And holy fuck, did I want to see that.

"Pull your dress up, sweetheart. I want to see what I've been fantasizing about." I spit in my hand and gripped the head of my cock, circling the tip with my thumb, never once taking my eyes off her.

Willa reached down and pulled the material of her dress up her thighs so slowly, I thought I was going to die from the anticipation. "Don't tease me, Willa."

I was so enthralled with the reveal of her thick thighs that I almost forgot what I really wanted to see was her reaction to what I was doing for her. I dragged my gaze from her lush skin up to her face. Her lips were parted, and she was staring directly at my hand.

"What if what I want is to tease you?" Her voice was raspy and sexy as fuck.

Oh god of debauchery. That did something to my brain that sent fucking electricity straight to my dick, and I gave it a long, slow stroke that ended with a pearl of precum beading at the tip. "It's about what you want, sweetheart. If you want to tease me, do it."

What the fuck was I saying? My mouth and brain were on a whole other track from my body. My cock was screaming at me to push that skirt up and push myself so deep inside of her that I wasn't ever getting back out. But my head said letting her call the shots was going to be so much more rewarding.

"Do that again," she whispered. "Stroke it like you did before, like the way that you said you're pretending it's... me touching you."

Jesus Christ almighty, she really was going to kill me. I spit in my palm again and fucked my hand slow and hard. Normally I'd be closing my eyes and imagining her, but this time I didn't have to. I couldn't look away from her face, the way her heart was beating in her throat, and the way she couldn't take her eyes off me either.

"Give me something, flower." I ran my hand up and down my shaft again, trying really fucking hard not to make myself come. She was just starting to get into this, and I had to make it last. "Let me see if your panties are wet for me."

She smiled, and I knew I was in for some trouble. "Now what kind of a tease would I be if I did that?"

That tension she'd been holding in her hands and arms relaxed. Finally she was letting go. Thank god. Instead of hiking her dress up higher, she yanked one side down to cover more of herself, but she stuck her hand inside the folds of fabric on the other side. I caught the tiniest glimpse of black panties as she slid her hand down, down, down.

"Mmm, I'm definitely wet." She closed her eyes for just a moment and her hand bobbed under the material. She was touching herself and my brain went haywire.

"Let me see, Willa." I growled out the words, my need taking over.

"No." Her eyes popped back open, and her soft, hazy gaze found me frantically stroking and trying to make this experience last long enough that she came with me. "I'm having too much fun being in charge."

That's all I needed to hear. My hand flew over my cock, and I groaned out her name. "Willa. Fuck. That's so god damned hot."

Her hand sped up under her dress and I prayed to whatever gods were listening that she was close to coming. But everything I'd read or watched said that a woman needed a lot more foreplay and time to reach her climax. I didn't think I'd even been jerking my cock for her more than five minutes. No way she was ready, and I could come any second now.

"I'm too fucking close. I'm going to—" I gripped the base of my cock to hold back my orgasm. She needed me to prove I could please her in bed and coming before she was even hardly warmed up was not the way to do that.

"Don't come yet, Hayes." The motions of her hand and arm sped up and she lifted her skirt just a little more so I could just see the bottom edge of her panties and the hint of her hand bobbing up and down inside of them. "Don't come until I tell you to, but don't stop touching yourself either."

The tingle of my balls tightening up, ready to spill, pulled at my will power. More precum dripped from me, and I'd never fucking been on the edge like this for so long. I wasn't used to doing much more than giving myself a good jerk in the shower and enjoying the rush of it.

Willa was changing everything.

I threw my head back and gritted my teeth trying to think of anything but the way she was touching herself watching me suffer. I recited stats from this year's games in my head, but completely lost the ability to think of any meaningful numbers after the first pre-season game.

All I could see in my head was the how I imagined her fingers looked wet and glistening, sliding over her clit. "Willa... I... fuck, Willa."

She stayed silent until I looked back down at her. She took a shuddered breath and said, "Say please."

Fucking hell. I was fully ready to beg her to let me come. "Please, babe, let me come on your thighs, let me see my cum on your skin. Please."

She arched her back and moaned so beautifully. "Yes. Oh god yes. Come for me."

Watching Willa bring herself to orgasm was more than I could handle, so it was a good thing this was what she wanted, because there was no stopping my own. I jerked my hand up my shaft and let out a guttural moan from deep inside as I let go, spurting a trail of my release onto her thighs.

The sounds of Willa moaning out my name and the

sight of my seed on her body had my cock and balls tightening even harder, and I squeezed my cock again, more cum spilling from me until my body ached and I had nothing left.

I breathed hard, not able to do anything besides stare at how beautiful Willa looked, her cheeks and throat pink, her own chest heaving with her gasps for air, and her hand still in her panties, with my cum all over her body.

With a huge lungful of air to recover, I sat back on my heels and reached out, touching her thigh, smearing my fingers through the slick trails of my seed on her skin. Willa pulled her hand from her dress and her wet fingers met mine.

I grabbed her hand and brought both to my mouth, sucking her fingers and mine into my mouth. I tasted the essence of us both on my tongue and I'd never forget the salty sweet flavor of us till the day I died.

Willa moved so she was up on her knees with me and pulled me down to her, pushing our hands aside and replacing them with her kiss. She sighed so softly as I pushed the flavor of us from my tongue onto hers, and I relished the sound. Because she was happy, she was relaxed. She was... Willa.

She broke the kiss before I was ready to, but she laid her head on my chest and traced lazy fingers across my bicep. "Thank you for that, Hayes."

"I'm pretty sure I'm supposed to be saying that to you."

She quietly laughed at my echo of her words from earlier. "It was... exciting to feel like I was in charge for once in my life. I think you maybe unlocked a new kink in me."

"How'd you even know to say those things to me, babe?" I clearly had not done enough research because the idea of controlling your partner's orgasm had not come across my feed. "I thought my head was going to explode when you told me not to come."

She shrugged and then surprised the shit out of me. "Romance novels."

"I'm definitely going to start reading those. They are clearly more educational than porn."

"They're a fantasy too." I got her warning not to take everything in the stories as gospel. "Most of the ones I read, it's usually the guy telling the girl what to do. I would have thought that's what would turn me on."

"Would it?" She may have realized a something new about herself, but my new kink was finding out what turned her on. "I'll try bossing you around in bed if it would do for you what it just did to me."

"I don't know." She smiled up at me in a whole new way than I'd ever seen before. There was nothing between us, nothing hiding the truth of her happiness from me now. "But I'm willing to find out."

I had a lot of reading to do.

WELCOME TO THE COWGIRLS

WILLA

Hayes Kingman unlocked something inside of me, and I didn't just mean a new kink. While that part was fun, it wasn't what lit a fire under something inside that I hadn't even realized had been banked for a very long time. I wasn't a hundred percent sure I understood what had happened or what it meant, and I was going to need some time to think about it.

Snuggling in his arms while he occasionally snored but held me so tight against his chest that I couldn't smother him with a pillow was more comfortable than I imagined it would be. And instead of getting all up in my head about it, I leaned into it, this feeling of being... content.

It wasn't about the sex either. Technically we didn't even have sex. The way he so blatantly wanted me and shared himself with me so unabashedly was not something I'd ever experienced before. It was so much more about intimacy, and I wondered if he even knew that's what he did so naturally.

Although, to be fair, it was a little bit about the sex. In the morning, I was definitely making him demonstrate exactly what it looked like when he thought about me in the shower. That's what I hoped to dream about as I fell asleep.

The next day's reality of being the almost-girlfriend of a professional football player was crazeballs.

Jules led me into the VIP suite that the Kingmans and freaking Kelsey Best had reserved for the game. There was a whole-ass buffet with hot foods in silver serving trays and was that an ice cream bar? Wait, wait, and an actual bar with a bartender? This did not feel real, but if I had to watch a football game, this was definitely the way to do it.

"Willa," the other women all called my name in unison, and I instantly got a warm feeling in my chest, like we were all old friends meeting up for a beer. Then they introduced me to a few other people who were joining us for the game including the freaking Manniways and plus-size supermodel Sara Jayne Jerry.

Every single one of them acted like I was cooler than the other side of the pillow. Marie Manniway even handed me her card and acted like we were already best buds. "I hear you have a coffee shop. Perhaps we could talk about you hosting some of the Cowgirls and Cowpals get-togethers, which I have a feeling we'll be inviting you to very soon."

What was a Cowpal? "Oh, yes, that would be amazing. We're up in Thornminster, if that works for you."

She nodded like it was no big deal to come to my hole in the wall coffee shop in the suburbs from her fancy-ass mansion in Peachy Creek. "Anywhere the Kingmans and their partners and lovers hang out works for us."

Aha. I bet pal was short for partners and lovers. But why Cowgirls and Cowpals and not Mustang Girls and Pals? Oh. Oh wait, I got it. Because cowgirls ride mustangs, and she was being inclusive knowing that not all Mustangs were into women. I was going to like Marie.

"Want to try the alcoholic root beer float with me, Willa?" Sara Jayne Jerry held out a frosty mug to me.

"Like I'd say no to that." Or say no to anything she offered me. I took it, took a long sip through the straw, and gave myself a brain freeze.

"Good, right?" She ordered two more and held all three in one hand. When I raised my eyebrows at her skill, she smiled and said, "I used to work the beer tents at Oktoberfest back in the day, before all of this." She waved her hand around to indicate the suite and its utter decadence. "I thought I had to have it all figured out back then. I'm sure glad I didn't."

She walked away and foisted the two other mugs off on Mr. Kingman and the man sitting next to him. Then gave that guy a kiss on the cheek, which he returned with a pinch to her butt. Cute.

Here I was, surrounded by football royalty, the unrivaled queen of pop, and a goddess of a supermodel, and they were all treating me like I was one of them.

We grabbed plates for the snacks, and normally, I'd just grab one or two things, having been trained under the watchful judgment of my mother about my eyes being bigger than my stomach. But Jules, Pen, Trixie, and Kelsey all loaded their plates, and no one looked at them funny. If they could, I could too. Those nachos looked bomb.

I sat right in front near the windows next to Jules, who nudged me with her elbow, her grin wide and knowing. "Badass, right?"

I huffed out one awed laugh. "Very. I've never experienced anything like this."

Trixie leaned over, her smile warm and reassuring. "You'll get used to it. Trust me, the Kingmans have a way of making you feel like family in no time."

They already had. Except my family had never made me feel so comfortable, like I belonged. Not like this.

I glanced at Hayes's dad, who was deep in conversation with Sara Jayne Jerry's guy, who I think I'd heard was somebody's agent. Mr. Kingman caught me looking and gave me one of those sports guy head nods, with a wink and a smile. I hadn't even talked to him and felt a rush of gratitude for the easy acceptance he'd shown me. It meant more than I could say.

The game finally kicked off, and where I'd normally be pulling out my Kindle, my eyes were glued to the field, searching for that familiar figure in his away-game white, blue, and orange. The Mustangs had the ball first, and after the kickoff return, they were right at the fifty-yard line. The first couple of plays only got them a few yards, but at third and six, Chris threw a pass right to Hayes.

I watched, transfixed, as he spun away from a defender and leaped, snagging the ball out of the air like it was the easiest thing in the world. Before I knew what I was doing, I was on my feet, screaming and pounding on the glass with both hands. "Run, you beautiful butthead, run."

He raced down the sideline, his movements fluid and powerful, and I couldn't stop screaming or jumping. Football had never been this exciting before. Who fucking knew?

"Touchdown, Mustangs!"

The suite erupted in cheers, everyone jumping to their feet in celebration. In one of the craziest moments of my life, I found myself chest-bumping Kelsey, her joy and laughter infectious as all of us ladies danced in happy circles.

Jules gave me a high five too, but with an added smirk and some teenage snark. "Beautiful butthead, huh?"

"I mean," I shrugged, "am I wrong?"

She laughed. "No, you are not."

The stadium's Jumbotron replayed the touchdown, but then it showed another view, and the cameras were trained on our box. Of course, with Kelsey here, they'd want to capture every reaction. But as I caught sight of my own face splashed across the hundred foot wide screen, my stomach dropped right down through the floor, making its way to the basement of the stadium.

Xander. What if he was watching? What if he saw me, here at the game, celebrating with the Kingmans?

I tried to push the thought aside and pretend it wasn't a big deal. If we'd been on TV, it would have been for all of, like, four seconds. Unless we ended up on replays, InstaSnap, FlipFlop, and a whole variety of other media outlets that liked to show international popstars at their fiancé's football games.

Crappity crap. I checked my phone quickly, and so far, no angry face emoji from Xan. Okay, good. Maybe he wasn't watching. I decided to focus on the game and the incredible display of athleticism happening below and worry about Xan finding out I was betraying him later. Much, much later. Like never, if possible.

But every time the Mustangs scored, every time the cameras panned our way, the worry gnawed at me, a constant undercurrent to the excitement of the day. By the fourth quarter, I was hiding by the buffet, my nerves were frayed, my bottom lip raw from worrying it between my teeth, even though the Mustangs were absolutely dominating the Sharks.

Thank goodness for that ice cream bar. I gave alcoholic root beer floats an A plus for drowning one's anxiety. Jules caught me staring at the remaining food, sucking on said drink. Except I hadn't noticed I was just standing there spacing out until she threw a chicken nugget at me.

"Willa? We haven't scared you off already, have we?"

I forced a smile, shaking my head. "No, no, of course not. This has been more fun than I expected. I think I'm just all worn out."

Penelope joined us and gave me an all too knowing look. "Wouldn't have anything to do with why you didn't rejoin the pajama party last night, would it?"

"Shh. I don't want to get Hayes in trouble." I glanced over to Mr. Kingman, who, of course, was definitely eavesdropping on us. Thankfully he laughed and went back to watching the game.

Jules saw that exchange and shook her head. "Don't

worry about my dad. Not that I want to talk about my brothers' sex lives, but everyone knows the Kingmans play better ball when they're getting laid."

Trixie and Kelsey came over to join in the gossip too, because why not? Apparently, there were no secrets among the Kingman queens. Trixie loaded up her plate again, grabbing a slice of red pepper and shaking it at Ms. Know-It-All with a giggle. "Jules."

"What?" Jules gave her a smug look. "I noticed Chris's game is on fire today too. Enjoy your visit to the locker room?"

Trixie turned the color of her snack. "If you must know, I did. You don't think I'd mess with the quarter-back's pre-game routine. They are as superstitious as it comes."

Kelsey snickered. "I think you were the one coming."

Trixie took a bite of her pepper and nodded with a dreamy smile on her face. "Hmm. Yeah. Twice."

"If I wasn't so happy to be getting more girls in this family, I'd be retching right now." Jules stuck her tongue out at the three of us.

Wait, she thought I was joining the family? Hayes and I weren't even actually dating. And we weren't going to. I needed to remember that the next time he made eyes at me that made me go all weak in the knees. I was leaving in a few more months. The last thing I should be doing is making friends with his sister and his soon to be sisters-in-law.

This day had to be a one-time thing. Or did it? I didn't have to know everything about how our future was going to play out, and it was probably better if I didn't.

"And I couldn't help but notice that Everett was not at the top of his game today," Jules continued, "Who are we going to find to make the love guru, a.k.a. man whore, fall in love?"

Penelope made an abrupt turn toward the bar. "One margarita, please. Extra shot of Patrón."

Our girl gossip got diverted by the crowd outside suddenly going wild. We rushed back to the windows to catch a particularly spectacular play happening on the field. Hayes was racing down the sideline, the ball tucked securely against his chest, two defenders hot on his heels.

Time slowed as one defender dove to catch him, and he danced away as the guy hit the ground. Hayes was approaching the end zone, but the second man was gaining on him. Then Everett smashed into the other guy, sending them both onto the sidelines. Hayes put on another burst of speed, and the roar of the crowd doubled. But for me, it faded to a dull hum in my ears. I held my breath, my heart in my throat, as he crossed the goal line, the ball raised triumphantly over his head.

The suite exploded, everyone screaming and hugging, but I couldn't tear my eyes away from Hayes. He was pointing up at us, at me. The stadium of people disappeared, the sound of a suite filled with family and friends celebrating dissolved, and there was only the two of us. Even as his teammates lifted him up on their shoulders and he ripped off his helmet, he stared up at me. I pressed one hand to the glass, wishing I could touch him, be with him, right now.

The worry, the fear, the uncertainty of how I was going to make this work, none of it mattered. All that mattered was this man, this incredible, talented, kind-hearted man, and the way he made me feel seen, cherished, wanted.

If I was going to get attached to someone in this world, it was Hayes Kingman.

The final seconds ticked down and the Mustangs secured their victory. I knew I should have been celebrating with the others. But all I could think about was getting to Hayes, of throwing myself into his arms and never letting go.

I barely registered the trip down to the family meet-up room, my feet just moved on autopilot, following the other girls. And then he was there, his eyes finding mine across the crowded space, and everything else faded away.

There were reporters everywhere, and of course they were all surrounding Hayes. He said something to the one he was talking to, patted her on the shoulder, and then pushed by all the rest of them, coming toward me. I ran to him, leaping into his arms with a laugh that was half sob. He caught me easily, his arms banding around me like he never wanted to let go.

"You were incredible," I murmured into his neck, my fingers tangling in his damp hair. "I couldn't take my eyes off you."

He pulled back just enough to look at me, his gaze soft and wondering. "I was playing for you, Willa. Every moment, every play. All I could think about was making you proud."

Tears pricked at the back of my eyes, my heart so full it felt ready to burst open and spew out rainbows and unicorns and cotton candy and kittens. I had no words for how that made me feel, so I kissed him, pouring everything I felt, everything I couldn't quite say, into the press of my lips.

Here, in this moment, wrapped in the arms of the man I was falling in love with, nothing else mattered.

Let the cameras capture that.

BUNCH OF DICKS

HAYES

We walked into my house, Willa's hand clasped tightly in mine. I had every intention of taking her directly up to my room, stripping her naked, and finding a whole lot more of her kinks. I'd already downloaded a half dozen romances so that I could properly study what turned her on. I acquired them upon Trixie's recommendations, and she guaranteed they were what she called spicy. Chris assured me that was an incredibly good thing.

"Look, superstar." Willa pulled my hand to stop me from going up the stairs. "I know exactly what your plan is right now, and I am equally excited, but all I've had to eat today is very fancy junk food and alcoholic childhood drinks, so if you don't feed me something with actual nutritional content and protein, I will either pass out on you or throw up on you. Neither of which is particularly sexy."

While she was right about my sole focus being to take her to bed, a deep sense of contentment washed over me at her request that I feed her. The weekend in Miami had been a whirlwind of emotions, both on and off the field, but having her want something so... domestic from me made everything feel even more right.

"So you're saying a bowl of cereal isn't going to cut it?" I usually ate out on Sundays with the guys, and the service I paid for meals prepped specifically for professional athletes didn't deliver until tomorrow. Which meant I had diddly squat in the fridge and cupboards.

"I am definitely saying that. I was thinking poké?"

She was never anything but interesting. "I don't know what that is, but you haven't steered me wrong with the other international cuisine you've subjected me to, so let's do it."

"It's basically a sushi bowl." Willa shrugged.

Huh. Interesting. "Right. Cool."

Willa gave me some side-eye. "Hayes, are you telling me you haven't ever had sushi?"

I was more of a chicken and rice guy, but I liked fish fine. Salmon and trout were pretty common in my diet. Although that was cooked. "I hear it's good protein."

We'd barely settled onto the couch, takeout menus pulled up on our phones, when a knock at the door popped our peaceful bubble. Frowning, I disentangled myself from Willa's legs across my lap and padded over to answer it.

Alexander Fucking Rosemount stood on the other

side, a six-pack of beer dangling from his hand and a too-bright smile plastered on his face. "Hey, man. I was just in the neighborhood and thought I'd stop by to congratulate you on the big win."

Caught off guard, I stepped aside to let him in. Xander's gaze landed on Willa, and I saw a flicker of a few too many emotions flash across his face for me to read before he quickly masked it with a sheepish expression.

"Oh, hey, Willabean," His tone was forcibly casual, and I hoped it was because he really was trying to come grips with me dating his sister. "Didn't expect to see you here."

Willa shifted uncomfortably, and she scooted to the other side of the couch. "Yeah, we just got back from Miami. Hayes invited me over to get a bite to eat. We were about to order poké."

"Right, of course." Xander hefted the six-pack, his eyes never leaving mine. "Well, I brought some tasty beverages that would go with the food."

I exchanged a loaded glance with Willa. I knew it would mean a lot to her if Xander and I weren't at odds with each other. He saw every second of that and rubbed a hand along the scruff on his chin.

"And you know, it's been ages since we've hung out, and I figured I ought to be the one to, uh, fix that."

I just wasn't sure I trusted that this peace offering was the true nature of Xander's impromptu visit. But what could I do? Telling him to get out because I had plans to make his sister come half a dozen times while I learned exactly how she liked her pussy eaten was probably not the right move here.

So, with a resigned sigh, I gestured for him to take a

seat. "Yeah, it has been a while. I'm always down to catch up with an old friend."

Xander gave me a tentative smile and cracked open a couple of beers for us. Even though he knew I didn't drink much and never during the season. It was a peace offering and I'd take it. He launched into a story about our high school glory days, and Willa excused herself to the kitchen.

"Let me get some glasses for the beer, Xan. We're grownups and drinking legally now." I shot him some finger guns, trying to act all casual. I was anything but as I followed Willa into the kitchen.

"I'm so sorry," she murmured, taking a step back when I tried to draw her into my arms. "I had no idea he would just show up at your house like this. But I should have guessed he'd do something. No way he didn't see me at the game today."

I gave her the space her body language was screaming at me to allow her. This was not how I thought this evening would go either. "It's not your fault. Maybe he's actually trying. That would be good, right?"

"Maybe." She rubbed her chin in exactly the same way Xan had. "He's actually a good guy when he wants to be."

I gauged the look on her face, and when I got a hopeful smile back, I pressed a kiss to her hair, breathing in her sweet scent. "Then let's hope he wants to be."

I grabbed some tall glasses out of the cupboard, and we rejoined Xander in the living room.

"Let's get some of Willa's fancy pants fish food, huh?"

As the night wore on and the beer flowed, mostly into Xander's glass, he grew increasingly nostalgic, rehashing old memories and inside jokes. It was clear he was trying to remind me of our past bond.

When Willa yawned, the exhaustion of the weekend catching up with her, I seized the opportunity to send Xander on his way.

"Hey, man, it's been great catching up, but Willa and I had a long weekend. We should probably call it a night." I stood and extended a hand to help him up from the couch.

Xander blinked up at me blearily. "Oh, yeah, totally get it. I should... I should go."

He stumbled as he stood, nearly knocking over the coffee table. Shit. He was drunk. I should have paid more attention to how much he was drinking.

Willa shook her head and stood up, inserting herself under his arm to act like a crutch. "Actually, Xan, why don't I take you home? You're in no shape to drive."

Xander waved her off, his words slurring slightly. "Nah, 'm fine. I can... I can crash here, right, Hayes? Jus' like old times?"

Fuck. I hid my grimace, hating the situation he'd just created. But one look at Willa's pleading face and I knew Xander was sleeping here, in my house. I couldn't take her upstairs and fuck her brains out with him here, no matter how much I wanted to.

"Of course, man. Let me just grab you some blankets."

I stomped off to rummage through the hallway closet. I wasn't even sure I had any random bedding. Eventually, I found a Mustangs logo blanket still in the package that I must have gotten as part of my welcome to the team. This would have to do.

I heard Willa's soft murmurs as she helped Xander settle onto the couch. She was the one who was good. She knew just as well as I did that her brother was probably here to sabotage what we had going, and she was still kind to him in his inebriated state. I was feeling less kind. He'd better not puke on my carpet.

When I returned with the blanket, Xander was already snoring softly, his beer-induced slumber claiming him. Willa looked up at me, her expression a mix of apology and exhaustion. "I should probably just go home."

I nodded, understanding even as disappointment curled in my gut. "I'll walk you over."

The short trek through my backyard to Willa's house was silent, and I seriously contemplated asking her if I could stay with her tonight. We were greeted at her door by Seven, who instantly wrapped himself around her legs and meowed like he was telling her about every little thing that had happened while she was gone. She picked him up and cuddled him in her arms.

I was not jealous of a cat. I was not.

"This isn't how I wanted tonight to go." She had the cutest little pout.

I cupped her face in my hands, my thumb brushing across her pouty bottom lip. "We'll have plenty of other nights, just you and me. Xander's antics can't change what we have happening between us."

She leaned into my touch, a shaky sigh escaping her lips. "I know. I just... I feel like now he's trying to put you in a position to choose between him and me."

I shook my head, my gaze fierce and unwavering.

"There's no choice to make, Willa. It's you. It will always be you."

I kissed her, pouring every ounce of love and certainty into the press of my lips. I only broke the kiss when Seven squirmed between us and howled out a warning meow. Once again, Willa had me breathless and flushed. I rested my forehead against hers.

"Get some sleep, flower. I'll call you in the morning." And every morning until I didn't have to because she was in my bed.

She nodded and turned but spun back, dropping Seven and pulling me down, stealing one last kiss before slipping inside. I walked back to my house, breathing in cold November air to cool the heat beating through my veins.

Xander's interference, whether it was well intentioned or not, was a complication I hadn't anticipated, a wrench in the gears of my carefully laid plans.

I was falling in love with Willa, and I wasn't going to let anyone, not even one of my oldest friends, if that's even what he was, stand in the way of our happiness.

Game on, brother. Game on.

The next morning, I woke up with Seven between my knees. "Are you trying to remind me of what I missed out on with your owner last night, cat?"

Rude.

Also, I was giving up on trying to figure out how he kept getting in my house. He clearly went where he wanted to regardless of the opinions of the humans who cared about him. He stretched, and I shot my hand down to protect my junk and/or thighs from his claws. He happily stuck them into the flesh of my fingers. Good thing I had callouses from years of catching footballs.

I padded downstairs with Seven in tow, quietly in case Xander was still zonked out on my couch. But it seemed he left before I even got up. I wanted to believe he was working through his issues with me, but the text from Willa I woke up to didn't bode well.

Willa: I think Xan's really mad I went to Miami with you.

I got Seven a bowl of water and a handful of treats I'd ordered off Amazon because I thought they'd probably come in handy. Then I showered, grabbed my gear, and in fifteen minutes flat, I walked into Willa's coffee shop before practice. Partly for her weak coffee, mostly because I wanted to see my girl to start my day off right.

Willa looked up from the chalkboard sign she was making with cat-themed drinks for the upcoming date with the rescue organization. I'd almost forgotten about that. She flashed me a smile that did more for me than any caffeine ever would. "Hey, you."

I leaned across the counter for a quick kiss. "Morning, beautiful. Your cat is at my house, and I figured I'd just leave him there. I put out a bowl of water, but I guess I should get some cat food if he's going to be a frequent visitor."

She sighed and chuckled. "I think he's trying to assimilate you. Xander still passed out on your couch? I don't think he'll be feeling too great when he wakes up."

I shook my head, sliding onto a stool. "He was gone when I got up. I'm... not sure he was as drunk as he seemed."

Willa reached across the counter, taking my hand in hers. "Xander's a dick, but he's going through some stuff this year, and the idea of us together is stupidly tough for him."

"At least we don't have to sneak around anymore." I ran my thumb across her knuckles, marveling at how perfectly her hand fit in mine. I was dying to see what other parts of us would fit together.

Her eyes flared and she waggled one eyebrow at me. "That part was kind of fun. But I'd trade it if Xander could see how happy you make me."

Zings of electricity zipped up and down my spine. Hells to the yeah, I made her happy. Touchdown Mustang.

"He will." I brought her hand up to press a kiss to her palm. "I promise to give him lots of opportunities because I'll be right here, being the best boyfriend I can be to you."

Willa's eyebrows shot up, a surprised, awkward laugh escaping her. "Boyfriend, huh?"

Oh, she wanted to tease me again, did she? Too bad for her because I'd recently discovered I liked it. I dropped my voice and lowered my mouth to hers but didn't quite kiss her. "Tell me I'm not your boyfriend, Willa. Just try it and see what happens."

"Why are you so freaking hot? It makes it very hard to resist you." She gave a soft contented hum and pressed her cheek against mine. "I'm just going to focus on living in the moment, you know? Not put too many labels on things."

Wait... was she teasing? It certainly didn't have the same effect as her teasing in the bedroom. Damn.

The bell above the door jingled, and a man in a blue

jumpsuit stepped inside, a toolbox in hand. "Ahem, hope I'm not interrupting anything, but do you need an espresso machine repair?"

"Yes, I do." Willa gave me a quick kiss on the cheek... the fucking cheek, and then waved him over. "I'm so glad you're here. We're already behind on reopening."

"I'm gonna head to practice." And figure out what the fuck just happened. "Call you later?"

She blew me a kiss. "Definitely. Have a good practice, superstar."

Was Willa really still being resistant to making things official between us? Did she not see a future with me? But she'd just told me I made her happy.

I needed advice, and not from a book or website this time. Back to the love guru for me.

The moment I got to the locker room, I sought out Everett immediately. He took one look at my face and sighed, slinging an arm around my shoulders.

"Alright, little bro. Lay it on me. What's got you looking like someone just told you they discontinued your favorite protein powder?"

I took a deep breath, steeling myself. "How do you know if a girl is in love with you or not?"

His eyes widened, a slow grin spreading across his face. "Well, well, well. You've finally decided to quit ignoring my relationship advice, huh?"

I elbowed him in the ribs, hard. "Don't make me regret this."

He laughed, holding up his hands in surrender. "Alright, alright. Tell me what's going on with you and the lovely Willa."

I started telling him, but before I got very far into the story, Chris and Dec had joined us too. This was a whole damn team meeting, but if there was anyone I trusted, it should be the men I looked up to, and at least two of them had found the loves of their lives.

When I finished talking about how Willa had started off telling me not to get attached because she wasn't going to be around long, and how Xan was acting like a dick, and that damn no-labels comment this morning, it was quiet for a long moment.

Declan laid a hand on my shoulder. "Take her up to the cabin and don't let her out of bed until she's had a hundred and two orgasms. Worked for me."

"Nah." Chris shook his head at us both. "You don't need to take her away. Just bend her over the kitchen table, or the couch, or her desk, or—"

I held up a hand. "Dude, I get it."

Dec and Chris looked at each other and chuckled. Everett rolled his eyes at both of them. "Like these two chuckleheads didn't come to me begging for help to win their girls over, and was my advice for them about sex?"

They each shook their heads. Bunch of dicks.

"Hayes, I'm gonna be straight with you." Everett sat on the bench and laced up his cleats. "Relationships are messy, complicated things. There's always going to be obstacles, whether it's disapproving friends or family members or just fucking life getting in the way."

I sighed. This was not what I was hoping to hear. Maybe I would take Chris's advice. I didn't think we could get away with a trip up to the mountains. I ran a hand through my hair. "So what do I do?"

Everett stood and grabbed his helmet, and then shoved mine at me. "You fight for her, man. You show her every day that she's your priority, your endgame. And most importantly, you communicate with her. Tell her how you feel, what you want. Don't let fear hold you back."

Well... fuck. Yeah, that was the right plan, and we all knew it.

I loved her, and it was time I made sure she knew it.

That lightning struck me again, this time directly to the chest, burning through every cell in my body, lighting me up like a firecracker. I fucking loved her.

I. Loved. Willa Rosemount.

This wasn't some crush, and it certainly wasn't a fling. I was in love, and tonight I was going to tell her... while I bent her over the kitchen table and gave her a hundred and three orgasms.

WILD CHILD RIDES AGAIN

WILLA

I stared at the depressingly empty coffee shop, the ticking of the clock on the wall a mocking reminder of yet another slow day. I probably shouldn't have closed over the weekend even if we couldn't make lattes. I might have capitalized on the Mustangs fans still coming in to see if there were any Kingmans here.

Although, real fans would have known they were all in Miami over the weekend, and honestly, I wouldn't trade that trip and the time I got to spend with Hayes and his family for anything.

I needed to remember that because the sight of the espresso machine, now repaired, sitting idle, and the pastry case with it's no day old donuts looked ridiculously forlorn. I don't know how Liam did this day after day. Except that he loved this place almost as much as George loved the Mustangs.

I missed them.

I must have sent some intentions out into the universe with those thoughts because just as I was about to start cleaning up for the day, my phone buzzed with an incoming FaceTime call. The Guncles' smiling faces filled the screen, and I couldn't help but grin back.

"Willa, darling!" George exclaimed, his voice tinny through the speaker. "You'll never guess where we are."

He turned the phone and showed me some kitschy port market on what I was guessing might be a Caribbean island. "Ooh. I'm not jealous at all. We're supposed to get snow next week."

To be fair, it was almost December, and so far, I'd lucked out and only gotten the mildest part of a Denver winter. I was not looking forward to February and March when it snowed the most. Even if that still meant once or twice a month and it all melted away three days later.

For the next few minutes, they regaled me with tales of their adventures, showing me snippets of exotic landscapes and bustling shopping districts. Their joy was infectious, but it also made me miss both of them and being out in the world doing crazy fun things too.

"Enough about our world tour," Liam said, his eyes crinkling with concern. "How are things going back home? How's Cool Beans? How's Seven, how's the fam? You're the first one we called."

"Oh, you know, everyone's fine." I was not getting into whatever was going on with Xander, and I hadn't even talked to my parents in days. Just like when I was abroad. "The coffee shop is... it's going."

Liam gave me some side-eye at those answers. He always saw right through my tough girl facade.

With a sigh, I confessed my fears about the shop's struggling business and my inability to turn it around. "I'm afraid I'm letting you both down," I admitted, blinking back tears.

"Nonsense," George declared, slapping the table they were sitting at. "Listen, Willa, don't you worry about a thing. I'm more than happy to keep paying the bills. The most important thing is that you're there, holding down the fort."

I noticed Liam's slight grimace at George's words and realized that he didn't entirely agree. He caught my eye and gave me a subtle nod, a silent encouragement to keep trying.

Their belief in me, even in the face of my doubts, sparked a flicker of determination in my chest. I couldn't let them down, especially not Liam. I had to find a way to make this work. "I do have the first playdate with the cat shelter this week, so I'm sure that will bring in business. It should be fun."

"Good, that's the spirit, kiddo. Now," George waggled his eyebrows at me. "How's the plan to make me an adopted Kingman because you're marrying Hayes coming along? I saw the Miami game highlights even though I'm not supposed to have the internet while we're on the ship."

That was something I could smile about. "The game was really amazing. I got to fly out on their jet, and I met Kelsey Best, who is actually super nice, and the Manniways, and Sara Jayne Jerry."

And did some serious fooling around with Hayes at the hotel. But they did not need to hear that part.

"Right, right, right," Liam said waving away my brushes with fame. "I want love life deets, baby girl. Are you officially seeing Hayes Kingman?"

Okay, so they did want to hear that part. "I... am?"

"Honey, don't answer like it's questionable." Liam frowned, leaning closer to the screen. "Willa, what's wrong? You know you can tell us anything."

George glared through the phone. "He's not being some sports star asshat, is he? I expect better of a Kingman."

"No. Hayes is perfect. Not a single red flag. I'm the one being an asshat," I confessed. I was the one who said we shouldn't have labels this morning when he was clearly so excited to call himself my boyfriend. Who did that? Scaredy cats, that's who.

"I'm scared of getting too attached when I'm supposed to be leaving in a few months. I'm afraid I'm already..." I almost said that I was already in love with him. But I wasn't ready to admit that out loud. "I already have some serious feelings for him."

Liam leaned back and smiled softly at George. "Willa, let me tell you something. Love, when it's real, is always worth the risk. Don't let fear rob you of something beautiful. Something that can make your life so much better than it ever could be alone."

George's bottom lip wobbled a little and he wrapped an arm around Liam. Then he cleared his throat and said, "Embrace love and happiness wherever you find it, darling. Life's too short to do otherwise."

Their words settled into my heart, a comforting warmth chasing away the chill of my doubts. if anyone knew about love, it was these two.

I full-well knew how to take risks. I told my parents I wasn't going to college even though that's all they'd ever wanted of me. I moved to foreign countries without knowing a single soul or a word of the language. I taught six-year-olds around the world how to read! Despite them having no idea what I was saying.

I was fearless... in everything but love. It was time to stop holding back and fully commit to this wonderful, terrifying, exhilarating thing I had with Hayes.

"Ooh, look at her face, Liam," George sing-songed, "She is having a moment. Go get 'em, wild child."

We said our goodbyes and I looked around the empty shop with fresh eyes. It was time for a change, time to take some risks of my own. If I was going to make this thing with Hayes work, I needed to make some plans too.

I started brainstorming ideas on how to make the coffee shop profitable, scribbling them down in a notebook. I could partner with local bakeries for fresh pastries. Offer specialty seasonal drinks. It was easy enough to update the menu, but what we needed was more customers.

What made people like to hang out at a coffee shop, besides the food and drink? What did I even like to do when I hung out here? The comfy chairs tucked in the corner by the very small lending library caught my eye.

I liked to read.

And then it hit me. A book club. Ooh, even better, a spicy romance book club. I could host it right here in the shop, creating a fun, flirty atmosphere that would be perfect for coffee and steamy reads.

Excited by the prospect, I scrolled through my contacts, looking for the perfect person to help me spread the word. Trixie. She was writing a romance novel, and she was a former librarian. I'm sure she had connections. I sent her a message.

A dozen ideas of drinks I could pair with books I'd read flew around in my head. That would make for great social media posts. Gasp. I could do the same with the cats from the cat shelter. That would be fun too. I was going to need a brand new InstaSnap and a FlipFlop account for Cool Beans.

But one book club and one playdate with shelter cats wasn't going to be enough to really make the business profitable. I could ask Hayes to do something with the Mustangs again. Or, yes, Marie Manniway had specifically given me her card and said she wanted to host a Cowgirls and Cowpals meeting here. If I could make that a regular thing, that would bring in a whole crowd of women who could afford fancy coffees and teas. This could be the perfect opportunity.

I fired off a text to Marie, finally following up on her request, asking if she'd be interested in stopping by the shop this week. Her enthusiastic response came minutes later, and I did a little victory dance right there behind the counter.

Watch out, Denver. Willa Rosemount was about to make her mark, one latte at a time.

The rest of the day passed in a blur of list making, graphics creating, and my first few social media posts.

Even if I only had two whole customers that afternoon, I was still hyped. By the time the bell above the door jingled that evening signaling a new customer, I was so engrossed in my plans that I almost didn't look up.

But I'd know those footsteps anywhere. Hayes, freshly showered, sporting a Mustangs hoodie and swagger that made me swoony crossed the shop to lean across the counter and steal a kiss. "Hey, sweet thing. Ready to close up shop? I've got plans for you tonight."

I grinned against his lips, my earlier worries and fears melting away in his presence. "Just about. What kind of plans?"

He shrugged, his eyes twinkling with mischief. "Oh, you know. Just wanted to see if my girlfriend wanted to come home with me and spend the night."

A brand new thrill zipped through me, like the warmth of hot cocoa laced with Bailey's, at the way he said girlfriend.

"All night?" I batted my eyelashes at him. "Whatever will we do?"

"Like I said, flower, I've got plans for you. And they involve you calling my name as I make you come for, oh, let's say the dozenth time."

"Oh really? And how many times are you going to come?"

"As many as you say I can." His eyes went dark with an instant shimmer of arousal that had me going all squidgy on the inside too.

"That is an excellent plan indeed," I said softly. "But what if Xander shows up again?"

Hayes grinned, looking entirely too pleased with

himself. "Already taken care of. I called in a favor with Flynn and Gryff. The captains of the team just happen to be calling a mandatory meeting tonight. We won't be interrupted."

I laughed, shaking my head in amazement. "You're something else, Kingman."

"And you love me for it." He said it jokingly, but there was a hint of vulnerability in his eyes, a silent question.

I swallowed hard, my heart racing like I was the one running down the field slipping past defenders and scoring touchdowns.

"I do," I whispered, holding his gaze.

The wattage of his answering smile could have powered the entire city block.

He literally leaped over the counter and kissed me, and kissed me, and kissed me. I melted into him and lived fully in this passionate moment, not worrying about the future, how we were going to make this work, where I would be in a few months, or what anyone wanted except for the two of us right here, right now.

Hayes grabbed me around the waist and lifted me up, placing my butt right on the counter, then pushed his way between my knees. He reached for the buttons on my coffee shop polo but changed his mind and dropped his hands to the button on my pants.

"Whoa there, Mustang. We are not having sex on the coffee shop counter, especially not while that little neon sign over there says that it's still open." I slapped his hand away when he popped my pants open anyway. "Do you know how much disinfectant I'd have to use to clean up if we had sex right here?"

"I will buy you a new counter." I had no doubt that he could. But that wasn't the point. "Besides, I have it on good authority that I could get you to say you love me out loud if I bend you over this counter."

Was that what this franticness was really all about? I'd implied the words a few moments ago, but this sweet, adorable man needed to hear them from me. I was sorry I hadn't already said it.

I placed his cheeks in my palms and gave him a soft, slow, lingering kiss. "Hayes, I've fallen in love with you. I'm sorry if I made you doubt those feelings earlier today."

Relief and joy and love bubbled up in his eyes and he lifted me up again, spinning me around and around, making me dizzy with his excitement. I wrapped my legs around him and squealed, exactly like a little girl on a park merry-go-round, loving the thrill of it all. Loving him.

"I fucking love you so much I felt like I was going to explode if I didn't get to tell you." He slowed and set me on the counter again and leaned in for another kiss.

I slid my hand between where our mouths would have met. "You'd better save that exploding for the bedroom, mister."

He laughed, and, my god, was his happiness infectious.

"Help me lock up, and then take me home, Kingman." I slid back off the counter and handed him a towel to wipe the counter off with. "You've got a busy night counting orgasms ahead of you."

This wasn't really about the sex or how many orgasms either of us had. The rush of feelings flowing through me was like nothing I could even describe, and it was far better than any sex.

But to be fair, I hadn't had my brains fucked out by Hayes Kingman yet.

BOOK BOYFRIENDS ARE BETTER THAN PORN

HAYES

We stepped up to the front of my house and I scooped up the box from Amazon off my steps. I tossed it onto the kitchen counter when we got inside because packages could wait. I could not.

However, Seven had other plans. He jumped directly onto the box and began singing the song of his people. By which I mean yowling his head off. Willa's eyes widened and she pointed to the box. "What exactly is in there?"

Something that had better occupy Seven or I was going to feed him to a Klingon Targ. I slashed at the top of the box with my house key and sliced that sucker open. Willa gasped and then giggled at the sight of the cat food cans and disposable litter trays, and the reason for the yowling, a spilled container of something called Kitty Crack, which was really just some reportedly strong catnip. "Hayes, what...?"

I grinned, rubbing the back of my neck. "I figured if Seven's going to be a regular visitor, I should be prepared."

She turned to me, putting a whole hell of a lot of extra emotion onto her face, and only laughed twice before she said, "You are... the most wonderful cat dad ever. You know that?"

Seven crawled inside the box and made himself at home, rolling around in the catnip.

I pulled her close, my hands settling on her rounded hips. "Do I get extra points if I say that cats rule and dogs drool?"

"Yes."

Our lips met in a slow, deep kiss that sent sparks dancing along my nerve endings. I poured every ounce of love and longing into that kiss, my fingers sliding beneath the hem of her shirt to caress the soft, warm skin of her waist.

Willa sighed into my mouth, her hands fisting in my hoodie. "But I'll have to award those points later, because right now, Hayes, I need you. Naked."

I scooped her up bridal-style, relishing her squeal of surprise and the way she clung to my shoulders. "Then let's not waste any more time."

I carried her up the stairs to my bedroom two at a time, never happier that I'd chosen the athletic life that allowed me to carry my girl to bed. She taunted me every step of the way with her lips nibbling along the skin at my throat and my jaw.

When I laid her gently on the bed, her dark hair

fanning out across the pillows, I had to take a second just to look at her.

She was breathtaking, all curves and softness and everything I'd ever dreamed of. This time I was not going to miss out on seeing every inch of her skin. I pushed my hands under the hem of her shirt and slid it up, up, up, until she had to lift her arms so I could pull it over her head. But remembering the romance novel I sped through this morning, I trapped her arms in the fabric of the shirt and held her hands up there so I could look my fill.

I traced a finger along the faint stretch marks on her belly, marveling at their delicate beauty, then bent my head and followed that same path with my tongue. “God, Willa. You're so fucking perfect.”

She flushed and squirmed, but I didn't let her free. Not yet. She could be bossy all she wanted to later, but it was my turn to touch her and taste her.

“I'm not, Hayes. I've got plenty of flaws just like anyone else.”

I shook my head, pressing a kiss to the top of each of her rounded breasts. I was going to lose myself between them. “All I see is the woman I love, in all her gorgeous, sexy glory.”

Willa let out a husky, watery laugh. “Okay, Casanova. You've been reading romance novels, haven't you? You don't have to seduce me you know. I'm a sure thing at this point.”

I grinned unabashedly. “Guilty on the romance novel part. What did you think I did when you went home and Xander sawed logs on my couch? I wanted to learn what you liked.”

"Oh, man, I hope you were reading rom-coms and not dark romance, because I swear to god, if you try telling me to crawl to you, or start stalking me... I promise that red flags and morally gray heroes are only sexy in fiction, Hayes."

Noted. "Where do dragon shifters fall on your book boyfriend scale?"

She laughed again. "I like the kind you can ride. Now let me up so I can show you exactly what kind of riding I mean."

I leaned in for one more searing kiss while I had her captured. Her tongue tangled with mine and she moaned so softly it was almost a whimper. I wanted to hear that sound over and over, and I was gonna try everything I'd studied to make sure I did.

When I broke the kiss and she looked up at me with those dark, glassy eyes that had so much need in them, I thought I'd die if I didn't fulfill every one of those desires I saw there.

I let her go, tossing her shirt aside, and we both shed the rest of our clothes in a flurry of roaming hands and heated kisses. When we were finally skin to skin, I had to take a steadying breath. The feel of her, all silky warmth and thick, enticing curves, threatened to short-circuit my brain.

But this was about her, about showing Willa just how cherished and desired she was. I trailed my lips down her throat, pausing to lavish attention on her tits that I could get lost in they were so big. But my real goal was the soft, plush belly, that curve of a pooch just above her pussy. I had fucking fantasies about licking it and biting it and coming all over it.

I kissed my way from her belly button to the peak of her stomach and indulged myself with just a nibble of that soft belly. I wanted to taste each blessed inch of her body.

When I reached the apex of her thighs, I glanced up at her, "Tell me to go down on you, Willa. Let me hear you say it."

Her fingers tangled in my hair, guiding me closer. "Holy hell, yes. I need your mouth on me."

"More, Willa. Tell me to fuck you with my tongue." Making her tell me what she wanted was the best way I knew of to ensure she wanted everything we did together.

She licked her lips and the grip of her fingers of my scalp went tighter. "You've got a dirty mouth. Use it to make me come, Hayes."

Mmm. Hell yeah. With a groan of pure male satisfaction, I set about learning every secret place that made her gasp and writhe, committing each breathy moan to memory. I'd read about and studied whole-ass charts about how the clitoris wasn't just the sexy as fuck little nub in front of my face. So even though I wanted to suck it between my lips, I opted to go for swirling my tongue around and around to see if that's what she liked.

That first taste of her blew my fucking mind. My dick went so damn hard I was going to poke a hole through the mattress.

"Oh god," she panted, her hips rocking against my face. "Hayes, right there."

Hell yeah. I doubled my efforts tasting and teasing her. But I wanted to drive her higher and higher. This was the opportunity to bring in the secret weapon. Romance novel sex scenes. All three of the heroes I'd read about really got their women going crazy when they use their fingers along with their mouths.

I pressed one finger at her entrance and teased it while I gave her a long slow lick, and I was rewarded with another of those whimpering gasps. Carefully, I pushed one finger inside so slowly I almost came right there on the sheets when she clenched down on me.

"Holy... oh... god," Willa panted out the words and tightened her grip on my hair again, sending tingles through my scalp. "Don't stop, more, god, yes."

If she wanted more, I'd give her all she ever wanted. I slipped my finger out and pushed in a second this time, and I sucked the tip of her clit I'd been aching to taste into my mouth. Willa arched her back, pushing my fingers deeper into her pussy, and shattered, her inner muscles pulsing around my fingers, her thighs clamping around my head. I barely heard her cry out my name.

Best. Earmuffs. Ever.

I held my position through the aftershocks, only pressing soft kisses to her trembling flesh until her muscles unlocked and she released me from her hold. I crawled back up her body, dotting kisses on her thighs, belly, and breasts along the way, while seeing stars. Making her come like that had sent every drop of blood I had straight to my cock.

Seeing her eyes closed, her soft gasps as she sucked in air, and then the whoosh of a satisfied exhale, made me feel better than any touchdown, good grade, or other accolade. She was soft and languid, and a gentle smile grew on her lips.

I'd done that for her. I made her happy.

She dragged her eyelids open and then grabbed my face, pulling me down and crashing her lips to mine, kissing me deeply. I groaned with a whole new burst of lust knowing she was tasting herself in my mouth.

“That was... God, Hayes. You really are good at everything. What the hell?”

I grinned, nuzzling her nose with mine. “I told you, I've been studying.”

She reached between us, her hand wrapping around my straining length. I hissed at the contact, my hips jerking instinctively. “Willa...”

She silenced me with a kiss, her hand stroking me with maddening slowness. “I want to feel you, Hayes. All of you.”

My heart threatened to beat out of my chest. “I'm going to come in your hand right now if you so much as even move a centimeter.”

Her tongue poked out and swiped across her top lip before she sucked the bottom one between her teeth. “I like watching you come.”

“Jesus, Willa. I swear to god, I'm not going to last even a second if you don't give me a minute and keep that tongue of yours inside your mouth.” I wasn't kidding. My brain and my dick were on overload.

This time she licked her lips back and forth and then ran her tongue across her teeth. She knew exactly what she was doing. It was the most delicious torture yet.

“Fucking tease.”

She slowly stroked up my cock, not with her fist, but with her nails. "It's your fault. I had no idea I liked it so much until you got turned on by it."

I closed my eyes and gritted my teeth, willing my balls to hold on for a little while longer. "Just you wait, sweetheart. I'm going to find the kink that turns you to putty in my hands, and then your ass is mine."

"I've never tried that, so we'll have to wait and see." Holy fuck, was she suggesting we try anal?

"I haven't even been inside your pussy yet." I wrapped my hand around her fist to stop her stroking. "I really want to be inside of you, Willa. I want to feel you coming on my cock this time."

Shit. I was letting my fucking libido get the best of me. This was supposed to be about her. "Tell me how to make that good for you. Because I still need to make you come at least a dozen more times."

She smiled and shook her head at me. "Alright, overachiever. In my limited experience, that's not actually how this works. I got my orgasm, it's your turn now."

I was not some fuckboy that went down on her once just so I could get my rocks off. I was proving my feelings to her. I was showing her all that love we'd declared to each other. She would feel my love, god dammit. "The fuck it is. Tell me what you want, Willa, because I am going to make you come again."

Willa narrowed her eyes at me and pushed against my chest playfully. When I didn't move an inch, she wrapped her thigh around mine and, in a move worthy of a professional wrestler, flipped me the fuck over so she was on top, and I was against the mattress. "What I want right now, Kingman, is for you to fuck me. I want to see your face when you slide into my pussy for the first time. And then whether it's three strokes or an hour's worth of fucking me, I want you to beg me to let you come inside of me."

Holy shit. Four alarm fire. The electricity she ignited in my body set my brain ablaze. "It's definitely going to be more on the three strokes side, babe."

"Good," she said with a sly smile on her face that sent more power surging through my cells, but it quickly turned to something softer and sweet. "Because I've never been on top before, and I know my hamstrings are not going to hold out."

I gripped her hips tight and flipped us back again, which had her squealing with a giggle. "I can beg just as well from up here, flower."

No way I'd ever make her work hard to get me off. I kissed her and reached between us, stroking her in the same ways I'd licked her, wanting to make sure she was ready for me.

"Stop stalling and put on the condom, Kingman." She jerked her chin to the box on the nightstand. But then she said something that changed this all from a game to something so much more. "Show me how much you love me and let me show you."

I pulled in a long, deep breath. She got it. She understood everything I was trying to do, to show her, to be for her. This wasn't just about sex for me, and Willa was right there too, wearing every emotion on her face, shining through in those gorgeous fucking eyes.

"I do love you, Willa." And I never wanted to love anyone else.

She touched my face, rubbing her palm down my cheek. "I tried not to, but somewhere along the way, you made me fall in love with you too. You're the love of my life, Hayes."

I thought hearing her say something like that would make my heart pound out of my chest, or honestly, have my dick exploding. But instead, the deepest sense of contentment seeped into my bones, my blood, my very soul. This was what it meant to be loved by this woman.

I reached for a condom with shaking hands. This was really happening. I was about to fuck the woman of my dreams for the first time, and in this moment, I sincerely hoped she was the only woman I ever fucked.

As I slid into her, our bodies joining for the first time, I swear I saw lightning bolts flash through my vision, and because I knew she was watching, I hid nothing from her. I stared into her eyes and let her see all of me. "Fuck, Willa. I fucking love you."

Nothing had ever felt so right, so perfect. I withdrew in a long slow stroke, wanting to make this last as long as I could. But as I pushed back inside, Willa made one of those whimpers that drove me wild, and I was a goner.

My hips moved on their own accord, finding a fast, hard rhythm, made only better when she wrapped her legs around my ass so I couldn't pull out if I wanted to. I poured every ounce of love and devotion into each thrust, each kiss, each whisper of her name.

Willa met me every step of the way, her body rising to meet mine, her nails scoring my back, her breathless cries mingling with my own. My universe became her, the way her body gripped mine, the way she said my name, until I couldn't take it anymore.

"Please, Willa, please let me come inside of you."

She shook her head. "Again."

Fuck. "Please."

Her eyes fluttered shut, but she breathed out a shuddered breath and then stared all the way into my soul. "Say it again."

And I knew what she wanted to hear.

"Please, Willa, I love you, please."

Her pussy clenched down on me, and she arched her back, keening, "Yes, Hayes, god, I love you."

I came so hard inside of her, I think I blacked out, except instead of darkness I saw the beautiful blue of Willa's eyes. My hips jerked a few more times all on their own, but I was already floating in hazy bliss that was just for me and her.

It took everything in me not to just collapse on top of her and ride this high. But all the romance novels and the better sex sites preached the importance of aftercare. Which I would do. In a minute.

The best I could do for now was kiss her. She returned my kiss with a soft, satisfied moan, and that was my second favorite sound she made during sex.

"Hayes?" she whispered, her eyes still closed and a smile etched across her face.

"Yeah, baby?" She was fucking beautiful like this, and I could hardly wait to see her this way night after night in my bed.

"Why are you so good at this on your first try?"

Touchdown Mustang. If I had a football, I'd spike it. I pretended she hadn't just made my day with her compliment and said, “I had help.”

She cracked one eye open and peered up at me with a question in her gaze.

I gave her another kiss and a cocky shrug. “From your romance novels. Book boyfriends definitely do it better than anybody in porn.”

CAT DADS

WILLA

I couldn't stop smiling. Even as I stood behind the counter, steam from the espresso machine fogging up in front of me, I was grinning like a fool. Every time I closed my eyes, I saw Hayes's face, felt his hands on my skin, heard his whispered words of love.

Last night had been... well, there weren't words. It had been everything I'd ever wanted and so much more. The way Hayes had worshipped my body, the reverence in his touch, the unbridled passion in his kisses, it was enough to make a girl go weak in the knees or the brain.

Wait, had he fucked my brains out? Sure felt like it, because there was nothing up there but ooey gooey mush.

"Earth to Willa," Trixie's amused voice snapped me out of my daydreams. She and Marie were standing at the counter, matching Cheshire grins on their faces.

I felt my cheeks heat, but I couldn't wipe the smile off my face. "Sorry, ladies. What can I get for you?"

Marie leaned forward, her eyes sparkling with mischief. "Oh, I think we'd rather hear about what's got you looking like the cat that ate the canary."

I bit my lip, my mind flashing back to the feel of Hayes's mouth on me. "I have no idea what you're talking about."

Trixie snorted, exchanging a knowing look with Marie. "Please. You're practically glowing. I know that look. That's the 'I just had mind-blowing sex with a Kingman' look."

I nearly dropped the mug I was holding, my jaw falling open. "Trixie."

Although, she would know. I'd Googled her and Chris since I got home, and that was quite the fun sex scandal and subsequent sex positive messaging they'd dealt out in return. I actually really admired her for it.

Trixie held up her hands, laughing. "Hey, no judgment here. I'm simply happy to see you and Hayes finally got your act together. According to Chris, that boy's been pining for you."

I couldn't help but smile at that, my heart fluttering in my chest. "I guess I just needed a little push to realize what was right in front of me."

Marie reached across the counter, squeezing my hand. "We're happy for you, sweetie. I told you I thought you'd be joining the Cowgirls sooner rather than later. Now we have to help support your small business."

There was no denying I was officially a lover of a Denver Mustang now. Hayes's fame didn't matter to me personally, but already it was opening up networking opportunities to help the coffee shop.

"It's not actually mine, you know." I pointed to the picture framed along with their first dollar bill from their first sale that hung near the cash register. "My uncles are the real owners. I'm just temporarily running it while they're on an extended and well-deserved vacation."

"That is very generous and amazing of you." Marie folded her arms and studied me for a moment. "And do you have plans for after they're back?"

Gulp. "Not yet. Right now I'm living in the moment. I want to do everything I can to make this place a success so when they get back, it's a healthy business for them."

Trixie nodded but tipped her head to the side. "But aren't you a teacher? You said something about living abroad before. Maybe you could look for a teaching position here, you know, after your uncles get back."

I wasn't ready to think about all of that, much less talk about it. "I'm not that kind of teacher. I didn't go to college or anything. I just teach English as a foreign language to little kids."

"There's no just about that," Marie said. "We need those kinds of skills in Colorado too, dear."

Umm, I hadn't really thought about that. But just hearing that there could be a job for me in Denver kind of gave me the heebie-jeebies. A job here meant being stuck here.

Nope. No. I was not thinking about that now. I was living in a happy brains-fucked-out bliss for today, tomorrow, and the rest of the near future. "Right. Sure.

But let me show you the plans I have for what we can do for the Cowgirls and Cowpals here at Cool Beans."

I spent the next few minutes telling them about my plans for the coffee shop, including the upcoming cat adoption event. I knew Marie Manniway was famous for doing philanthropic work, so I hoped that would appeal to her. Trixie was particularly thrilled to hear about the spicy romance book club idea and promised to not only spread the word but participate. She said she might even know some published authors who would send swag for the readers, or even Zoom in to say hello and answer questions.

That would be incredibly cool. Authors were my rockstars.

Before they left, a woman from the local bakery arrived with the orders I'd placed for the new cat-themed pastries to go with the cat-themed drinks. They were my secret weapon for the day the actual cats that were coming to hopefully be adopted came in. I took pictures and posted them to the shop's new InstaSnap, tagging the bakery.

Marie went on and gave the post a heart and commented that she'd be at the event in a couple of days. Which, to my surprise, made my phone blow up with notifications.

Over the next couple of days, I did not get to see Hayes as often as I wanted. I only slept over twice. Although Seven slept over every night. At this point he was basically living at Hayes's house. Hayes even ordered him a very elaborate cat tree that now stood next to his live streaming and gaming set up in the living room.

One of the nights my mother called and insisted she wanted to take me Christmas shopping, and we met Xander out at The Mall of the Rockies. We stayed until closing, which, since it was December, was ridiculously late. While Hayes insisted he had plenty of stamina and didn't need a full eight hours of sleep, I knew better. He was a professional athlete who needed his rest. So instead of going over, I texted him a picture of my boobs and told him to have sweet dreams.

Strangely, the next night, my dad asked for my help picking out a present for my mom, and we once again met Xander, but this time downtown at the fancy pants Peachy Creek Mall. I was definitely missing the small shops that the rest of the world bought their things at instead of these giant American islands of mass consumerism.

I'd never known my parents to care so much about getting their shopping done. The last few years while I was abroad, they just put money into my account. Xan said it was because this would be the first Christmas all of us could be together since I'd gone galivanting around the world.

Hayes and I did make up for lost time when he did as promised and bent me over the desk in the back room after closing the shop one evening. Another new kink unlocked that night when I learned I really liked it when he wrapped my hair around his fist and pulled on it while he was fucking me from behind. Good times, good times.

Cool Beans was busier than it had ever been, the tables filled most mornings with chattering customers, and the line at the counter was steadily growing. But it still wasn't enough to get the numbers out of the red. I did have someone call to book our first after-hours event on Sunday night.

Thankfully it would be after the Mustangs' game. The guy who called said something about a family game night and wanting room to spread out and snacks that he didn't have to make. The shop would be perfect for that, and they were going to pay my shiny new café rental rate of a hundred bucks an hour plus the cost of food and beverages.

That Friday was the cat adoption event, and my day dawned bright and early, this time in Hayes's bed. He came with me to the shop before sunrise to help set up the play area for the cats and make sure everything was perfect.

"Good luck today, babe. I'll be back early, it's just run through of a few plays for the KC game."

I gave him a slightly distracted kiss on the cheek. "Okay, I'll see you later. Don't be surprised if we accidentally end up with a new cat."

He stopped dead in his tracks and grinned like a loon.

"What?"

He jogged back over to me and gave me a ridiculously hot kiss. "I just like that you're thinking about us doing things like that together."

Was I? I guess I was. Instead of the idea of making a commitment like that with him scaring me, it made me feel all warm and fuzzy on the inside. "I'll make a cat dad out of you yet."

Just as long as he didn't get ideas about being a baby

daddy anytime soon. No way either of us were ready for anything like kids.

When the shelter volunteers arrived with a dozen adorable felines in tow, I couldn't help but let out a little squeal of excitement. They were just so darn cute.

"Thank you so much for coming to do this." I shook hands with the woman who was my contact. "I'm very excited to have the cats here."

"We're excited that Cool Beans is still willing to host."

Still willing? "Umm, did something happen to make you think we wouldn't?"

"Oh, you know, just that time when one particularly feisty tabby managed to escape the play area and led us on a merry chase around the shop." She shook her head and laughed. "But once we got him safely out of the espresso machine, things ran smoothly from there."

Well, that explained a lot.

It was a good thing I'd added extra staff for today because we were packed from the moment the shop opened. It probably helped a ton that Marie Manniway stopped by first thing and posted a shot of a fluffy cat named Princess Moondrop sitting on the table next to her Calico Cappuccino with the cat design in the foam and a slice of almond bis-cat-i.

So many customers came in and cooed over the playful kittens, falling in love left and right. My cat-themed drinks and bakery items were a huge hit. To my surprise, the Tabby Tea Latte with orange pekoe sold out because it was so popular.

By midday, we'd already had six adoptions and the shop was purring with a happy, lively energy that made my heart swell. This was what I thought the shop should be like all the time.

I was just saying goodbye to a newly adopted black cat and his new owner who promised to come to the spicy romance book club when, to my surprise, Xander walked in. He was grinning from ear to ear, his eyes taking in the festive decorations and the playpen full of frolicking felines.

"This is pretty cool, Willabean. I don't think I've ever seen the place this busy." He pulled me into a big bear hug, lifting me off my feet. "I had no idea you could pull off something like this."

"Thanks." I think. "It was a lot of work, but I'm so glad it's running so well."

Xander released me, his expression turning serious. "Listen, sis. I know you're probably going to the Mustangs game on Sunday and all, but I was sort of hoping you might come to my game on Saturday."

I didn't know what to say. Maybe he really was trying to be good about Hayes and I being together. Even if he hadn't said another peep to Hayes since the night he crashed on his couch.

I had been planning on sneaking into the hotel again, since this was a home game and I didn't have to close the shop for the whole weekend to be with him. But if Xan was really offering an olive branch, I was going to take it. "Sure, I haven't been to one of your games in years. It will be... weird."

He grinned, ruffling my hair like he used to when we were kids. "Yeah, yeah. Don't go getting all mushy on me.

Now, how about you introduce me to these furry little matchmakers?"

As I watched Xander cradle a tiny orange kitten, making silly faces at it, I couldn't help but feel like everything was falling into place.

The shop was thriving, my relationship with Hayes was stronger than ever, and now, even Xander was coming around.

Life was good. Really, really good.

And as I looked around at the smiling faces of my customers, the playful antics of the cats, and the love and support of my friends and family, I knew one thing for certain.

I was exactly where I was meant to be today.

The bell above the door jingled again, and my heart skipped a beat when I saw Hayes walk in, a big palm in a pot under his arm. Why did I just know he'd done the research to know that ponytail palms were cat safe before bringing it on cat day at the café?

He caught my eye across the room, his smile brighter than the sun. But before I could make my way over to him, Xander intercepted me, the kitten still nestled in his arms. "Willa, you've got to see this little guy's trick. I think I've found my new best friend."

I laughed, indulging my brother as he showed off the kitten's ability to give a tiny high-five. It was adorable, sure, but I had a twinge of impatience. Hayes was here, and all I wanted was to be in his arms.

Xander kept on chattering about the cats, the shop, and everything in between. "You think I'd make a good cat dad, don't you, Beanie?"

"Sure. Why don't you adopt this one and name it Dragon or Mustang?" I tried to step away to go greet Hayes, but Xan didn't seem to notice I was trying to end our conversation.

"He looks more like a Dragon to me, don't you, little guy?" Xan bopped the kitten on the nose, and it mewed at him. "See how fierce he is already?"

I looked and scratched the spot between my eyes. "I think that one is a girl."

"Ooh, Dragon Slayer then. Killer of men's hearts everywhere."

Was Xan having girl problems? I wasn't going to ask. From the corner of my eye, I saw Hayes waiting patiently near the counter. He could have just come over here, but somehow, I knew he was trying not to engage with Xan. I didn't blame him.

"Mommy, look, an orange kitty. It matches daddy's hair. Can we get this one?" Xander's attention was diverted by this little girl who clearly had her heart set on his Dragon Slayer. When he knelt to show the kitten to her, I took my chance, slipping away and making a beeline for Hayes.

"Hey, you," I murmured, rising up on my toes to press a kiss to his lips. "I'm so sorry about that. Xander's weirdly enamored with the cats."

Hayes shook his head, his smile understanding. "It's okay, Willa. I get it. He's your brother, and he wants to spend time with you."

I sighed, taking the plant from him, and carrying it to the sink behind the counter. "Yeah, you're right but... I feel like I've hardly gotten to spend time with you at all this week."

He pulled me close, his arms wrapping around my waist. "We've got all the time in the world, sweetheart. I'm not going anywhere."

I leaned into him, breathing in his familiar scent. How did he always know just what to say?

Over Hayes's shoulder, I caught a glimpse of Xander watching us, his expression unreadable. Please let him finally be happy for me for once.

"Hey, boss," Javier, my most reliable employee who'd actually volunteered to work the cat rescue shift with me, stuck his head out from behind the espresso machine. "It's doing that thing again. I think it's gonna blow."

"Shit." I dashed over to the backline and hurried to examine the machine. The repair guy had given me a couple of tricks to do if it started acting up again. I went through a few of them, but in the end, I gave it a swift smack to the side, and the rattling it was making stopped.

"Phew. Crisis averted." Javier snorted at me. "I don't think it's used to working this hard."

I helped him catch up on the orders for the waiting customers, and while I was putting the fancy cat foam topper on a latte, I noticed Hayes and Xander standing near the door talking.

Xan said something to Hayes, too low for me to hear, but I saw Hayes's jaw tighten almost imperceptibly. When he didn't reply, my brother slapped him on the arm and walked out the door, without so much as a goodbye wave to me.

After I got Javi caught up, I made my way over to Hayes. "What was that about?"

Hayes shrugged, his smile not quite reaching his eyes. "Nothing important. Just guy stuff."

I didn't believe that for a second. These two were the most important men in my life and I was going to sit on one or the other to find out what had just happened between them. One I was going to smack around in the way only a younger sister can, and the other... I decided I'd start with Hayes, because sitting on certain parts of him would be a lot of fun.

Starting with his face.

SO ALIVE, SO DEAD

HAYES

My girl was a force of nature, and watching her in her element, charming people, and cats for that matter, making her dreams come true, only made me fall deeper in love with her.

But what the fuck was I going to do about Xan? He may have Willa fooled that he was trying to be a good guy, and I did not want to hurt their relationship, but I loved her, and I wasn't going to let anyone stand in the way of our happiness.

After the last customer left with their brand new cat in a carrier under their arm and a tea latte to go, I locked the door behind them and pulled the cord on the neon open sign. Willa looked beat. Happy, but exhausted.

"That was a crazy day," she murmured, giving me a hug, and nuzzling into my chest. "Tell me you're here to carry me home to bed. Who knew cat wrangling mixed with coffee making would be so exhausting?"

"That's the very next thing on my to-do list." I was insisting she get some extra sleep, which was not my original plan. Although, a couple of really great orgasms could send her off to dreamland.

I made her leave some of the cleanup for the morning and put her into my car. She yawned and laid her head on my shoulder as we drove the few blocks back to my house.

"You wanna sneak into the hotel with me tomorrow night, sweetheart? I promise not to accidentally on purpose knock on Coach's door this time. Unless, of course, the thrill of getting caught is on your kinks list."

She didn't look up at me and gave my arm a soft squeeze. "I promised Xander I'd go to his game tomorrow night. He asked me to be there, and I don't want him to think I can't support him just because we're together, you know?"

I nodded, trying to ignore the little twinge of unease in my gut. Xander's challenge had me on edge. *"You're good, Kingman. But you'll never be good enough for her."*

I couldn't tell Willa that. Not when she was so hopeful about rebuilding her relationship with her brother.

"That's great, babe. I'm sure it'll mean a lot to him to have you there." I forced a smile, an idea forming. "We can go together if you want. Dad's box will have room for us."

Looks like I'd be sneaking out of the hotel instead of Willa sneaking in. But I'd probably get in less trouble for going to my brothers' college football game than getting caught with a girl in my room after bed check. And honestly, I'd be happy to pay that fine. I hadn't been to a Dragons game since I'd joined the Mustangs. Might be fun to hit the alma mater.

Willa bit her lip, looking torn, which surprised me. “That's really sweet of you, but... Xan said he already has a ticket for me, probably sitting with my parents. I don't want to ruffle any feathers, you know?”

I swallowed back my arguments, reminding myself that this was about supporting Willa, not giving in to my own worries. “Of course, babe. It'll be nice for you to hang out with them.”

She snuggled into my arm. “I haven't been to this many football games since high school. Two in two days? What have you done with the real Willa? Because this is a clear case of body snatching if ever I saw one.”

Willa had made a lot of changes in her life, and she hardly seemed fazed by it. “I've thrown her into a supernatural prison with no memory of who or what she truly is. But there are four wolf shifters there who will help her remember through the power of her magic va-jay-jay.”

She giggled and smacked me in the arm. “You read *The Fate of the Wolf Guard*?”

“Yep.” I hadn't read this much fiction in quite a while, but I'd always been a big reader. And honestly, I was learning as much from romance novels as I did the nonfiction I usually chose. Not just about sex either. Plus, it was fun to share a hobby with my girl. “I really enjoyed all the historical references. Not to mention some of those very interesting sex scenes. We should definitely try doing it outside in the woods under the full moon.”

"When in the world did you have time to read a whole series this week?"

We pulled into the garage, and I loved the naturalness of chatting while coming home together. When her uncles were back, I'd ask her to just move in with me. Then we could do this all the time. "The nights I wasn't spending with you."

Seven met us at the door and she scooped him up, giving him a snuggle. "At least somebody had fun. If I have to go Christmas shopping with any of my family members one more time this month, I'll cry. I don't know who thought malls were a good idea, but they need to be smacked around."

Her cat spent a long time smelling her up and down and rubbed his face all over her chest. Lucky bastard. At least with him, I could have Willa to myself by distracting him with a can of fancy cat food.

Afterward, I fed both her and her cat and took Willa to bed, indeed fucking her until she fell asleep after a couple of orgasms.

But as comfortable as I was with her laying in my arms, I was restless.

I left her sleeping peacefully and padded down to the living room, my mind churning, bouncing from one thing to the next. I hated not being able to focus.

There was some game tape I could watch, but for once, the thought of diving into football analysis didn't appeal. Instead, I threw on a hoodie and some Crocs, and slid the back door open. Seven sprinted out after me and took up residence on one of the lawn chairs. "Good call, buddy."

I picked him up and sat down, settling him in my lap.

The full moon stared down at me and Willa's words from earlier echoed in my head. "What have you done with the real Willa?"

It was a joke, of course, but the Willa I'd first met, the one who'd breezed into town with wanderlust in her eyes and adventure in her heart, had transformed so much in the past few months. She'd taken on the challenge of running the café with gusto, pouring her creativity and passion into making it thrive.

Willa slipped into any role with ease. She was a world traveler, a teacher, then a small business owner and a rescuer of cats. She went from the girl next door to instant friends with a pop star. She was a romance loving book worm who knew just as many football stats as I did.

Watching her come alive with this new purpose, this new direction, had been breathtaking. But it also stirred something in me, questions were coming up that hadn't even crossed my radar before.

She was so fucking joyful, colorful… alive.

What was I?

I'd had one goal my whole life, and I was living it now. I'd never allowed myself to ever think about anything but playing pro ball. I loved the game, lived and breathed it. The thrill of competition, the rush of adrenaline, the satisfaction of pushing my body to its limits, it was everything to me.

My life, my goals were always so black and white.

But seeing Willa embrace this whole new life, this new career path, made me wonder. What if football wasn't forever? What if, God forbid, I got hurt and couldn't play anymore? Who would I be then?

She was flexible, adaptable, and could so easily be whatever she wanted to.

I was a football player.

That was it.

How would that ever be enough for her?

Seven purred, probably his way of laughing at me for being a dumbass. I sighed, rubbing a hand over my face but giving myself a nose full of cat hair.

Life was good, great even. I had an amazing woman who loved me, a family who supported me, a career that most people could only dream of. I just couldn't shake the feeling that I needed to work harder. Do more. Be more, for all of them.

A snowflake drifted down in front of my face, and then another. This would make for a cold game for the boys tomorrow night, but it would probably be gone by my game on Sunday. It didn't snow as much here as people thought it did.

So many people hated the snow, but I'd always loved it. Some of my very first memories were of playing in the snow. For the first time in my adult life, a very old but familiar pang hit me right behind the eyeballs. It crept down my throat and made it go tight.

I wished Willa could have met my mom. I think they would have really liked each other.

Seven made a weird sort of chirping sound at me and then crawled up my chest and settled himself there like a soft, fluffy cat baby. I gave him a hug and it weirdly made me feel comforted. God, I really was turning into a cat dad.

I needed sleep, needed to clear my head. Reset and

focus on what was right in front of me. A girl I loved and a career I was really fucking good at.

I went back inside and slipped into bed, Willa instinctively curling into me, her warmth chasing away the chill of my thoughts. I probably shouldn't have, but I couldn't help it. I woke her with a series of soft kisses, and then fucked her gently until she was whimpering my name again and again. This time I made her beg me to make her come.

We were both a little bit extra tired the next morning, and Willa even had a couple of sips of my coffee before she went back to her house to change and get ready for her day. I was this close to telling her to just bring her clothes over here.

My head wasn't in it at practice that morning either. It wasn't like I didn't know these plays frontward and backward and sideways. I could do them in my sleep. Which was basically what I did.

My mind was already racing ahead to the DSU game tonight. I knew I shouldn't interfere, that Willa could handle her brother and her parents herself, but I couldn't shake the feeling that Xander was up to something, and I needed to be there.

Once Coach released us, I made a split-second decision, pulling out my phone and dialing my dad's number. "Hey, Dad. How do you feel about catching the Dragons game with me tonight?"

He'd be there anyway. Being the former coach and having three or four kids on the team at any given time meant it was his favorite past time.

"You asking me to contribute to the delinquency of a

Mustang, son?" His tone was deadpan, but I knew him better than that. Once a Dragon, always a Dragon, and we always supported our own.

"Yep." I crossed my fingers he wasn't as surprised by this favor as I suspected he would be.

He didn't say anything for a minute, and I thought maybe I'd read him wrong. "About time you broke a few rules, kid."

I... didn't know what to say to that. My life was and always had been about following the rules and doing what was expected. All eight of us learned real early that was the only way the household could function. Except maybe Jules. She was the exception to every Kingman rule. And we loved her for it.

A few hours later, after I'd checked into the hotel the Mustangs stayed at for our home games and then snuck out, I was settling into my seat in the Kingman suite. My dad, and fucking Chris and Declan sat on one side of me, and Everett and Jules on the other. Seemed I wasn't the only delinquent Mustang who liked to sneak out of the hotel to catch a Dragons game.

"Wondered when you'd get your head out of your tight ass and show up to one of these." Declan stole the hot dog I'd just grabbed and took a bite out of it.

What was this, razz the rookie day? "I'd have been here sooner if you dickwads would have told me this was a thing."

Chris shook his head. "No you wouldn't have. You were too busy running circles around the rest of us to even take a break, much less sneak out to relax for a minute."

My oldest brother was the last one I thought I'd ever hear that from. He was the one who twitched if you were two minutes late for anything. He was also the brother I'd idolized most growing up. He had everything, and I worked my ass off to be just like him.

"It still took most of the season to get him here." Declan shoved the other half of the hot dog into his mouth and did not wait to swallow before he continued. "Something brought you here and it wasn't to hang out with us."

Everett laughed. "It's got to be about a girl."

Oh god, save me from older brothers. "It's—"

Jules cut me off. "Duh. It's always about a girl with you lot. His girlfriend is coming to the game tonight."

Wait. When I prayed to be saved from brothers, I did not mean I wanted to be harassed by my one and only little sister.

"What I don't understand is why she isn't up here in the box with us." Jules shook her head at me like I really was a dumbass. "Who lets their girlfriend freeze in those cold, plastic seats in the snow?"

"She's sitting with her parents." I was about to go buy a ticket in the cheap seats too.

"You could have invited them, son." That was big coming from my dad. He didn't like having anyone but family in his box.

"I tried."

Every Kingman in the room turned and looked at me. Jules was the one to break the silence. "Uh-oh. Do her parents not like you? That's got to be a new feeling for our own personal golden boy."

I opted to look straight ahead at the football field. "The Dragons are looking good this season."

My dad was the one who let me off the hook. "They are, thanks in no small part to Flynn and Gryff's stellar performances. I expect they'll both go in the first round this year, along with your friend Xander Rosemount."

Did I say he let me off the hook? Why did I decide to come to this game again?

Chris leaned over and stage whispered to Declan, "I thought I was the golden boy of the family."

"No, you're confusing yourself with the Golden Girls," Jules leaned across me and Everett to not so quietly whisper back. "Of whom you will soon be joining because you're so old."

As my siblings continued to swap jabs and the minutes ticked by while the teams warmed up and the stands filled with fans, I couldn't stop my eyes from scanning the section below us where family members usually had tickets. When kickoff rolled around and there was still no sign of Willa, I started to worry. I pulled out my phone, shooting her a quick text.

Hey, babe. I decided to catch the game with my family too. You here yet? I thought maybe we'd all get a bite to eat after the game.

Her response came a few minutes later, and my heart sank as I read the words.

I'm here, but they can't find my ticket. Xan said he left it at will call, but no one seems to know anything about it. I'm stuck outside the gate trying to argue my way in.

I was on my feet in an instant, already moving toward the exit. "I'll be right back. Willa needs me."

I took the stairs two at a time, my mind racing. There was no way Xander had "accidentally" forgot to leave a ticket at will call for his sister.

When I finally spotted her standing forlornly by the ticket booth, my heart clenched. I jogged over, talked to Mrs. Bo, who, at a thousand and two years old still volunteered at the DSU ticket booth, and then waved Willa in.

She was shaking and I didn't know whether it was from the cold or if she was about to cry. I was going to kill her brother either way. I pulled her to me and rubbed her back and arms. "Hey, it's okay. I've got you."

She clung to me, her face buried in my chest. "I am going to murder him. I can't believe he did this. I mean, I can, but... I really thought he was trying. Do you know my parents aren't even here? I am going to kick Xan's ass. He thinks I can't do it, but I assure you, if I surprise him, I can take him down and sit on his chest so he can't fucking breathe."

Maybe I didn't have to get my brothers to help me bury Xander's body. We'd be too busy helping Willa do it. She was pih-issed.

I stroked her hair, trying my best to tame the savage beast, and pressed a kiss to her temple. "I know, flower. I'll help you bury the body later, okay?"

She was still seething as we walked up the stairs to the club level. "I'll plant columbines on his grave so it will be illegal to dig it up. I'll do it too. He's been a giant douche from the land of douchebags since I came home."

Note to self: don't ever make Willa really angry and keep her away from the state flower. "Let's go watch the game. We'll deal with him after."

Xander might be trying to come between us, but I don't think he realized how incredible his sister really was. He could doubt me all he wanted, but he was the one who wasn't good enough for her. He was her brother for fuck's sake. He should be taking care of her, supporting her.

I was going to enjoy seeing Willa take him down a notch.

DETAILED FRATRICIDE PLANS

WILLA

I slammed my front door and Seven hissed at me and ran away in protest.

"Sorry, poo poo. I didn't mean to scare you. I owe you a treat." I was getting one for myself anyway. A lot of Moose Tracks ice cream was in my near future.

Maybe I would have been able to calm down if I'd gone to spend the night with Hayes, but I knew I wasn't good company and honestly couldn't be bothered with the whole sneaking in and out of the hotel thing. I was feeling second place to everything in the whole wide world, and that wasn't fair to Hayes.

So I came home to sulk. I made my sundae, made a mini one with whipped cream and tuna for Seven, and flopped onto the couch. I needed some good old-fashioned escapism to forget my detailed fratricide plans.

I pulled out my Kindle, opened the book I was in the

middle of, and proceeded to read the same page three times. Gah. I couldn't even get into the book I was reading, and it was just getting to the juicy part. That made me even more irritated so I turned on the TV and navigated to my comfort episode of Star Trek Voyager.

It was the one where Janeway and Chakotay get stranded on an uninhabited planet and have to eke out a new life for themselves. It was the stuck-on-a-deserted-island trope I loved, and I wished I could escape to some tropical island where I didn't have to deal with anything but what kind of hut I was going to build and how to store all the coconuts.

The only company I could tolerate for the night was Seven, and for once he wasn't at Hayes's. At least I was important to my own cat. Could be the whipped cream and tuna that kept him by my side though.

How could Xander do this to me? Sure, he'd been a dick plenty of times when we were growing up, but he'd never been truly malicious. I didn't think I could handle talking to him right now, and this was not a text conversation. But I knew exactly where he'd be tomorrow morning.

Anytime he won a game, my mother made him old-fashioned cinnamon rolls the following morning. She'd never fucking made me any sort of baked good. Well, tomorrow I was going to my parents', and I wasn't just going to eat Xan's precious reward breakfast, I was going to flush it down the god damned toilet.

That made me a whole lot happier just thinking about it. I fell asleep on the couch with the TV on and had lovely dreams about my brother being assimilated by the Borg.

But I still woke up early enough to make it to my parents' house in time for the sweet scent of freshly baked cinnamon rolls the next morning.

"Xander." I marched over to him, right past my mom plating up the warm food, my hands balled into fists at my sides. "What the hell was that?"

He looked up, his eyes widening in surprise. "Willa? What are you doing here?"

"Oh, I don't know, maybe I thought some hot cinnamon rolls would help thaw out my frost-bitten fingers. The ones that turned blue trying to get into the game I was invited to last night. The one you conveniently forgot to leave me a ticket for."

"Willa, dear." My mother's voice was both syrupy sweet and chastising at the same time. "You don't like going to Xander's games. Why would you try to go to the one last night when it was snowing? Your father and I didn't even go in that weather."

Xander's brow furrowed, genuine confusion etched on his face. "What are you talking about? I left your ticket at will call, just like I said I would."

I scoffed, crossing my arms over my chest. "Well, it wasn't there. I spent half an hour standing in the snow arguing with the ticket office, trying to convince them to let me in."

He stood up, his expression a mix of concern and hurt. "Willa, I swear, I left that ticket for you. I would never intentionally keep you out of the game. Do you really think I would do something like that?"

I opened my mouth to retort, but the words died on my tongue. The look on his face, the earnestness in his voice... could I have been wrong? Had it really just been a mistake?

"I..." I swallowed hard, suddenly feeling exceedingly small. "I don't know what to think, Xan. It's just, with everything that's happened, the way you've been acting about, you know, Hayes, and everything."

He sighed, running a hand through his hair. "Willa, I would never betray you like that, and honestly, it fucking hurts that you would even think it. You never would have before you started spending so much time with him."

"You do spend a lot of time with that boy." I expected guilt trips from my mother, which was part and parcel of being her daughter. "I thought with you being back in Colorado, we'd see you more than when you were in god knows where."

Guilt twisted in my gut, a bitter taste in my mouth. Had I been so wrapped up in my own life, in my relationship with Hayes, that I'd neglected my own family? When was the last time I'd spent any real time with Xander, or my parents, without being coerced into it?

"I'm sorry," I whispered, blinking back the sudden sting of tears. "I should have known better. I've just been so caught up in everything, and I guess I haven't been a particularly good sister lately, have I?"

Xander's expression softened, and he pushed his plate over to me while my mom wasn't looking. "Hey, it's okay. We're family, Willabean. That means something."

I ate a bite of his cinnamon roll, my anger draining away, replaced by a hollow feeling of regret. He was right. Family did mean something, and I'd been taking mine for granted.

"Care-bear, why don't we head back to bed and have a little fun." My dad walked into the kitchen, not even noticing that Xander and I were there. "I was hoping the weather would clear up this morning and I could get a tee-time, but it's a no go."

Xander cleared his throat a little too loudly and for an extra-long time. I laughed and waved at my dad. "Hi, Dad."

"Kids, what are you two doing here? I thought I got rid of you both years ago." He came over like he hadn't just propositioned my mother right in front of us and gave me a kiss on the cheek and Xander a clap on the back. "Good game last night?"

"Yeah." Xander made a face. "But now I think I know why you and Mom didn't make it, you dirty old man."

My dad shrugged. "Rosemount men are virile, son. Don't ever forget that."

"Gross, Dad."

My dad grabbed the cinnamon roll I was eating and popped the rest into his mouth. "You'll thank me for it when you're in your fifties, kid. Trust me."

Strangely, my mother was silent through the entire exchange, but she did have a secret little smile on her face.

"I think I have to go throw up now." I slipped out into the hallway and pulled out my phone. I needed to talk to Hayes, to explain what had happened and the realizations I'd come to.

He answered on the first ring, his voice warm and soothing in my ear. "Hey, babe. Everything okay?"

"Yeah, I just…" I sighed. I hated being wrong, but it was worse being wrong and a bitch about it. "I talked to

Xander, and I think it was all just a misunderstanding. He swears he left my ticket at will call."

"Do you believe him?" There was no judgment in Hayes's tone, just gentle concern.

I leaned against the wall. "I do. And it made me realize how I've been neglecting my family. I feel like a terrible daughter, a terrible sister."

"You're not. Not even a little bit. I've seen you drop everything for your family, and they know that. Xan has been... challenging lately. We both jumped to the conclusion that he punked you."

"Okay. You're right." His words were like a balm to my battered heart, easing the ache of guilt. "Thanks."

We stayed quiet for a moment, just listening to each other breathe, and I needed that safe space with him. It made it easier to deal with everything else in my world. "Hey, do you think I could bring my family to your game today? It would be kind of nice for our families to hang out together."

"Of course, babe. That's a great idea. I'll make some calls, get them set up in the box. Be forewarned, no Kelsey today. She's got a music video to shoot or something."

Relief and gratitude surged through me. "Noted. I'll save that surprise for another day. Thank you. For everything."

"Anytime. Now, go enjoy the game with your family. I'll see you tonight."

"Not until later. I have that after-hours booking for the board game people at the shop tonight."

"Oh, right. Yeah. Gotta go, babe. Love you."

He clicked off before I could say it back. Weird. Probably had to make those calls to set up the tickets for the game. It was really last minute, and kickoff was in just a few hours.

I walked back into the kitchen with my good news. “Hey, so, do you all want to go to the Mustangs game today?”

My dad smiled, but my mom and brother exchanged a look. “Sorry, honey, but your brother and I have plans this afternoon. But why don't you take your father since he can't play golf?”

Sigh. I tried. “You up for it, Dad?”

“Since I'm not getting laid, I guess a Mustangs game will have to do.” He wrapped me in a one-armed hug, and we walked out of the kitchen. “Let me just grab my coat, hat, and gloves. It's gonna be a cold one. Should we grab some lunch on the way?”

I'd surprise him later with the fact that he wasn't going to need his cold-weather gear or lunch since it would be toasty warm and there would be plenty to eat in the Kingman box. “No, let's eat at the game. I love stadium food.”

“Beer and nachos for the win.”

An hour later, I stood in the Kingman suite at Mile High Stadium, my father already loading up on the nachos. He was delighted when I introduced him to Mr. Kingman, and they hit it off right away. Probably because Mr. Kingman started a conversation about Xander's chances in the upcoming draft. Funny how they'd never really met before. But my mom did like to control everyone in the family's life, so there was that.

The game kicked off and the players took the field,

and I couldn't take my eyes off Hayes. He was all power and grace and determination. Every time he made a play, I felt a thrill of pride and love so strong it took my breath away. Plus, I think he might have changed his workout routine, because his butt was looking fi-ine in those tight pants today. Better than usual. He was moving up my mental list. He might even make it into the top ten this year.

Jules and Trixie plopped down on either side of me, which were open since my dad was totally engrossed in his new BFF. I couldn't quite shake the feeling of being an outsider in my own life. Jules gave me a knowing and empathetic look.

"Been there, done that, got the I'm-the-only-girl-here t-shirt. But don't worry, I got you, boo. I'm collecting a whole girl gang if you hadn't noticed, so none of us have to be wallflowers at these things."

Trixie raised a finger. "I've been collected."

"Jules," I shook my head and stole a handful of her popcorn. "I don't believe for a second that you've ever been a wallflower."

"Yeah, but everything is a competition in my family, including who's the center of attention. You'll see." She winked at me. "Later."

I didn't know what that meant but the Mustangs scored their first touchdown of the day, a pass from Chris to Everett, and the crowd and the box went wild, so I didn't get the chance to ask. It was a really intense game, especially when Hayes got tackled really hard and it took him a second longer to get up. Ooph. I didn't like that.

I had to leave a few minutes early to make sure the

coffee shop was set up for the small event tonight. So I sent a text to Hayes to tell him how great he was and that I'd see him later, and I called an Uber so my dad could stay for the whole game.

As I hurried through the quiet streets of Thornminster, my mind buzzed with plans and ideas. This event could be a good test for the shop, a chance to see if I could cross that red line into the black with after-hours events like this.

I was so lost in thought that I almost didn't notice the figure huddled by the front door of the shop until I was nearly on top of them.

"Xander?" I frowned, taking in the cardboard box at his feet and the distressed look on his face. "What are you doing here?"

He stood up, running a hand through his hair. "Willa, thank god. I need your help."

A muffled mewling sound emanated from the box, and my eyes widened. "Are those... kittens?"

Xander nodded, his expression pained. "I took Mom to the shelter today, thought she might like a cat for Christmas. You know, after seeing how much fun you had with the adoption event."

I raised an eyebrow, a sinking feeling in my gut. "Let me guess. She wasn't thrilled with the idea."

"That's an understatement," he muttered, kicking at the ground. "But that's not the worst part. When we were leaving, there was this woman in the parking lot, crying her eyes out. She had this box of kittens and was freaking out about the shelter euthanizing them."

I pinched the bridge of my nose, a headache beginning

to throb behind my eyes. "Xan, the shelter is a no-kill facility. They wouldn't have euthanized them."

He threw his hands up, his face flushing. "Well, I know that now. But in the moment, I just... I couldn't leave them there. So I said I'd take them."

"And now you're here," I finished, my tone flat. "Xander, I can't take a box of kittens right now. I have an event starting in..." I checked my watch, my stomach dropping, "less than thirty minutes."

His eyes pleaded with me, his bottom lip jutting out in a pout that had always worked on me when we were kids. "Willa, please. I can't take them back to the dorm, and the shelter's closed now. I don't know what else to do."

I stared at him, my mind racing. I wouldn't just leave the kittens to fend for themselves, but I also couldn't have them running around the shop during the event. It would be chaos.

But as I looked at my brother, at the genuine desperation and fear in his eyes, I knew I couldn't turn him away. Not after all the bridges we'd started to rebuild.

"Fine," I sighed, my shoulders slumping in defeat. "Leave them here. I'll figure something out."

Relief washed over his face, and he pulled me into a quick, tight hug. "Thank you, Willa. I owe you one."

"Yeah, yeah," I grumbled, pushing him away. "Just go, before I change my mind."

He flashed me a grateful smile before jogging off, leaving me alone with a box of mewling kittens and a rapidly approaching deadline.

I carried the box inside, my mind whirling with possibilities. Maybe I could set up a play area in the back room or...

The jingle of the bell above the door interrupted my spiraling thoughts, and I spun around, ready to apologize to my early guests.

But the words died on my tongue as I took in the sight before me. The entire Kingman clan, from Bridger to Jules, even Trixie, Kelsey, and Penelope, were piling into the shop, their arms laden with board games and weirdly embroidered pillows.

"Surprise!" Jules called out, her grin wide and mischievous. "I'm the one who booked the coffee shop for family game night. We do not fit into the living room anymore now that there's a girls' team, and we needed a bigger space. I figured this way, we could support your business and get you to join us."

I gaped at her, my heart swelling with a mixture of gratitude and overwhelming affection. "Jules, this is... I don't even know what to say."

She shrugged, her eyes twinkling. "You're almost family, Willa. And family looks out for each other."

As the Kingmans began to set up, chattering and laughing and filling the space with warmth and love, I felt a lump form in my throat.

This. This was what I'd been missing, what I'd been searching for all these years. A sense of belonging, of unconditional acceptance.

And as I watched Hayes walk through the door, his eyes finding mine across the room, I knew I'd finally found it.

I was home.

The kittens chose that moment to let out a chorus of plaintive mews, drawing everyone's attention to the box in my arms.

"Uh, Willa?" Hayes raised an eyebrow, amusement, and curiosity warring on his face. "Is there something you want to tell us?"

I laughed, the sound bubbling out of me like a spring. "It's a long story. But first, who wants to help me wrangle some kittens?"

KINGMAN FAMILY GAME NIGHT - NOW WITH KITTENS!

HAYES

As my family basically took over the coffee shop and set up for game night, I couldn't keep the grin off my face. Seeing Willa's surprise and delight at Jules's secret plan made all the whispered conversations and covert planning worth it.

"I hope you're ready for this, sweetheart, because you have no idea what you're in for. Kingman family game night is intense to say the least."

She laughed, rising up on her toes to press a quick kiss to my lips. "Bring it on, Kingman. I think I can handle a little friendly competition."

As if on cue, a shout rang out from across the room. "Dibs on the lucky pillow!"

I whirled around to see Flynn clutching the faded green cushion to his chest, a triumphant grin on his face.

"No fair!" Jules pouted, her arms crossed over her chest. "You got it last time!"

Flynn stuck his tongue out at her, hugging the pillow tighter. "Snooze, you lose, little sis."

I shook my head, chuckling under my breath. The lucky pillow, handmade by our mother years ago with the words "In this house, we bleed green" embroidered on the front, was the subject of much contention at every game night.

Legend had it that whoever sat on the pillow was guaranteed victory, and my siblings would stop at nothing to claim it as their own.

"Alright, everyone." My dad clapped his hands, his voice booming over the chatter. "Time to pick your teams and your kitten mascots!"

There was a mad scramble as my brothers, all grown men who towered over six feet, dove for the box of kittens like they were fumbling for a football.

"Dibs on the orange ball of chaos!" Everett shouted, scooping up a squirming ball of fur. "And I choose Pen as my partner in crime." Pen blushed and took the kitten from Everett as she sat down next to him.

Chris cradled a tiny tuxedo to his chest, his face softening in a way I rarely saw. "This one's ours, Trix. He looks like a winner."

She laughed and smiled at him. "Only if we can name him Obi Wan Catnobi."

Even Declan, the most competitive of us all, couldn't resist the charm of a fluffy orange and white striped one. "You and me, little guy," he murmured, stroking the kitten's head with a gentleness that belied his size. He turned to his fiancée and said, “Kelsey, meet Winnie the Purr.”

She frowned at him. “No, Declan, no.”

“Meow-ore?” He gave the cat a sad face.

“No.” Kelsey was having none of it.

“Meowl.”

Kelsey shook her head again and gave him a warning wag of her finger. “Declan.”

“A. A. Mewln?”

Kelsey took the cat from him and cuddled it to her chest. “Why does he tease us like this Tigger?” She mock glared at Declan. “T-I-double Puh-urr.”

It was a lucky thing there were nine kittens in the box, because it almost came to fists over the remaining kittens. Willa leaned into me, her eyes shining with laughter. “I never thought I'd see the day when the Kingman brothers were brought to their knees by a bunch of kittens. Is it always like this?” she murmured, her eyes wide with a mix of awe and amusement.

I grinned, squeezing her hand. “Pretty much. Just wait until the games actually start.” This was nothing compared to when the competition really heated up. “It's about to get real. Real crazy.”

And start they did, with a fierce intensity that would have put any football rivalry to shame. Teams were chosen, kittens were claimed as mascots, and the battle began.

And real it got, with the first casualty coming mere minutes into a heated round of Footballopoly.

“No!” Isak cried, lunging for his sleek gray kitten as it

darted across the board, scattering houses and hotels in its wake. "Vito Catlione, come back!"

Penelope dissolved into giggles, leaning against Everett for support. "Vito Catlione? You named your kitten after the Godfather?"

Isak shot her a sheepish grin, finally capturing the wayward feline. "This is clearly a kitten you can't refuse."

As the game progressed, so did the kitten-induced chaos.

Jules's cat kept swiping the dice whenever anyone rolled, and it was hilarious to see her mock outrage. "Now, Marie Purrie, that is no way to win the hearts and minds of the people."

But it was Willa's kitten, a tiny tan fluffball she'd named Captain Purrcard, who stole the show. With a mischievous glint in his eye, he pounced on Flynn, sinking his tiny claws into my brother's ass, which had him jumping to his feet, giving Gryff a chance to steal the pillow right out from under Flynn.

"Oh no, Captain!" Willa laughed, trying to detach the cat from his prey. "You must honor the football butts, not destroy them."

Watching Willa with my family, seeing the joy and love that radiated from her, only made me fall harder.

Gryff's tabby, dubbed Catzilla, made a break for the snack table, upending a bowl of popcorn and leaving a trail of buttery paw prints in his wake. That's when Willa declared a short break for everyone to feed their charges with the kitten food she had DoorDashed to us.

As the night wore on and the kittens began to doze off in our laps, the trash talk and laughter gave way to whispers and giggles, none of us wanting to disturb their slumber, and we switched gears into a game of silent charades.

It was in those quieter moments, watching Willa cradle a tiny ball of fluff against her chest, her face soft with tenderness, that I felt the most comfortable. She made me laugh, made me think, made me want to be a better man.

"Alright, team," my dad whispered, cradling a sleeping calico against his chest. "We've got this. Kingmans see the game through, even at a volume level suitable for napping kittens. But if any of you wake up Catsanova here, you're out of the game."

The lot of us exchanged silent grins, our competitive spirits rising to the challenge.

What followed was a battle of wits and stealth, with exaggerated gestures and barely suppressed laughter filling the room. Trixie and Penelope proved to be masters of the silent clue, while Jules's interpretations bordered on the surreal, and Kelsey literally guessed every single charade before everyone else.

But it was Willa who awed me, her face alight with happiness as she acted out clue after clue, her movements fluid and graceful even in the confined space. I'd never seen anything more beautiful.

The final round drew to a close, Declan and Kelsey were declared the winners, and the kittens began to stir, so we called it a night. Everyone gently returned their cats back to the box, now made more comfortable with several scarves to line it.

Isak almost snuck out with Vito Catlione, but my dad

caught him and made him put the furball back with the others. He and Jules were the last to leave.

"Thank you," Willa murmured, her arms tight around Jules. "For everything. I've never felt so..."

"Loved?" Jules finished, her smile soft and knowing. "That's because you are, Willa. You're one of us now."

I swallowed past the lump in my throat, my eyes stinging with sudden emotion. Jules was right. Willa was a part of this family, a part of my heart.

And as we gathered up the kittens and said our goodbyes, I knew I'd do whatever it took to keep her there, right by my side.

Where she belonged.

We drove the few blocks back to my house, the streets quiet and dark, and I couldn't keep the grin off my face the whole way. This night, this perfect, chaotic, wonderful night, was everything I ever needed.

When we got out of the car, Willa paused at the door from the garage to the house. "I'm not sure how Seven is going to react to having all these kittens around. We might have to keep them in your room and him out."

"Ooph. He isn't going to like that." When we got inside, the box under my arm, Seven was perched on the back of the couch like he'd been waiting for us all night. Except, he didn't give either Willa or me a second look. His eyes fixated on the box.

"Let's see what he does." Willa sat on the couch and had me hand her the box. She carefully opened the lid and Seven looked down and then very carefully crawled inside and laid in the middle of the sleeping fuzzbutts.

"Well, would you look at that," Willa laughed, shaking

her head in amazement. “I think someone's feeling paternal.” Seven began to groom the nearest kitten, his rough tongue smoothing over downy fur.

“I'm pretty sure he's decided those kittens are his.”

I knew the feeling.

There was something about tonight that had me feeling possessive of Willa. Not like I thought anyone could ever steal her away from me, more like I wanted to make sure she knew she was mine and that I was hers.

She made me feel so damn alive, and I didn’t want to lose that feeling. Tonight, having her by my side, being a part of my family, and bringing a whole new excitement to our fun was like a trip to Oz where everything was colorful, and bright, and crazy in all the ways I didn’t even know existed.

No way I was ready to go back to Kansas.

I wanted something special that was only between the two of us, something to hold onto when I had to go back to the responsibilities of my everyday life. I didn't yet know what that was. Maybe she would.

I led her upstairs and pulled my shirt over my head the moment we were in the room, tossing it into the laundry basket. Her sweet smile turned spicy as she licked her lips and motioned with her finger for me to come to her.

I stalked toward her. It was fun and a phenomenal turn on when she took charge, but that wasn't what I needed tonight. I grabbed her wrist and pulled her to me and crashed my mouth down on hers.

“Strip for me, Willa. I want to watch you as you show me every inch of what I want to fuck tonight.”

A new blush I hadn't seen before rushed across the

tops of her cheeks, and she drew in a sharp breath. For a second, I thought I'd made her mad, but then she blinked, and her eyes sparkled like starlight on broken glass. "I think it might be your turn to be bossy in the bedroom, because that was sexy as hell and definitely just flipped a switch for me."

Well hot damn. There was something so perfect about the way, without even saying a word, we were on the same page. I let her go and then sat in the chair across from the bed. "Take it off, slowly. I want to see every single inch of you."

I also knew what she wanted. I unbuckled my pants and pulled my dick out, giving it a few short strokes. Willa's eyes flared and her lips parted. "I'm going to fuck that pretty mouth later. Now stop stalling and let me see what else I'm going to fuck."

She smiled and undid her jeans, wagging her hips back and forth as she pushed them down her thick thighs. I swear to god, I wanted to drop to my knees and sink my teeth into that first curve of her inner thigh, right where it was the widest, below her soft pussy. But that wasn't the game right now.

Willa was giving me what I wanted, and it was my turn. I spit in my hand and gripped my dick harder, sliding my hand up and down. Her eyes were transfixed on me, and she clenched her legs together.

"That look on your face is doing things to me, Hayes. In my belly and between my thighs."

"Show me. Take off those damn panties."

Instead of just shoving her undies down her legs, she turned around, and then she looked back at me with a cheeky smile. I was already feeling feral for her, but when I realized, once again, she was wearing my jersey, my number, my name on her back, something darker and needy broke free inside of me.

Willa did that same hip waggle, scooting her panties down inch by inch, going slowly like I'd told her too, but I was done waiting. I stood, shucked my pants and boxers, and then I was on her, bending her over the side of the bed.

"Oh god, Hayes." She let out that soft whimper that drove me crazy. "I don't know what's gotten into you, but I'm loving it."

"I'm glad you are, sweetheart, because I don't think I can hold back. Not tonight." I wanted to mark her, claim her, make her mine. But I wasn't an animal, and I took a couple of deep breaths to find my control. "But if I push a boundary you're not ready to cross, just say so. Okay?"

"I will. But I trust you. You know that."

I did and it made me want her even more.

I shoved one of my thighs between hers and pushed her legs open wider, but they would only go so far. Her damn underpants weren't even past her knees. I grabbed the soft material and was this close to ripping them off her body but decided I wanted to keep these ones for later. They were special and I was going to take them with me to games when she couldn't be there so I could jack off in them.

I yanked them down and tossed them onto the chair. Then I grabbed each of her butt cheeks, one in each hand, and scraped the tips of my fingers along her skin, opening this part of her body to me.

"Fuck, I love your ass. I have dreams about this ass."

She dug her fingers into the blanket and took a couple of shuddery breaths. "You know that's weird, right?"

"No, no. These dreams are definitely not weird." Nothing felt weird with Willa. It all felt abso-fucking-lutely perfect. "They're very, very erotic."

"Tell me."

My girl wanted some dirty talk? I could provide that for her easily. "I dream about licking my way between these cheeks and getting you nice and wet. I dream about sliding my fingers into your cunt and drawing your juices back to make you even wetter and then pushing my fingers inside your tight little asshole."

I grabbed one of her arms and moved it so she had her own hand on her ass, helping me hold her open. "Have you ever done that before?"

My name and number stared up at me as I waited for her answer. I was going to fuck her from behind while she wore my jersey all the fucking time. She was my girl, and I was going to prove it to her over and over.

"No. Never." Her voice was little more than a whisper.

"No one has ever fucked you here?" I slid two of my fingers between her butt cheeks and flicked them across her asshole. Her body instinctively clenched and my dick begged me to take her fast and hard. I wouldn't, because if we were going to do this, I wanted her body ready, and I wanted her to come harder than she ever had before.

She shook her head again.

"Then I'm claiming this for myself, Willa. This is just for you and me. I want to fuck your ass so we can both see what it's like for the first time, together."

YSAGGFTMBCSW

WILLA

Good god. Did everyone else know that the sweet ones were the spiciest? Hayes Kingman had a dirty mouth, and he knew how to use it. I don't know who took my sweet virgin boy and replaced him with this filthy, needy man, but they were getting a Christmas present from me.

At some point I'd want my softy green-flag boyfriend back, but... later. Much, much later.

"Sweetheart," the word was a growl, his voice huskier than I'd ever heard it before. "I don't want to hurt you so I'm going to need you to give me a yes or no when I check in with you. Got it?"

"Mmm hmm."

He gave my butt a little swat that sent all kind of tingles through me. "Yes or no, Willa."

"Yes, Hayes, I want this. Yes."

"That's my girl." He crouched down and put a hand on each of my inner thighs, pushing my legs farther apart. He kissed the lips of my pussy and then gave me a long lick, dipping his tongue inside. But he quickly replaced it with two of his fingers, sliding them in and out. "Yes, or no?"

He felt so good, I clenched around them already feeling the build toward what was going to be a really intense orgasm. "Yes, more, please."

He put his mouth on me again, and this time licked up, up, up and proceeded to tongue my asshole. I had no idea something like that would feel good.

"Yes, or no?" With every request for my consent to continue, his voice got deeper, darker.

"Yes. Don't stop." My own replies were getting breathier, and I was really going to have to concentrate to make sure I actually voiced the words the closer we got to him being inside of me.

Hayes licked me again, but then pulled his fingers from my pussy and smeared the wetness around my tight pucker. Then he licked it all back up.

Holy shit. This was way more erotic than I ever expected. I didn't think I'd be into assplay, and honestly, don't think I would have been had this been anyone other than Hayes doing it with me. Because that was the key here. He wasn't doing this to me. We were absolutely together, and I was so happy I'd never done this with anyone else.

He drew his fingers up again, and I wasn't sure I'd ever been so wet in my life. I thought I was probably going to leave a wet spot on his blanket before we were done. This time he didn't follow with his tongue. No, instead I felt the light pressure of his finger slipping inside of my ass. "Fuck that's so hot. Yes or no, baby?"

I barely got my answer out. He wasn't the only one who thought this was hot. "Yes, Hayes."

Gently, he pushed that finger in deeper and withdrew so slowly I thought I would scream. But I groaned or moaned or both. He did that one more time, then withdrew and pulled more of my juices from me and slid a second finger in this time. "Yes?"

I pushed myself back, driving his fingers deeper. "Yes, yes."

"Jesus, fuck. Ride my fingers, just like that."

I gripped the blanket and rocked my hips, doing exactly as he said, letting his fingers slide in and out of my body, sending shockwaves through me. Hayes reached around with his other hand and found my clit with his fingers. Just two little flicks and both my pussy and my ass were clenching.

"God, Hayes, I'm going to come."

He pulled both hands from me and smacked my ass again. "No you're not. Not until I'm inside of you. You're going to come on my dick while I'm buried inside of your ass."

God, he fucking owned me right now, and all I could do was whimper.

"Yes or no, Willa?" My name sounded like it came through gritted teeth, and I loved that he was as heated by this as I was.

"Yes. I need you, yes, yes." Before I even finished my bevy of yeses, I saw him reach for the condoms on the bedside table and heard him rip one open. Just the sound of it, the anticipation of knowing what he was about to do had my muscles clenching, almost spasming, waiting for him.

Hayes shoved his fingers back into my pussy and pulled my body's own lubricant up, smearing it around, pushing just the tip of his fingers inside, then repeated that twice more. "I should have gotten lube for this, but I don't have it, so I want you as wet as I can get you, baby."

His fingers slid inside me even more easily this time, and he fucked my asshole faster, scissoring his fingers inside of me. "I want your body ready for me to fuck you."

I was ready. I was so ready. "Yes. Now. Please."

He pressed his hips against me, but he didn't withdraw his fingers. Was this my punishment for teasing him, making him wait to come?

Nope. I felt his cock at the entrance to my pussy, and he buried himself deep with one thrust. I whooshed out a groan and then another one as he took one stroke, then another.

"I can fucking feel my cock moving inside of you. God damn. If I didn't want to know what being inside of your ass felt like so badly right now, I'd fuck you just like this."

"Next time," I whined. "Please, I want to know what if feels like too."

"I'm going to fuck you with my fingers in your ass a lot, honey, don't you worry." He pulled his cock and his fingers from me and then leaned down, covering my body with his. With his lips against my ear, he snarled, "But first I'm going to claim this ass. You're mine, Willa. Mine."

He pushed his hand between my thighs again and circled my clit. I groaned, my legs shook, and my stomach muscles pulled tight. The head of his cock pushed at the tight ring of my asshole, and he slid in, barely breaching me.

"Yes?" he gritted out.

"Yes," I choked on the word.

His fingers moved, sliding over my clit over and over, as he pushed his cock deeper inside of me. "Relax, Willa. I'm going as slow as I can."

I couldn't relax. I couldn't breathe, my chest was so tight. All I could do was feel.

And trust.

I trusted Hayes so intensely in this moment that it was far past simply having faith in him, beyond love even. In this moment, I fully surrendered. I was his, and I never wanted to be anything else.

"That's it, baby. Fuck." He buried himself all the way inside of me, never once stopping the slick glide of his fingers in my pussy.

"So... big." My words sounded garbled even to my ears, and I gripped the blanket tighter, holding on for dear life as he just as slowly withdrew.

"Yeah, I am, sweetheart, and you're such a good girl for taking my big cock so well."

Holy gods of porn, I didn't think his mouth could get any dirtier, but his absolute alpha male confidence in this moment made me love him even more. He moved so slowly, thrusting deep, driving us both into harsh pants and moans.

"Fuck, you're so tight." His voice was strained, and I thanked the universe because he had to be close to coming. I was ready to tumble over that edge and trying my best to hold on so we could come together.

His hips jerked and he made a sound I'd never heard from him before, so ferocious in his pleasure. "Are you ready to come for me? Yes, or no?"

He pinched my clit between his fingers and the blue-white heat exploded inside of me as the orgasm of all orgasms seared through me. I cried out my yes, gasping for breath, the pleasure ripping me apart until I was nothing but bliss floating around on storm clouds and tornadoes.

But in the haze, I heard his own guttural moan and felt his dick ripple inside of me. He jerked against my ass and grunted out my name before collapsing on top of me. He crushed me into his mattress, and I reveled in the weight of him on top of me. I wanted to stay that way forever.

Hayes sucked in a gasp of air and then rolled us both, so I was cradled against his chest. "Holy fuck, Willa."

I could do nothing more than hum from the sex high I was riding in that moment.

"That was amazing, baby." He stroked my arm and pressed a kiss to my neck. "Are you okay?"

"Yes. I'm..." Blissful, euphoric, satisfied beyond belief, contented more than I'd ever been in my entire life. "in love with you and your big dick."

Hayes laughed, the rumble coming from deep in his chest. He was lighter than when he pulled me into the bedroom, and I think he got whatever it was he needed tonight. I rolled in his arms and propped my head in one of my hands.

"Are you sure you were a virgin? Because that was some next level fuckery you just did to me, Kingman."

A soft blush rose across his cheekbones, and I nearly died from how dirty he could be one second and adorable the next. "I'm sure. I can't imagine doing that with anyone but you, babe."

"How is that even possible?" I mean, I know he said he'd studied and watched porn, but how could someone this good in bed have kept himself from the world for so long? If I wasn't directly benefiting from his loving right now, I'd declare it a travesty and, honestly, a tragedy for all of womankind.

"I didn't have sex because I didn't make time for a love life." He shrugged and stared up at the ceiling for a minute. "I saw a lot of guys get all up in their heads because of a woman and that messed up their games. That would have thrown off my plan. So I opted to focus on my family, football, and school. In that order. That was more than enough. Until you."

Aww. He was making me go all soft and squishy for him. "Your plan?"

I knew he'd been gunning for the pros since he'd played with Xander in high school. But this sounded like more than that.

"Since I was five, the plan was always get a scholarship to DSU to play for the Dragons, get drafted to the Mustangs."

Okay, maybe it wasn't that complicated. But there was something in the way he recited it that made me think there was more he wasn't saying.

"When you were five?" He had to have been reincarnated or something to know what he'd wanted practically from birth like that. "I was painting with my fingers and wished I was a unicorn who pooped marshmallows when I was that age."

He smiled at me and rolled us again so we could get under the covers. "That is also a noble plan, and I'm sure you can still be a marshmallow pooping unicorn if you really put your mind to it and work hard."

I slipped out of the Mustangs jersey I'd been wearing. "Umm, I think I'd rather work on something else hard right now."

"That is a much better plan." He pulled me closer and gave me a long, lingering kiss.

But I still couldn't get over the idea of an adorable little five-year-old Hayes thinking about getting a scholarship to a well-known football school so that he could go pro. Sure, we all wanted to be like the stars we idolized in our youth, but scholarships weren't usually a part of that fantasy. "But really? Five? What happened at such a tender age to give you grown-up goals?"

He stared at me for a breath or two, like he was deciding exactly what he should or shouldn't say.

Wait. Had something happened?

Oh. Oh fuck. I knew, and I was such a dumbass. "It's okay, you don't have to talk about it if you don't want to. I'm sorry I was just being... I didn't put the pieces together."

"No, it's okay." He looked up at the ceiling again, but then brought his eyes back to mine and my chest got tight with the amount of trust he was putting in me right now. "I don't usually talk about it much. Most people don't really think a five-year-old could understand what was going on, but I did."

"You can talk to me about it if you want. I'll understand."

"I know you will, and I love you for it, Willa." He took a deep breath and then said the words I knew he would. "My mom died when I was five, and everything in our world changed overnight."

He swallowed and blinked a few times. "I do remember her, but a lot of it is more a feeling of being loved than real memories, you know? But what I do truly remember from back then is how fucking devastated my dad was. And somehow, he still kept going."

I did the math in my head really quick. He'd have had to, because Mr. Kingman had eight kids at that point, at least two or three not even in school yet. "He's amazing for the way he was able to raise all of you as a single dad."

"That first year, we all spent a lot of time at DSU football practices." He chuckled for a moment. "There's this one picture of him on the practice field with Jules in one of those Baby Bjorn things strapped to the front of him with big orange earmuffs protecting her ears that I swear were made for the guys on aircraft carriers. My dad is clearly chewing some player's ass, and Jules is grinning from ear to ear."

And where was a five-year-old Hayes for all of that?

"Football saved us," he said. "It brought us all together, gave us goals, gave us something to do and look forward to when our lives were in pieces."

I laid my head against his chest and hugged him so tight, because I didn't know what else to do. Nothing had ever been that important to me in my whole life. This one moment in time had defined him, and I still didn't even know what I was looking for in life, or, really, who I was.

"So, yeah. I knew at five what I needed to do to help my family, and be the best Kingman I could be." He wrapped his fingers into my hair. "And that meant not having time for girls. Until now."

"I'm not sure I've ever felt lucky in my life. I mean, everything growing up was fine, you know? But nothing was ever extraordinary." Family, school, even traveling the world and becoming a teacher was all fine and dandy, but none of it was ever truly fulfilling. "Except for seeing you, naked, holding up my cat to return him to me on the very day I came home."

I hadn't realized it then, but that was a perfect moment, and I was going to try really hard to hold onto what I had with Hayes for as long as I possibly could.

Even though I could never truly be good enough for him. My whole life had proven that to me. But my life and my world had changed when I'd let him in, let him love me, let myself love him. And I wasn't letting go.

I fell asleep clinging to him and woke later to an empty spot in the bed beside me. I blinked a few times and heard a soft humming in the dark.

Hayes was sitting at the end of the bed, illuminated only by the light from the moon outside shining through the window. He was singing something softly and had a kitten in his arms.

"Hush little kitty, don't say a word. I'm gonna buy you a baby bird." He held one of the squeezy tubes of kitten food I'd had delivered to the coffee shop earlier, and the kitten was lapping it up, looking blissed the hell out.

Same, kitten, same.

One minute he's banging my brains out so hard I think I lost consciousness with the power of the orgasms—plural—and the next he's feeding an abandoned baby kitten at four in the morning, while singing a freaking lullaby to it. How could I not be in love with him?

And how could I not be worried someday he'd figure out that he was the focused, accomplished, achiever, with a family who loved him as much as he loved them, and I was the... the opposite. As lost in the world, needing to be claimed and taken care of, as that kitten.

FIGHT FOR HER

HAYES

The next few weeks were a blur of bliss, a whirlwind of stolen moments and endless laughter. Willa had become such an integral part of my entire being, woven into the very fabric of my heart and soul, that I could hardly remember what it was like before she'd waltzed into my life and turned it upside down.

And in bed? Fuck. I don't know how I'd lived without a woman like her rocking my world. We took turns being in charge in the bedroom, and every time I felt like we discovered another layer of ourselves in each other.

I'd never had more fun in my life, ever. Even playing football. Although, according to my brothers, a well-laid Kingman in love was always on top of their game. I certainly was. I felt fucking invincible.

So fucking alive.

I gave Seven a scratch on the head, but he couldn't be

bothered with me. After the incident with the kittens, he'd taken to picking up my socks, carrying them around the house meowing, and then dropping them into the corner of the room where he'd spent that happy night with his brood. "I know buddy. I promise we'll get you some kittens to foster for real in the off-season, okay?"

He wasn't buying it. I'd have to pick him up some new toys or treats or something to win back his love. Maybe after my date with Willa tonight. I'd never gone on dates before, and I had one planned for a new horror movie, where I had visions of her crawling into my lap when the film gave us a good jump scare.

My phone buzzed with an incoming text, and my heart sank as I read her message.

> Hey babe, I'm so sorry but I have to cancel tonight. Xander and my parents just showed up with one of those family four packs of tickets to the Miners game. Raincheck on the movie.

I stared at the screen, my jaw clenched. This was the third time in as many weeks that Xander had swooped in with some last-minute plan that derailed our alone time.

Last weekend, it was a family dinner that he insisted Willa couldn't miss. The week before, an impromptu visit to her grandparents in the Springs. And now this.

I tried to push down the growing unease in my gut, to remember that family was important. But as I tossed my phone onto the couch with a sigh, I couldn't shake the feeling that there was more to Xander's sudden attentiveness than met the eye.

The next day, I was going to follow Everett's advice to fight for her and decided to bring it up, but casually. I gave Willa a wave as I entered the shop because she had a line of customers here for her new concoctions from the increasingly cat-themed menu. I went over and stretched out on the couch. Today had been particularly rough practice, and I was happy to sit down for a minute. This week's rescue cats instantly crawled all over me, and I gave them all the attention they wanted.

Trixie and Jules were here too. They'd made the coffee shop a regular haunt for working and homework. Trixie had her laptop open, her brow furrowed in concentration as she typed away, while Jules had a textbook and a stack of notes spread out in front of her. But I knew full well they were both world class eavesdroppers. Even more reason to keep my questions about Xander casual.

A few minutes later, Willa brought over a mug of something that smelled Christmassy and flopped down beside me, instantly curling up. "You have great timing. This is the first real break I've had all day."

"Good. So, how was the basketball game last night?" I asked, trying to keep my tone light.

Willa's eyes lit up, her smile wide. "Oh, it was weirdly great. The game moves so fast, and I find it completely bizarre that I'm turning into a sports girlie."

I nodded, my own smile feeling stiff on my face. "That's great, babe. I'm glad you had fun."

She gave me a look that said she saw right through me. "I missed you though. I hate canceling on you."

I swallowed past the lump in my throat. God, I was being a jackass. Of course she should spend time with her family. Family was life. I'd never ask her to choose between them and me.

I just... wished I could be her family too. But she felt like mine. It wasn't that. No, I guess I wished her family wanted me to be a part of their lives. Mine had pulled her right into the fold, but hers held me at arm's length like some kind of intruder.

The bell over the door jingled and one of Willa's bakery partners walked in with a stack of boxes under her arm. "Oh, gotta go. The cookies for the Besties' listening party that Pen is hosting this weekend are here."

I watched her walk away, savoring the way she swayed her hips, but also bummed that this was all the time I got with her. See, jackass?

Before I even had a second to wallow, Trixie and Jules grabbed up a cat on either side of me and plopped down in their places on the couch.

"Hey, guys," I said, sitting up straighter, awaiting the Kingman inquisition I full-well knew was coming. "What's happening?"

Jules stared at me like she was trying to read my mind. "I know that look. What's wrong?"

I sighed, running a hand through the hair of the cat on my lap. "It's nothing. Just... Xander and Willa's parents."

Jules stole the drink Willa left for me and took a long sip. "Yum. Now, what about them? Is her brother still giving you a hard time?"

I glanced over at Willa who was, as usual, charming the wits out of the person she was talking to. They'd probably offer to bring her cookies for life by the time she was done with them. But that also meant she'd be too occupied to hear, and I really needed to talk this out. Might as well get advice from some smart and savvy women about my woman problems. "Not exactly. It's more like, he's always around, you know? Constantly making plans with Willa, monopolizing her time."

Trixie frowned, scratching the ears of the cat crawling up her leg. "That's weird. I thought Chris said he was starting to come around."

I shrugged, my gut twisting. "I wanna believe he is. But it feels like every time Willa and I make plans, Xander swoops in with some family thing that she can't say no to. And I'm pretty sure I'm being a dick thinking she has to spend all her time with me and not them."

Trixie exchanged a look with Jules, her expression thoughtful. "First of all, you're the least dick-ish guy I know. But have you talked to Willa about it? Told her how you feel?"

I shook my head, picking at a loose thread on my jeans. "I don't want to upset her. She's so happy. The other day she said something about how she feels like they're actually grownups now, and not acting like little kids anymore."

Jules leaned forward, her eyes serious. "Hayes, I get that you want to be supportive. But if Xander is purposely trying to come between you two, Willa needs to know."

"Maybe he's not doing it on purpose," I argued, even as the words rang hollow in my own ears. "Maybe he really does want to spend more time with her. She has been out of the country for the past few years."

Trixie raised an eyebrow, her expression skeptical.

"And he has to do that by constantly interfering with your plans? Come on, Hayes. You're smarter than that."

I sighed, my shoulders slumping. "I know. I just... I don't want to be the guy who makes her choose between me and her family."

Jules reached across the table, squeezing my hand. "You wouldn't be making her choose, Hayes. You'd be asking her to set healthy boundaries, to make your relationship a priority."

Our relationship was a priority to her already, wasn't it?

"Jules is right," Trixie chimed in, her voice gentle. "And honestly, it's not just Xander. Carin Rosemount has always been kind of... manipulative, especially when it comes to her kids."

My head snapped up, my eyes widening. "What do you mean?"

Jules nodded, her expression grim. "Don't you remember back in school, she was always pulling stunts like this. Making Willa and Xander feel guilty for having lives outside the family, for wanting to do their own thing. Willa especially. If she wasn't at every one of Xander's football games, her mom made her feel like dog shit."

A cold sense of dread settled in my stomach as the pieces started to fall into place. The constant last-minute plans, the guilt trips, the way Willa's face would fall every time she had to cancel on me.

"I never realized," I murmured, more to myself than to them. I'd spent long hours hanging out with Xander in high school, but almost all of them had something to do with football. I just always figured he was as focused on the sport as I was. And my family was always at my games, so it hadn't occurred to me Willa was being forced to be there. "I didn't have a fucking clue."

Trixie reached out, patting my arm. "Of course you didn't. You were just a kid, and the Rosemounts are good at putting on a show. But trust me, there's a reason Willa was so eager to get away, to see the world."

I sat back in my chair, my mind reeling. All this time, I'd been so focused on being the supportive boyfriend, on not rocking the boat, that I'd missed what was really going on.

Willa's family, whether intentionally or not, was slowly but surely pulling her away from me. And if I didn't do something soon, I was going to lose her.

Jules, as if actually reading my thoughts, leaned in, her expression serious. "Hayes, have you talked to Willa about Christmas yet? About her spending it with us, at the game? I'm pretty sure her dad would enjoy it. He had a lot of fun at the last home game."

I blinked, still thinking about how much I'd fucking missed about my own friend's and now my girlfriend's lives. My answer was absent minded. "Not yet. Why?"

She exchanged a loaded glance with Trixie, her jaw tight. "Because if I know Mrs. Rosemount, she's already got some elaborate family Christmas planned. One that Willa won't be able to say no to without a huge guilt trip."

My heart sank as I realized she was right. If I didn't talk to Willa soon, make our own holiday plans, I might very well end up spending Christmas without her, while she was off being forced to play happy family with her parents.

"Okay," I said, my resolve hardening. "Okay. I'll talk to her tonight, make sure she knows to ask her family to join us, and how much it would mean to me to have her there at the game."

Trixie smiled, her eyes soft. "Good. And Hayes? Don't be afraid to fight for her. Willa loves you. She just needs to be reminded that she gets to choose her own happiness."

I nodded, my chest feeling tight.

That evening, as Willa and I sat curled up on my couch, I decided to broach the subject, hoping this went better in person than it had in my head.

"So, I've been thinking about Christmas," I started, like this was going to be any average conversation. "We've got a home game on Christmas Day, and it's going to be a bit different this year, with me playing and all."

Willa tilted her head, her brow furrowed. "Oh. Right. I hadn't really thought about how there's always football on Christmas Day. I guess that's your family playing. So you don't do Christmas?"

I took a deep breath, choosing my words carefully. "We do. The whole family gathers in the suite at the stadium, whichever we're playing in. We watch the game, exchange gifts, eat way too much food. It's kind of our thing."

She smiled, her eyes soft. "That sounds amazing. I love that you all have that tradition."

"It's silly, but... we have this white elephant gift exchange. And everyone always saves the worst gifts for whoever is playing, as a kind of joke. We save them for when everyone is together that night."

Willa laughed, her nose crinkling in that adorable way I loved. "Okay, that's actually hilarious. What kind of gifts are we talking?"

I grinned, memories of past Christmases flashing through my mind. "One year, Declan got a singing fish trophy. Chris ended up with a 'Buns of Steel' workout DVD. And Everett... let's just say there was a bedazzled jockstrap involved."

She snorted, her body shaking with mirth. "No way. Please tell me there are pictures."

"There are definitely pictures. Blackmail-worthy pictures." I sobered, my smile fading. "I guess I'm just feeling a little left out, knowing I'm going to miss all of the fun up in the suite, while I'm on the field, this year."

I cleared my throat, my heart pounding. "And I was hoping... I mean, I would love it if you were there. With me. With us."

Willa's smile faltered, a flicker of uncertainty crossing her face. "Hayes, I... I don't know. It's just, my family..."

I reached out, taking her hand in mine. "I know, and I understand how important your family is to you. I would never want to take you away from them, especially during the holidays. They're invited to come too."

She relaxed slightly, her fingers intertwining with mine. "Thank you for understanding. It's just, it's been so long since we've all been together for Christmas. My mom's been planning this big family dinner, so I don't think they'd..."

I fought back the sinking feeling in my stomach, Trixie's and Jules's words echoing in my head. "Of course. I get it. But Willa, I want you to know that you have a choice here. You don't have to do anything that doesn't feel right to you, even if it means disappointing your family."

Willa blinked, surprise flashing across her face. "What do you mean?"

I sighed, gathering my courage. "I just... I've noticed how much pressure they put on you sometimes. Xander with all his last-minute plans, your mom with her expectations. It's like they don't want you to have a life outside of them."

She stiffened, pulling her hand away. "That's not fair, Hayes. They're my family. They love me."

"I know they do," I said quickly, trying to backtrack. "And I'm not saying they're doing it on purpose. But sweetheart, you deserve to be happy, to make your own choices. Even if those choices don't always line up with what your family wants."

Willa was quiet for a long moment, her expression conflicted. "I hear what you're saying," she said finally, her voice soft. "And maybe you're right. Maybe I do let them pressure me sometimes, let their needs come before my own. I just don't want to be a disappointment to them."

I reached out, cupping her face in my hands. "You have such a big heart, Willa. It's one of the things I love most about you. There's no way you could ever disappoint anyone. But you have to take care of yourself too."

She leaned into my touch, her eyes glistening. "I know. And I want to be there for you, Hayes. I want to start our own traditions."

I felt a rush of relief, of love so strong it stole my breath. "Yeah?"

She nodded, a small smile tugging at her lips. "Yeah. So here's what I'm thinking. I'll go to my parents' house in the morning, do the whole presents and breakfast thing. But then I'll come to the game, be there to cheer you on and kiss you senseless when you score the winning touchdown. And save the best worst white elephant gift for you."

I laughed, joy bubbling up inside me. "That sounds perfect. And Willa? Thank you. For hearing me, for being willing to find a compromise."

She leaned in, brushing her lips against mine.

I kissed her back, pouring all my love, all my admiration into the press of my lips. "Always," I murmured against her mouth. "I'm always going to fight for us, Willa. For you. No matter what."

Part of that fight meant that I let her family have her as much as they wanted Christmas morning, knowing I'd get her at the Christmas Day game and that night. Our next game was away, and I didn't even ask if she could travel with me. But you'd better believe we fucked like rabbits the days I did get her.

Maybe there was something to the idea of playing better being in love. Christmas morning I texted Willa, who'd stayed over at her parents the previous night, that I loved her and to have a good day. And then I ran onto the field ready to have a killer game.

And a tough one it was. The Dawgs were out for blood, specifically mine. Their defense was a wall of muscle and aggression that seemed impenetrable. We were well into the fourth quarter and tied at three each.

But I was in the zone, my mind crystal clear and my body humming with adrenaline. I hoped Willa was having fun with my family and I loved knowing she was watching, like a warm glow in my chest urging me on.

The clock was ticking down, and it was time to make something happen. In the final seconds, with everything on the line, Chris called the play.

He looked right at me and gave me a nod. "Hayes, this is it. Make it count."

I nodded, my jaw set with determination. This was my moment, my chance to win the game for us, and I was going to push myself to the limit to make it happen.

The ball snapped, and I was off, my legs pumping and my heart pounding. I dodged one defender, then another, turned and looked up, knowing Chris's pass would be right where it should be. I snagged the ball out of the air, my eyes locked on the end zone. I was so close, the roar of the crowd a distant echo in my ears. I saw the big-ass defensive lineman coming for me, but I was so damn close. I cradled the ball against my chest and dove for the endzone.

The hit came just like I knew it would, a bone-crushing tackle, and then came another, and another as we all hit the ground really fucking hard.

The air left my lungs in a rush, my vision blurring at the edges. But even as I ate that grass, I knew I'd made it. I'd crossed the line, the ball clutched tight to my chest.

Touchdown.

The last thing I saw before the darkness claimed me

was the bright blue of the Denver sky, a perfect mirror of Willa's eyes.

And then... nothing.

I came to in a haze of pain and confusion, the concerned faces of my brothers swimming into view above me.

"Hayes? Can you hear me?" Chris's voice was tight with worry, his hand gripping mine. Everett was on my other side, waving to the sideline frantically.

But that was the last thing I saw before I lost consciousness again.

WHILE YOU WERE SLEEPING

WILLA

I sat on my parents' couch, my eyes glued to the TV screen as the Mustangs took the field again. The familiar sight of Hayes in his dark blue home uniform sent a pang through my chest, because I should fucking be there.

But instead, I was here, trapped in a stuffy living room with my mother, grandfather, and Xander, all because they'd guilt-tripped me into staying for some "quality family time." If quality time meant no one even talking to each other and the occasional cheers and boos at the television, yeah, then that's what we were having.

I couldn't even imagine what I'd missed by not hanging out with his family today. They would have at least talked to me. Some of them might have even been happy to see me.

God, I missed my Guncles. They'd been the best thing

about this family for years, and while I had no idea what was going to happen to this weird new life I'd carved out over the past few months when they came home to their coffee shop and house, I'd much rather claim them as family than anyone in this room.

I tried to focus on the game, on the way Hayes moved with such grace and power, but my mind kept drifting to our last conversation, to the way he'd been worried for me. He'd called it when he said I needed to break free from the way my family's expectations weighed heavy on me. Today demonstrated that more than anything else ever could.

The thing was, I had been free. Living abroad and only coming home for one visit a year had given me the space to be who I was, not the version of Willa they all expected from me. I didn't regret volunteering to help George and Liam, but I wished I'd... I didn't even know, maybe remembered who I was when I wasn't around the rest of the Rosemounts all the time.

I really needed to get out of Denver.

The commercial break ended, and the game came back on. At least I actually cared about the outcome for once, and that gave me something to pay attention to. This one was a nail-biter, the score tied and the clock ticking down. I leaned forward, my heart in my throat as I watched Hayes catch the ball, his legs pumping as he raced toward the end zone.

A defender came right at Hayes, slamming him into the ground. How he did that every day and got back up so easily was beyond me. I watched and waited while the entire Cleveland Dawgs defense that had piled on him slowly got up.

And there was Hayes, still clutching the ball to his chest. The announcer declared the touchdown, but I barely heard him.

Hayes wasn't getting up. He wasn't even moving.

"No," I whispered, my hand flying to my mouth. "No, no, no."

Chris and Everett jogged over to him, and Chris knelt beside him while Everett frantically motioned to the side-line for the medical personnel to hurry over to them.

The stadium that had erupted into cheers went deadly silent.

The announcer's voice was grim as he relayed the news. "It looks like the booth is calling a medical timeout, folks. And from what we can see, the staff are calling for the stretcher and the cart. Looks like they're going to skip the med tent evaluation altogether and take Kingman straight to the locker room."

A second announcer said the last thing I wanted to hear. "That could indicate a serious injury. The League's concussion protocol states that if a player loses consciousness they have to—"

I was on my feet before I even realized I was moving, my heart pounding a frantic rhythm in my chest.

"I have to go," I said, my voice shaking. "I have to get to the stadium."

Xander scoffed, his arms crossed over his chest. "And do what, exactly? It's not like they're going to let you in. You'd just be in the way."

I whirled on him, my eyes blazing. "Give me your keys, Xander. Now."

He blinked, taken aback by the venom in my tone. "What? No. He just got his bell rung, the big baby. He'll be fine."

Something inside me snapped, weeks of pent-up frustration and hurt boiling over. With a growl of rage, I launched myself at my brother, tackling him to the ground.

"Willa!" my mother shrieked, her hands fluttering uselessly. "What on earth are you doing?"

I ignored her, my fists pounding against Xander's chest as I straddled him. "You selfish, insensitive prick," I seethed, punctuating each word with a blow. "Why can't you just be happy for me? Why do you have to ruin everything?"

Xander struggled beneath me, his face red with exertion and embarrassment. "Get off me, you psycho."

"Not until you give me your damn keys and stop trying to fuck around with my life!"

My father's voice cut through the chaos, calm but firm. "Enough, both of you."

I looked up, my chest heaving, to see him standing over us, his expression unreadable.

"Michael, make her stop this right now." My mother fanned herself and gave me that look. The same one I'd seen a hundred thousand times. The one that told me she loved Xander a whole hell of a lot more than she did me.

"Let them work this out," my dad said, holding up a hand to silence my mother's protests. "This has been building for a long time. They need to get it out of their systems."

I clambered off Xander, my hands shaking as I pushed my hair out of my face. "I don't understand why you hate Hayes so much," I said, my voice cracking. "What did he ever do to you?"

Xander sat up, his jaw clenched. "You mean besides abandoning me, abandoning our team, to go play hero in the big leagues?"

I stared at him, shocked by the raw pain in his voice. "Grow up, Xan. He didn't abandon anyone. He worked his ass off to get where he is, and you should be proud of him. He was your friend."

"Proud?" my mother scoffed, her face pinched with disdain. "When Xander is clearly better than he is? Proud of a man who's just using you to make your brother feel worse about not being drafted?"

I reeled back as if she'd slapped me, my stomach twisting with hurt and disbelief. "What? How can you say that? Me being with Hayes has never had anything to do with Xander. In fact, I fucking hid my feelings for Hayes for far too long just so I wouldn't hurt Xan."

My mother scoffed. "And you just go around flaunting that you've gotten yourself a rich boyfriend. Well, you'd better hope you can rely on him to support you when you're a lonely old cat lady. Because we won't, and I won't have Xander helping you anymore either."

My father stepped forward, his expression thunderous. "Carin, that's enough."

He turned to me, his eyes softening as he fished his keys out of his pocket. "Go, Willa. Go be with your man.

I'll be there later. It appears I have some things to take care of on the home front."

I took the keys with shaking hands, my throat tight with emotion. "Thank you, Daddy. I'm sorry, I just... I need to be there for him."

He nodded, pulling me into a quick, fierce hug. "I know, baby girl. And I'm sorry too, for not seeing what was going on here. We'll talk later, figure out how to make this right."

As I raced out the door, my heart pounding in time with my footsteps, I couldn't shake the feeling that everything had just changed, irrevocably and forever.

But none of that mattered now. All that mattered was getting to Hayes, being there for him the way he'd always been there for me.

I'll admit to texting and driving, but only because I messaged Jules to find out what hospital they'd taken Hayes to. I swallowed down tears when she replied that they would be there waiting for me.

I burst through the hospital doors a few minutes later, my heart in my throat as I searched for a familiar face. The sterile scent of disinfectant and the steady beep of machinery assaulted my senses, but I pushed forward, my focus solely on finding Hayes.

As I rounded the corner, I spotted the Kingmans taking up all the available space in the waiting room, their faces all drawn with worry. Jules was the first to see me, her eyes widening as she jumped to her feet.

"Willa, you made it."

I was engulfed in a sea of hugs and murmured words

of comfort, the warmth of their embraces easing the icy grip of fear around my heart.

"How is he?" I asked, my voice raw with emotion. "Have you heard anything?"

Mr. Kingman shook his head, his jaw tight. "Not yet. The doctors are still examining him."

As if on cue, a man in a white coat appeared, and another in what looked more like a track suit. Both of their expressions were grave. The guy in the white coat called out, "Family of Hayes Kingman?"

We surged forward as one, our hands clasped tightly together. "That's us," Mr. Kingman said, his voice steady despite the tension in his frame. "How's my son?"

The white coat guy consulted his clipboard, his brow furrowed. "Hayes sustained a concussion during the game. We're following the League's protocols to the letter, and I want to keep him overnight."

Track suit held out his hand to Mr. Kingman. "I'm the UNC assigned to the Mustangs for today's game, Mr. Kingman."

I whispered to Jules. "What's a UNC?"

"Unaffiliated Neurotrauma Consultant. The League takes the concussion protocol really seriously."

Neurotrauma? I was maybe going to throw up. It was just a game. It wasn't supposed to be life threatening.

Mr. Kingman nodded. "You did the locker room comprehensive concussion exam? You've got his pre-season baseline neuro report?"

"Yes, sir. Since he lost consciousness, the team's head physician and I both agreed that we needed to get him to the EAP-designated trauma center for more advanced evaluation and treatment. I've assisted on the diagnosis."

The bitter taste of bile and my grandmother's Christmas goose rose up the back of my throat.

"We'll get him into the training room in a few days, but he's going to need to rest and avoid any strenuous activity for the time being."

I sagged with relief, tears pricking at the back of my eyes. Rest and avoid strenuous activity was so not what I thought he was going to say. I'd already spiraled into brain damage and learning how to walk and talk and feed himself again. Hayes was going to be okay.

"There's more," the doctor continued, and my stomach clenched with renewed fear. "He also dislocated his shoulder during the impact. We've reset it, but he'll need to keep it immobilized for a few weeks to allow it to heal properly."

Mr. Kingman nodded, his expression grim. "Can we see him?"

The doctor hesitated, glancing at the assembled crowd. "He's still groggy from the pain medication, so I'm only going to allow one visitor at a time."

Mr. Kingman squared his shoulders, and I was ready to look for a chair to wait. I just needed to hear from someone who knew him personally that he was okay. I could wait. I could. I would. I might die first, but I could wait.

But then Mr. Kingman turned to look at me. "Willa, you should go."

I blinked, surprised. "Me? But you're his father, you should be the one..."

He shook his head, a small smile playing at the corners of his mouth. "No, I'm sure he'll be asking for his fiancée sooner than he will his dad."

I stared at him, my mouth falling open.

Jules grinned, nudging me forward. "Go on, this isn't our first rodeo in a hospital waiting room." She motioned to her six other brothers. "I practically grew up here. We know the drill."

In a daze, I followed the doctor down the hallway, my mind reeling. Fiancée? What on earth had Hayes been telling his family? Or perhaps they were all just savvier than I was at the moment and knew they wouldn't let me see him if I wasn't considered family.

I stepped into his room and saw him lying there, his face pale and his arm strapped to his chest, and all other thoughts fled my mind.

"Hayes," I whispered, taking trembling steps to his bedside. "Oh god, baby. I was so scared."

His eyes fluttered open, but they were hazy with pain and probably some really good drugs. "Willa? Did you see me win the game?"

"Of course I did, you big lug." I wanted so badly to touch him, to hold him, but I was worried I'd hurt him more. "Maybe next time, do that without scaring me half to death."

He smiled, wincing slightly. "I'm fine, flower. Just got my bell rung, that's all."

I laughed, a watery, hiccuping sound. "That's exactly what Xander said."

His expression went hazy at the mention of my brother. Shit, I shouldn't have said that. He didn't need to know right now that I hadn't been at the game. I took his good hand and tangled our fingers together.

"You should go home, get some rest," he murmured, his eyelids drooping. "They're gonna keep me overnight, make sure I don't have any brain damage."

Gulp.

I shook my head, just barely holding back the tears, and opened my mouth to protest, but he cut me off with a gentle squeeze of my hand.

"I mean it, Willa. You look exhausted. And trust me, you're gonna need all your energy to deal with me for the next few weeks."

I frowned, confused. "What do you mean?"

He sighed, his eyes drifting closed. "Concussion protocol. No practice, no workouts, no nothing. I'm gonna be a real pain in your ass until they clear me for activity again."

Despite the worry still churning in my gut, I couldn't help but laugh. "Oh, joy. Just what I always wanted, a grumpy, stir-crazy boyfriend to babysit. You know no strenuous activity means no sex, right?"

His breathing evened out and the heart monitor beeped a steady rhythm, and I sat back in the uncomfortable plastic chair just watching him for a few minutes. I watched the rise and fall of his chest, the gentle flutter of his eyelashes against his cheeks, and I wasn't going anywhere.

I was really mad at myself for needing an almost tragedy to see that Hayes and the Kingmans were more family to me than anyone else in the world.

I cried silently for what I'd lost today, and for what I gained.

DOCTOR'S ORDERS

HAYES

The first week of my concussion protocol was a special kind of hell. I'd never been good at sitting still, at being idle, and now I was forced to do nothing but rest and recover.

It was driving me insane.

I couldn't practice, couldn't work out, couldn't even watch game footage without the pounding in my head intensifying to an unbearable level. I couldn't be there for my team.

All I could do was lie on the couch, staring at the ceiling and trying not to let the dark thoughts consume me.

What if this was it? What if I never fully recovered, never played again? Who was I without football?

Icy hot pinpricks curled through my gut. Football was my life, my identity, for as long as I could remember. The idea of losing that, of having to find a new path, a new purpose... it was literally painful. My head was going to explode.

Willa made her way over to the couch, perching on the edge beside me. "Hayes, I know this is hard. But you're doing everything you're supposed to do. Resting, recovering—"

"And going absolutely fucking stir-crazy in the process." I sighed, scrubbing a hand over my face. "Sorry. I'm just... I'm already sick of this, and it's only been five fucking days. I'm out for weeks, trapped in my own body, in my own head."

She wrapped her arms around me, and I leaned into her warmth. "I just feel so... useless. Like I'm letting everyone down."

She cupped my face, forcing me to meet her gaze. "You could never let anyone down, Hayes. You're so much more than just a football player. You're brilliant, kind, compassionate. Football is a part of you, but it's not all of you."

I swallowed hard, her words hitting me like a linebacker. "I don't know who I am without it. I've never had to think about anything else."

After a long moment, Willa kissed me on the forehead and cupped my cheeks in the palms of her hands, forcing me to look at her. "You listen to me, Hayes. I know you like your plans and your goals and forever exceeding everyone's expectations. And this wasn't part of the plan."

Ouch. I barked out a wounded sort of laugh.

"So change the plan." She brushed her lips softly across mine, like a little reward for the hard love she was giving me right now. "I know that makes you uncomfortable, but you're smart, you're the hardest working person I know, and you're also stuck thinking there's only one way for you to exist in this world. I promise that's not true."

"I don't... I can't—" I swallowed hard. Never once in my whole damn life had I ever said I can't. But my outlook was so damn dark. Nothing but black and white.

"You keep saying 'I', but you don't have to, nor should you try to, do this alone. I will be here for whatever you need, but I don't have a whole lot of experience with what you're going through, and I have to get to the coffee shop."

"You're saying I should ask for help, huh?"

She stood up and walked toward the front door but blew me a kiss along the way. "I got you, boo."

My Willa, she understood me better than I did myself. Because she didn't just walk away from me to wallow in my self-fucking-pity like a lot of people would have. She'd already called in backup.

On cue, the doorbell rang, and Willa, already there, answered it. All six of my brothers stood on my front porch, their arms laden with snacks and video games, and Willa gave me a wink and a wave as she headed out to work.

Chris held the door open as the rest of them filed in like the god damned marching band. "Willa called and said we needed to come over and pull your head out of your asshole."

I tried for a quarter of a second to open my mouth to protest, but Declan gave me one of those grumpy looks. "Don't make me smack you upside the head and give you another concussion. We're here to fucking cheer you up."

Flynn slapped a bottle of some healthy kombucha or something weird into my hand while he popped open a beer. "What's up, cracker head? Ready to get your ass whupped at Mario Kart?"

"Alright, little bro," Everett said, plopping down on the couch beside me. "Time for some good old-fashioned distraction therapy."

Isak already had the game queued up, and Gryff, who was the undefeated champion at this game, even let me be Mario. But an impromptu video game session was not going to cheer me up. I guessed it might distract me from the downward fear spiral.

And it worked for a few hours.

But it wasn't long before my head was pounding and I struggled to hold the controller with my injured arm, my fingers fumbling over the buttons. The frustration welled up inside me like a tidal wave.

"Damn it!" I growled, throwing the controller down as my character died for the tenth time in a row. "This is pointless. I can't even play a stupid video game."

Declan and Everett exchanged a worried glance, but it was Chris who spoke up, his voice gentle. "Hayes, it's okay. This isn't your first injury, kid, and it won't be your last. We've all been there. You're still healing. No one expects you to be at the top of any game right now."

I laughed, a harsh, bitter sound. Sure, we'd all had injuries before, but through the grace of the universe and the new and improved technology of helmets, none of us had ever had a serious concussion. So they hadn't been here before. I was the only one. "That's the problem, isn't it? I'm not at the top of my game. I'm not even in the game. I'm just fucking... useless."

My vision began to blur, and I realized with a start that it wasn't just from the headache that was now pounding behind my eyes. Tears were welling up, hot and stinging, and I couldn't even fucking wipe them away.

"Okay, boys, I think it's time to call it a day." My father's voice cut through the tense silence, calm but firm. I hadn't even noticed him come in. "Let me have some time with Hayes."

My brothers filed out, each one pausing to give me a quick hug or a pat on the back. When the door clicked shut behind them, I finally let the tears fall, my shoulders shaking with silent sobs.

Dad sat down beside me, his presence solid and comforting. He didn't say anything at first, just let me cry it out, his hand a steady pressure on my back.

When I finally pulled myself together, he stood up, making his way to the kitchen. "You hungry?"

I shrugged, wincing as the movement pulled at my injured shoulder. "Not really."

He nodded, pulling ingredients out of the fridge. "I'll make your favorite. Spaghetti and meatballs, just like your mom used to make."

The mention of my mother sent a fresh wave of grief washing over me, but it was tinged with warmth, with love. She'd always known how to make everything better, even on the darkest of days.

As Dad cooked, the familiar scents filling the kitchen, I found myself talking, the words pouring out of me in a rush.

"I was scared, Dad. When I woke up in that hospital, when they told me about the concussion, the shoulder... I thought that was it. I thought I'd lost everything."

He hummed, stirring the sauce with a thoughtful expression. "You know, back in my day, I was known as one of the meanest linemen in the League. I cracked my fair share of heads, maybe even ended a few careers."

I looked up, surprised. Of course Dad talked about his playing days, about the toll the game had taken on his body and mind. But I'd never heard him say anything like this.

"But you know what I realized after I retired?" He turned to face me, his eyes soft. "Football isn't everything. It's a big part of who I am, who we are, sure, but it's not the only thing."

I swallowed hard, my throat tight. "I don't know who I am without it. I don't... I don't want to let you down, Dad."

He crossed the room in two strides, pulling me into a fierce hug. "Hayes, listen to me. You could never let me down. You're my son, and I am so damn proud of the man you've become."

I clung to him, my face buried in his chest like I was a little boy again. "But all I've ever wanted was to be like you, to make you proud."

Dad pulled back, gently cupping the back of my neck. "Hayes, you are so much more than just a football player. You're brilliant, kind, compassionate. You could do anything you set your mind to, and I would be just as proud of you."

I said the thing I didn't want to. "What if setting my

mind to it and working hard isn't enough to get me back in the game?"

He gave a small nod acknowledging the pain I was admitting to. "Then so be it. To be honest, I sort of thought you'd do something else with that big brain of yours. You used to love to build things, and I don't know if you noticed, but you're kind of a genius. Grow some funny hair and you could be Albert Einstein."

I blinked, stunned. "But I thought... I thought football was what you wanted for me, for all of us."

He sighed, regret flickering across his face. "When your mom died, I did the best I could to raise you boys on my own. Being on the field with me was the only way I knew I could keep this family together without her. But I never meant for you to think that football was your only option, your only worth."

Damn it. I was going to start crying again.

"You did good, Dad. You gave us all a way to stick together." I didn't know if any of us had ever told him that. It could not have been easy to raise seven rowdy boys and one princess all by himself.

"You kids turned out all right." He cleared his throat and handed me a plate.

We sat down to eat, the spaghetti and meatballs just as delicious as I remembered, and that storm cloud hovering over me wasn't quite as dark for the first time since my injury. I was just going back for seconds when Willa came home, with her dad in tow.

"Mr. Rosemount," I said, surprised. "What are you doing here?"

He gave me a small smile, his eyes tired but warm, and

he shook my dad's hand. "I came to apologize, Hayes. For the way my family has treated you and Willa. It wasn't right, and I'm sorry I didn't step in sooner."

What the shit? I knew something had gone down with her and her brother at Christmas, but I'd been so wrapped up in myself, I hadn't asked her about it.

Willa's hand found mine, her fingers intertwining with my own. "I didn't tell you because I was busy making sure you weren't dead, but... I didn't make it to your game on Christmas. I came straight to the hospital from kicking my brother's ass and having a real blow out with my mom."

Jesus. I'd been a shitty man baby of a boyfriend. I should have known this. "Babe, I'm so sorry. I wish I hadn't been so whiny this week that you didn't feel like you could tell me. This is major."

"No, I don't want you to feel sorry about that. I wasn't really ready to talk about it yet. But Dad's been coming to the coffee shop this week to help out, and we had a really good talk today."

"Babe, that's great."

"I figured if I could call your family to come help you out, I should be able to call mine to help me." She looked up at her dad with a new, different smile. "I've never really done that before."

Mr. Rosemount nodded, his expression serious. "I'm sorry to both of you that you had to avoid our family instead of feeling loved and supported by us."

He looked over at my dad. "I thought I was raising a son more like your boys, but I failed Xander somewhere along the way. I'm not sure when that happened, but I realized it when I saw your family together that day at the game and mine didn't even want to do something fun together."

He clapped me on the shoulder, his grip firm. "You're a good man, Hayes. Don't let anyone tell you otherwise. I'm glad Willa found you."

I was incredibly glad too. I really did need to pull my head out of my asshole, so I never let her down again the way I had this week.

The next day, I headed into the practice facility to see the doc and the trainers. I knew they weren't going to clear me to play and not being able to travel with the team was going to fucking suck.

We went through the whole barrage of tests to see how the recovery was going, and it wasn't good news.

"I'm ready to move on phase two, Doc. I can do some light activity. I know I can." I was not spending another week staring at the ceiling.

The team's head doc looked around me to the two other trainers who I'd be working with. "Look, Kingman. Every concussion is different, and the recovery plans aren't some standardized list of do this and you're better. You've still got a ways to go before that. I'll upgrade you to light stretching and walks. That's it."

Fuck.

"I can't get better if I can't do the work to get better."

"This is the work, kid." He wrote something on his clipboard and shook his head at me. "You guys think I don't know you push through pain all the time. But there's a difference between being hurt and being injured. You push too hard, and you'll end up putting yourself out for the rest of the season, not just a couple of games. The last thing the team or I want is you on the injured reserves list."

Injured reserves. The fucking death knell of any pro player.

How the hell had I gone from the best rookie the League had ever seen to sitting on the fucking sidelines?

"See the trainers to stretch your arm, and then go home and rest. And I mean it when I say light activity. That does not mean working out, no running, absolutely no impact of any kind. Don't even think about trying to catch a ball, you hear me?"

"But—

Coach walked by Doc's room, and when I say walked, I mean stomped like an angry rhinoceros. "Kingman. Get your ass in my office, right the fuck now."

Shit. "Coming, Coach."

Doc gave me a told-you-so look more like the kind I got from my siblings when any of us was in serious trouble. Great.

I hustled into Coach's office and stood in front of his desk while he stared at me like a slug he wanted to pour salt on. He didn't say anything for an uncomfortably long time. I was not used to being on his bad side. "Kingman. Get your shit together. We are going to the fucking bowl this year, and if we lose that game because you didn't listen to the doc, I'm going to eat your fucking helmet for lunch—with your head in it. You got me?"

Okay, this was actually the first bit of good news I'd gotten. Not that we were going to the bowl. Unless we really fucked up during the playoffs, we had the best chance of any franchise in the League. Chris was the right guy to take us there. We deserved to be there with our undefeated season so far.

The good news was Coach was counting on me to be playing in that bowl. "I got you, Coach."

I did my stretching with the trainers, which both felt good and hurt like a son of a bitch. Then I headed home. But I stopped by a copy store to print something out first.

When I walked into the house, Willa was waiting for me. She knew how important today's checkup was. "So, what did they say?"

I shook my head. "I'm out for at least one more game. But they did send me home with this."

I handed her the note I'd printed out and looked anywhere but at her.

"Hayes. This is from Dr. Harry Beaver."

Yep, I did have the sense of humor of a thirteen-year-old. "Uh-huh. That's the team doc."

"I'm supposed to believe the Mustangs' team doctor wrote you a prescription for," she snickered and then cleared her throat to read the note aloud, "two doses of pussy a day?"

I took her hand and led her toward the stairs up to my bedroom. "If I want to get better, I have to follow my doctor's orders."

SPONTANEOUS COMBUSTION

WILLA

After Hayes had to miss playing in the New Year's Day game and the last regularly scheduled game of the year, I decided to make him come to work with me so he couldn't sit at home and stew. He was making progress, but, of course, it wasn't enough for him.

"You're not allowed to watch those game tapes for one more minute, mister. Look," I pointed to Seven who was sleeping on the couch next to Hayes, with his paws covering his face. "Even the cat can't stand to see the Bruins beat the Mustangs one more time."

"We might have won if I could have been there to help them out. One fucking game from having an undefeated season." He glanced over at me, noted my raised eyebrow, folded arms, and tapping foot. "Umm, but you're right. I've basically got every play memorized now."

"C'mon. You're coming to the coffee shop. I've got new

tea lattes I need a guinea pig to test out." I didn't, but I'd come up with some. I sat him down in the office to go over the coffee shop's books. That was something he was good at, and he promised if he got a headache looking at the screen, he'd take a break.

I didn't believe him for a second and brought him one of the tea lattes I was testing for the upcoming week's menu at least once every half hour, just to have an excuse to check on him. He'd been at it for about two hours, making charts and graphs and all kinds of fancy things. He ran the numbers, his brow furrowed in concentration as he analyzed the data. But if I was honest, he actually looked like he was having fun.

"Huh," he said, tapping his pen against the table. "Looks like two things specifically are making you the most money."

"You can tell that from all this?" I waved my hands at the colorful charts that didn't mean squat to me.

"Your POS system tracks the products you sell the most of, and it's easy to extrapolate the food costs to see which food and drinks are the most profitable. Your bizarro, uh, new and interesting tea lattes are where the money is at, babe."

"Really?" Those had only been a whim since I didn't like coffee.

"Look. It helps that your teas are coming from Heavenly Herbs over in Boulder. They're local, which helps, but even if they weren't, they're a better food cost per drink, overall. Your coffees are imported, and you can see, the costs there are increasing month over month."

God, he was so fucking smart. I understood everything

that he was saying, but I doubt I would have been able to look at the data and figure any of this out on my own. I kissed his head and gave it a couple of soft strokes. "We must do better at protecting your big brain, because I'm finding your smarts really freaking sexy right now."

He spun in the office chair and pulled me into his lap. "Are you now? Want me to start talking in algebra and calculus when we're in bed?"

"Hey, big boy, is that a quadratic equation in your pocket or are you just happy to see me?"

Hayes snort-laughed and shook his head at me. "Nope. Doesn't do it for me like it does for you."

"Boo. Fine." I stuck out my tongue at him. "You said two things are making us profitable. What's the other one. It's catpuccinos, isn't it?"

"You're not entirely wrong." He pointed to one of his charts. "The days you host the cat shelter events are by far the biggest income days. Like, by a lot."

I leaned over his shoulder, studying the figures. Then I blinked at them, because I had no idea what I was even looking for. But just thinking about how busy we were on those days, he had to be right. Even with the occasional feline-induced chaos, we were packed and often ran out of our specialties for that day before closing. Plus, who didn't like cats? Besides my mother.

Hayes grinned, nudging me with his elbow. "Maybe you should just turn this place into a cat café. Embrace your true calling as a crazy, sexy cat lady."

I laughed, but his words triggered a memory. Back when the Guncles were getting ready to leave on their trip, we'd joked about how funny it would be if they came home to find I'd transformed their beloved coffee shop into a cat café.

An idea began to take shape in my mind, equal parts exciting and ridiculous. I grabbed my phone, typing out a series of messages while Hayes was distracted with the spreadsheets.

A few minutes later, my phone buzzed with a string of responses. I bit back a grin, excitement bubbling up inside me.

"Hey, sugar pie honey bunch?" I said, trying to keep my voice casual. "How do you feel about a little impromptu trip?"

He glanced up, his eyebrows raised. "A trip? But what about the coffee shop, and I'm still on concussion protocol, and we've got the playoffs coming up..."

I held up my phone, showing him the messages. "Already taken care of. I asked my dad and Javi to cover for a couple of days at the shop. Jules is going to watch Seven. I cleared traveling with your doctor, Chris cleared it with your coaches, you don't have a game because the Mustangs are top seeded, so no wild card, and your brothers are letting us use the private jet. We leave in two hours."

Hayes stared at me, his mouth falling open. "What? How did you...? You have the team doctor's number? And everyone in my family?"

I grinned, feeling a rush of the old exhilaration I used to get when planning my own next adventures. "I've got my ways. Now, go pack a bag. We're going to Japan to check out cat cafés."

"Japan?" He said it with a look on his face like he'd

thought he was getting a bite of chocolate, but it was lemon-lime. "There's not, like, a Japan in Texas is there? I feel like there might be."

I gave him a side-eye but Googled it just for funsies. "Nope. I see a place called China, New York, and there's are towns named Norway, Lebanon, Peru, Mexico, Sweden, and Poland in Maine. Oh, actually there are eight states with a city called Lebanon, and ten with a city named after Peru. Indiana has both, and also an Angola, Brazil, and Morocco. Ooh, Georgia has a Budapest."

He raised his hands in surrender. "Okay, okay, so you're saying we are leaving the United States. How do you know I even have a passport? I've never left the country before."

I stared at him like he'd just admitted he was from Middle Earth or Asgard. "Never? Not even to like... Mexico or Canada?"

"Not a lot of football games in Mexico." He shrugged. "Or, well, not American football."

"Oh, my sweet summer Hayes. I'm about to rock your world."

He did in fact have a passport, and it was so fresh and crisp, with no stamps or visas or pages that were even flipped through. Mine was battered enough for the both of us. The flight was gonna be hella long, but goodness gracious, I wasn't going to miss ever having to fly coach again after this luxury. I didn't even have to worry about the disappointed or upset looks from strangers when they saw they were seated next to a chubby girl in the middle seat.

If my machinations went according to plan, we

weren't even going to be seated for most of the flight anyway. I happened to notice the last time we were on their jet that it had a small bedroom in the back. I couldn't keep the smile off my face.

We definitely hadn't been having as much sex since his concussion. Not because he didn't want to. He did. All the time. I was the one who insisted we not take any chances with his health. But I figured if the doctor okayed him for international flight, that had to include joining the mile high club.

"I can't believe we're doing this," Hayes murmured as we boarded with only our overnight bags in hand.

I traced my fingers along his jaw, loving the way he leaned into my touch, already anticipating dragging him into the bedroom once we reached our cruising altitude. "No plans, no expectations. Just you and me, exploring something new together. Like, for example, the mile high club?"

"I like the sound of that." He kissed me, deep and hungry, and I melted into him, as far as I could sitting in our seats buckled in for takeoff. But the moment the pilot's voice came over the intercom to say we could move about the cabin, we practically sprinted to the bedroom.

I made one quick stop for my bag along the way. Had to make sure Hayes was properly strapped in should there be any turbulence. And I was planning plenty of turbulence.

Hayes shut the bedroom door, and in an instant his hands slid under my shirt, his touch leaving trails of heat in their wake. I arched into him, needing to be closer, needing to feel his skin against mine. We undressed each other slowly, reverently, taking the time to explore each newly revealed inch of flesh.

When we were finally bare, his eyes darkened, his grip on my hips tightening, his eyes roaming over my body like he wanted to eat me up in the way that always made my heart go pitter with an extra pat. Nobody looked at me, or ever had, the way he did.

"Lay down on the bed," I whispered. "I brought a surprise."

His eyes crinkled with interest, and he crawled onto the bed, laying back against the pillows. He was so tall, his feet almost hung over the end. I unzipped my bag and pulled out three of his silk ties.

"Fuck, flower. Are you about to do what I think you are?" He spread his arms wide, palms up, and flashed me a big smile.

I suppressed my laugh at his delight. "You won't be so excited when you're blindfolded and tied to the bed, and I'm torturing you with my tongue."

He sat up, ripped one of the ties right out of my hand, and started wrapping it around his own wrist. "Oh the hell I won't be. Just remember, however you torture me, I'm going to give it right back to you when it's my turn. This is an awfully long flight."

After I gave him a leg trembling, begging, tied up, and blindfolded mile-high blow job, Hayes tied my hands over my head and moved over me, his weight a comforting pressure, his dick pressing against my thigh. I was so ready to go, so turned on already. But instead of rushing to go down on me like I thought he would, Hayes took his time, at first just staring down at me.

"I want you to watch as I worship your body." He took his dick in his fist, spreading my saliva that still glistened on his skin up and down. "Watch how hard it gets me to love every inch of your body, how I have to keep myself from coming when I'm touching and tasting you."

I swear he kissed and licked and nibbled me from toes to nose and back again. And not just the parts that made me moan in pleasure. He spent a long time working his way from one of my hips across my stomach, dipping his tongue into my belly button, licking my stretch marks, and then made his way back, all the while slowly stroking his cock.

He worshipped me over and over with his hands and mouth until I was trembling, until I was gasping his name like a prayer.

When he finally put on the condom and slid inside me, it felt like coming home. We moved together, our bodies perfectly in sync. Hayes's eyes never left mine, his gaze holding a depth of emotion that stole my breath. Stole my heart.

I felt cherished, adored, seen in a way I never had before. This man, this incredible, driven, loving man, had chosen me, even when I'd told him not to.

The knowledge was overwhelming, humbling, exhilarating. Hayes's thrusts grew more urgent, and my legs tightened around his waist, cherishing that love.

We came together in a blinding rush of ecstasy, Hayes's name falling from my lips like a reverent whisper. He collapsed against me, his face buried in the crook of my neck, his breath hot against my skin.

For a long moment, we just held each other, basking in

the afterglow. When Hayes finally lifted his head, his eyes were shining with a mix of love and wonder.

"You're so fucking amazing," he whispered, pressing a kiss to my collarbone. "I can't believe I get to love you."

A laugh bubbled up in my throat, joy and love and absolute certainty flooding through me. Here, in Hayes's arms, in this little cocoon of love we'd created at thirty-thousand feet.

When the plane touched down in Tokyo, the excitement to be somewhere new sang inside me like a kid who'd just rocked the junior high talent show. We'd finally arrived, and I couldn't wait to explore this vibrant city with Hayes by my side.

We made our way through the private airfield's passport control and customs and toward the exit. I noticed Hayes's brow furrowing, his shoulders tensing. "Uh, Willa?" he said, his voice tinged with uncertainty. "Where exactly are we staying? And how are we getting there?"

I grinned, pulling out my phone. "That's part of the adventure, isn't it? We'll find a place when we get into the city. And as for transportation, the trains here are supposed to be great. I know you're probably not used to public transportation because A, Denver is the worst, and B, I don't suppose you can just get on the light rail and not get mobbed by Mustangs fans, but I don't think you're as famous here. So it should be fine."

Hayes's eyes widened, a flicker of panic crossing his face. "Wait, you mean we don't have a hotel booked? Or any plans at all? Have you ever been to Tokyo before?"

I took his hand, giving it a reassuring squeeze. "Nope. That's half the fun of it. We'll figure it out as we go."

He took a deep breath, and I could see him struggling to wrap his mind around the concept. Hayes was a planner, a man who thrived on structure and certainty. This was so far outside his comfort zone, it might as well have been on another planet, and man, I loved him for trying. Freaking out a little but trying. For me.

"Okay," he said finally, his voice a little shaky. "Okay, I trust you. But please tell me you at least know where these cat cafés are that we're supposed to be visiting."

I bit my lip, feeling a twinge of guilt. "Well, not exactly. But that's what the internet is for, right? We'll do some research on the train."

Hayes closed his eyes, and for a moment, I thought he might actually pass out. But then he surprised me by letting out a laugh, shaking his head in disbelief.

"Willa Rosemount, you are going to be the death of me," he said, pulling me into his arms. "But god, do I love you for it."

I gave him a big old kiss, my heart swelling with love and gratitude. "I know this is scary for you," I murmured, looking up at him. "And I can't tell you how much it means to me that you're willing to go a little crazy with me."

Hayes smiled, brushing a kiss across my forehead. "For you, Willa, I'd leap off a cliff and trust you to be my parachute."

I laughed, warmth spreading through my veins. "I don't think it will come to that. But we might get lost a few times. But I promise not to lose you."

Hayes held my hand a little bit tighter as we made our way to the train station, ready to take on whatever adventures lay ahead. As we stood on the platform, waiting for our train, I couldn't stop smiling.

Sure, we had no idea where we were staying tonight, or exactly where we were going. But we had each other and a whole city waiting to be explored, and for the first time in months, I felt like the real me.

SWEET SUMMER HAYES

HAYES

Holy shit. I was completely out of my depth in these crazy-ass busy streets of Tokyo. The neon signs, the towering skyscrapers, the sea of people rushing past us—it was all so overwhelming, so different from anything I'd ever experienced.

I didn't realize how absolutely unworldly I was until we were in the thick of it. I felt like a country mouse in the city.

But Willa? She was a goddess taking me on an adventure.

All I could do was hold on tight and be absolutely awed by the way she confidently led us through the maze of streets, her eyes sparkling with excitement and her smile never wavering. She seemed to have a sixth sense for where to go and what to do.

"Babe, I think we might be lost," I said, trying to keep the unease from my voice as we turned down yet another alley. I always thought I had a pretty good sense of direction, but without my mountains to know which way was west, I didn't know my front from my back. "Are you sure this is the right way to the cat café?"

Willa just grinned, squeezing my hand reassuringly. "We're definitely lost. Also known as exploring. And look, I think we've stumbled onto something."

She pointed to a small, unassuming storefront, its windows adorned with cutesy illustrations of cats. The sign above the door read "Neko no Jikan" in both Japanese and English.

Willa held up her phone and used Google Lens to translate.

"Cat Time?" I read off her screen, raising an eyebrow.

Willa's grin widened. "Sounds perfect. Come on, let's check it out."

Inside, the café was a cozy oasis, filled with plush couches, colorful cat trees, and of course, dozens of adorable felines. The air smelled of coffee and floral teas and something distinctly furry, but not unpleasant.

A petite Japanese woman wearing cat ears, furry paw-looking mittens, with her face painted with whiskers, greeted us with a warm smile and a flurry of words I couldn't understand. But Willa, in her typical fashion, just smiled right back and managed to convey our intentions through a mix of enthusiastic gesturing and speaking slowly. "Can we buy drinks and meet cats?"

The woman smiled and shocked the shit out of me by

replying in perfect English. "Yes, of course. Please follow me."

Minutes later, we were settled on a couch, sipping matcha lattes, which tasted like milky grass to me, and playing with a pair of rambunctious pure white kittens.

"This is amazing," I said, shaking my head in wonder. "How did you know she spoke English?"

Willa shrugged, her eyes twinkling. "I didn't. But we're lucky that English has become the international language. It used to be French. Did you know that?"

Willa was so animated and excited. The only other time I'd seen her like this was when she was telling me her ideas to get more business to the café. She was so fucking happy right now.

"Nope. I took Spanish." Not that I could speak a lick of it. Guacamole, jalapeño, and tortilla was about it. Mmm. Colorado did have good mountain Mex food.

"Yeah, me too. A lot of people around the world study English in school, and not like we take Spanish and learn to say things like *'Dónde está el baño,' 'Una más margarita, por favor,'* and *'Mi burro es muy perezosa.'* Especially in a big city like this, and with younger people, you can usually find someone who speaks at least a little bit of English, or even someone who knows it better than we do."

"Your donkey is very..."

"Lazy." She scooped up a kitten, nuzzling its fur and cooing softly.

"Right. I'm sure it probably was. Donkeys are known to be like that." But not Willa. She told me I was hard-working, but I had to work hard. She was a natural at so many things, and I wasn't sure she even knew it.

She was... incredible. This woman, this amazing, adventurous, free-spirited woman, had chosen me. She'd brought me halfway across the world, pushed me way out of my comfort zone knowing I needed it, and in a few hours has shown me a side of life I'd never even dreamed of.

Another couple of cats came over to check us out, and one crawled right up on Willa's shoulders and wrapped itself around her like a travel pillow. She scratched its head like this was the most natural thing in the world. "But even if she didn't speak any English, it probably wouldn't be hard to figure out what we wanted to do in a literal cat café."

Willa smiled, so happy to be lost in Tokyo.

My stomach, chest, and head, everything inside of me went off kilter. I had the sensation that I was on a roller-coaster that had just hit the highest peak and was about to go flying down, spinning around, making everyone scream. And I was in the front row.

It wasn't the concussion either. It was this moment, and a realization that as much as Willa loved running the coffee shop, as much as she cared for her uncles and the community she'd built, it wasn't enough for her. She needed more, needed the thrill of the unknown, the challenge of navigating new places and experiences. She needed to be free.

Denver, with its familiar streets and predictable routines, could never fully satisfy her wanderlust. No, it wasn't just wanderlust. But lust for life, for all of the new and different the world had to offer.

Just like being at the top of a literal rollercoaster, for a split second, I was scared. I didn't want to be threatened by that realization, but I was.

I wanted to be the one to give her that. But how was I going to do that? I was tied to Denver, both by my family and my career.

Sure, I could get traded to another team and have to leave, but it would always be my home. I wasn't sure Willa even needed a home.

"Thank you," I said softly, reaching out to tuck a strand of hair behind her ear. "For bringing me here, for showing me this side of you. I know it's not always easy for me to let go of my plans and just... trust the journey. But I'll always try."

She smiled, leaning into my touch. "You're really having fun? I haven't freaked you out?"

"I think maybe you freaked me in. Because I am all in for you."

Willa leaned in close. "I don't know what the rules for public displays of affection are in Japan, but if you don't kiss me right now, I'll die."

I kissed her and would have continued to kiss her if the cat lying on her hadn't decided he wanted kisses too and stuck his nose in my face. As we sat there, surrounded by the playful antics of the cats and the soft murmur of conversation, a new determination seeped into me.

I would find a way to be her partner in adventure and in life. I wanted to learn from her, to grow with her, to chase our dreams together, wherever they might lead. I couldn't see the way to do it yet, but I would. I had to. Because I wasn't ever letting her go.

After a few more hours of exploring the city, visiting

two more cat cafés, and eating some really strange, but weirdly delicious street food, we were both exhausted. It might only be early afternoon in Tokyo, but it was midnight dark thirty back home. The jet lag and the overwhelming newness of everything was catching up to me, and all I wanted was to find a soft bed, fuck my girl into oblivion, and sleep for a hundred years.

"Please tell me you have some kind of idea of where we're going to sleep tonight, and that it isn't in a park under a tree or something."

Willa laughed like that was ridiculous, but I wouldn't put an experience like that past her. "No, I made a reservation at a ryokan with a private onsen while we were at the last café."

"I like the word reservation and private, but other than that, I have no idea what you just said. Is it a hotel?"

She grinned, shaking my head. "Trust me, this will be so much better. More authentic, more immersive. And the couple who runs it are supposed to be the sweetest."

Willa guided us through another trip on the subway and then a few minutes' walk where we came up to what looked way more like some samurai's enormous house than a hotel. "We aren't staying at these people's house or something, are we?"

"It's a traditional Japanese inn." She tugged my hand. "Come on, you're going to love this. I promise."

She led me inside, where we took off our shoes and put on some slippers, which honestly did feel good after walking around all day. Then we were met by a Japanese woman who bowed in greeting. "Welcome, Mr. Kingman, Ms. Rosemount. Please come this way."

Inside the inn was a balm to my country-mouse soul. It was quiet and peaceful, with only the sound of trickling water instead of the hustle and bustle of the city. I didn't think it could get any better, until the hostess slid open the door to our private room. I literally fucking gasped.

I'd been in luxury hotels plenty of times. But they all felt sterile and boring compared to this. The space was a stunning blend of traditional Japanese aesthetics and modern luxury, with sleek lines, natural wood, and soft, diffused lighting.

But what really caught my eye was the private porch just beyond the sliding glass doors. There, nestled amid meticulously arranged rocks and lush greenery, was a steaming, inviting hot tub.

"Here are your nemaki, and your private onsen is ready whenever you are." The hostess motioned to some cotton looking bathrobes, and then to the hot tub outside. "I will bring dinner at seven. Please do not hesitate to let me know if you need anything else."

It was like a scene from a dream, the water glistening under the soft glow of lanterns, the rising steam promising warmth and relaxation. My mind immediately jumped to carrying Willa right into the soothing heat of the water, our bodies intertwined and our worries melting away. I glanced at Willa, seeing my own excitement mirrored in her eyes, a sly smile playing at the corners of her mouth.

Oh, the things we could do in that onsen. I was getting one of these put into my backyard the second we got home. The jet lag and hours of exploring faded into the background. All I could think about was getting Willa into that water, of losing myself in her.

The hostess said something else, her words a gentle hum in the background, but I barely heard her. I was too focused on Willa, on the heat in her gaze and the promise of what was to come. The door slid shut behind us, leaving us alone in our private oasis, and I reached for her, my hands already aching to touch her, to claim her.

We stripped faster than ever, and she giggled as I chased her across the room to the porch. But this was one of those nights I needed something more from her than a fun romp. We stepped into the round stone bowl of swirling water, but before she could sink down, I grabbed her hips and turned her to face away from me. "Hands on the side of the tub, Willa, ass in the air, with your legs spread."

This was one of those times when I was feeling so possessive of her. But this time I recognized it was because of a change in our relationship. She didn't know it yet, but I did. We wouldn't be the same when we got back to Denver, and I needed something to hold on to, if only for one more night. For one more night, I needed to know that I was alive. I only ever felt alive when I was with her.

She sucked in a tiny gasp and leaned against me, pressing her cheek against my chest and moving her arms back to grip the top of my thighs. "You have no idea how much I need you right now."

That was exactly what I needed to hear. How did she always know? Because she was my girl, my Willa.

"Good, because I want to fuck you fast and hard. Hands on the tub. Now."

She did as I told her to, as I needed her to, but not without a little tease. She pressed her plump ass back against my dick and wiggled it back and forth. As if I wasn't already hard for her. I gave her a smack for her troubles and then again when I saw how it made her ass and thighs jiggle and her skin pinken. "Yes, or no, Willa?"

"Oh fuck. Umm, yes."

Hmm. "Are you saying yes because you think I want it, or because you do?"

She looked over her shoulder at me and the love and lust in her eyes just about brought me to my knees. "Because I think you need it."

Damn. I sunk down into the water, scraped my teeth across that pink spot I'd left on her ass, and then grabbed her hips and pulled her down into the water with me. Good god, the heat of the water and her weight on my lap felt so fucking perfect.

I nuzzled her neck and pressed my lips to her ears. "That's not how this works, love. However we fuck, and however we make love, it's because we both want and enjoy what we do to each other, how we make each other feel. We're in this together."

She relaxed into me, and we were both quiet for a few minutes.

"Hey," Willa whispered, her fingers tracing gentle thighs on my chest. "What's going on in that head of yours?"

I sighed, staring up at the unfamiliar sky. The words felt heavy on my tongue, weighed down by the fears I'd been carrying. But if there was anyone I could talk to, it was her. “Your uncles will be back eventually, and they'll take over the coffee shop again. And I know Denver isn't enough for you, Willa. You need this, need the world and all its adventures.”

I swallowed hard, my throat tight. “But I don't know how I fit into that. My family, my career, they're all tied to Denver. Even if I got traded, I'd just be in another city, not... not out here, living life the way you do.”

The thought of losing Willa or holding her back from the life she was meant to live made my chest ache, and the only thing that made if feel better was having her held tight against me.

“I... don't know the answer to what's going to happen when they get back.” She tried to turn to face me, but I couldn't let her. Not yet. She sighed and let me have my way. “I wish I could say I'll just stay, but I can't. And it's not because I don't love you. I do. I love you more than I've ever loved anyone in the whole wide world.”

“I know, baby. I know.”

“And...” Her voice cracked, and damn it all to hell, I'd made her cry. “I know you've been expecting me to stay, but—”

“No, baby. No.” I refused to break her like this. I grasped for the right thing to say to her. “No expectations. Just you and me, exploring something new together.”

Her words to me were the only thing I could come up with that fit. She let out a broken sort of cry-laugh, and I buried my face in the crook of her neck. “If the last twenty-four-ish hours have taught me anything, flower, it's that when I'm sure we're lost, you find a way. We will find a way to make this work. It might not look like whatever I thought it would, but I swear on my life, we can and will be together."

Willa sniffled and I reached, wiping her tears away. "Yes, or no, Willa?"

"Yes. So, so much yes."

NEVER LET ME GO

WILLA

Hayes had brought up the fears I'd been ignoring, because he was strong and confident that we could face them together and figure it all out. Of course he was. He was a Kingman. He'd never met a challenge he couldn't plan and execute his way out of.

I'd been raised to avoid talking about problems and run away from them if possible. I was really good at that. I'd run all the way to Europe and then Asia to avoid the expectations of my life in Denver.

But we'd just made a promise to each other. No expectations. And falling in love with him had been the adventure of a lifetime. I had to believe that we would find a way to be together that didn't mean either of us felt stuck.

But I had to be fair and admit that the way I wanted to exist in the world would mean he'd have to make compromises. It's me, hi. I'm the problem, it's me.

I grabbed his hand from my cheek, where he'd tried to wipe my tears, and brought it down into the water between my legs. "Tell me again how much you love me. Then show me."

He groaned and pushed his fingers into my pussy, touching me in the way only he knew how. "I do love you. So fucking much."

"I know." I needed these words to affirm our feelings. I wanted to feel utterly possessed by him. Like I had the night he'd taken my ass. He'd been so feral, and I relished that side of him.

I grabbed his other hand and brought it up to my chest, where he played with my nipple, stroking, and pinching, and teasing. But it wasn't enough. I wanted more.

I dragged his hand up, wrapping his fingers around my throat, feeling my pulse beating under his thumb. His breathing was harsh and coming so fast, and even as I soaked in his need for me, I had to have more.

"I need you fuck me like this. I want to know you have me, all of me."

"I've got you, sweetheart. Always." He pressed two fingers inside of me. "Ride my fingers, Willa. Let me feel you come."

It wasn't enough. "Please fuck me, Hayes."

"I don't have a condom. I don't even know if it would work in this hot water."

"We don't need it. I've been on birth control for years, and I promise I'm clean." I was not above begging. "Do you trust me enough to fuck me without one, to come inside of me?"

"Jesus, Willa." His voice was hard like gravel now. "You know I do."

"Then take me. Make me feel like I belong with you and no one else." I arched my back, moving my hips backward, searching for his cock.

"Hold onto my arm." His grip around my throat went just a hair tighter, and he used his other hand to pull my core farther back. With his fingers still in my pussy, I felt the tip of his cock press against me, and for a moment as he slid in, I forgot how to breathe.

"Fu-uck, Willa. Holy fuck."

Exactly. I had almost reconnected my lungs and brain when he wiggled his fingers, sliding them out and his cock in deeper, and we both moaned.

"Christ, you'd better be close to coming, baby, because I'm going to fuck you hard. Are you ready?"

"Uh-huh." I was lucky I got those two sounds out.

He didn't even really wait for my reply before he jerked his hips against me, sliding in and out, hitting new places inside me I never even knew existed. I squeezed his hand around my throat tighter, wanting him to do the same.

"This throat is mine, Willa. Just like your pussy, just like your ass." He pressed his thumb against my pulse, and it sent tingles all through my brain. "Later I'm going to fuck your throat, because we'll both like it when I do."

Yes. Yes. This was exactly what I needed. Dirty talking, possessive Hayes. Because he was the one who would never let me go no matter how hard I tried to make him.

He fucked me even harder and swirled his fingers

around my clit, making me shudder. "Is that what you want, baby? Yes, or no, Willa. Don't say no."

"Yes, please, Hayes. Yes."

Please don't ever let me go.

As if he heard the thoughts inside my head, he tightened that grip on my throat and growled in my ear. "Good girl, because I'm never letting you go. You're mine. Fuck, you're mine."

I didn't just come at his words, his declaration, his claiming of me, I came apart. Every cell in my body exploded and then froze somewhere in space and time. I heard Hayes from some distant, faraway place, whispering my name, or maybe he yelled it. I didn't know.

The only thing I did know was the way he said it meant that I belonged to him and he belonged to me, and I had to find my way back to him to make sure he knew it too.

I fell back against his chest and his hand that had been around my throat dropped across my collarbone, holding me tight against him. His other came up to join it, and I wrapped my arms around his, never wanting to let go of this possessive hug he had me in.

We sat together in the onsen, soaking up more than the healing waters. We soaked in each other's love.

When the sky turned shades of gold, then blue and purple, Hayes picked me up, princess style, and carried me to the bed. I grabbed up the towels and slowly dried us both off, then brought over the cotton nemaki robes for us to put on.

That night we both slept like the dead, and I was sure I had some dreams, but I couldn't quite put my finger on what they had been about. Hayes was quieter than usual in the morning, and I wanted to say it was because of the jet lag, but I knew better.

We went to the small dining hall for breakfast where we were served miso soup with freshly cooked rice, grilled fish with rolled egg omelets, nori, and pickled vegetables. I was starving and tucked in, but Hayes mostly picked at his eggs. I'd never seen him not eat so this wasn't a good sign.

"I got a message from my dad this morning." I was trying for some semblance of how we'd felt yesterday. "He wants us to stop at a particular shop to pick up something he's ordered for the family."

"That sounds good." He stared at his food. "Maybe I can pick up some souvenirs for my family. At least something for Jules anyway."

"We can go straight to the airport if you want to."

His head snapped up. "I don't want to leave. If I could, I'd stay in this perfect little bubble with you forever, Willa."

I didn't know what to say to that. "You're not upset that I..."

"I will never be mad at you for being honest with me, especially not about what makes you so incredibly you." He grabbed my hand and rubbed his thumb over my knuckles. "I'm just trying to work out how to make our lives work together. I want you to believe me when I say I'm not letting you go. You're mine, Willa. Not in some, I own you way, but—"

"In a soul deep, cosmic kind of way."

He nodded and his shoulders relaxed. "Yes."

"I know. I'm putting all my faith and trust in that smart brain of yours to figure it out for us." I touched his forehead softly. "So don't go and crack your head again, okay?"

He smiled, and it was almost shy, like in the early days. "I'll do my best."

"I'm counting on it."

We headed back into the city center to the address of the store my dad provided. The item he wanted us to get was a big, heavy box with zero markings on it, just a pre-filled customs slip. "I hope we didn't just become drug mules for the Yakuza or something."

"Oh my god, don't even joke about that." He took the box and carried it under his arm like it weighed no more than a football. My adorable little rule follower.

The flight back should have felt long, but it went by much faster than I wanted it to. Worry churned in my chest and stomach, aching. I had a feeling that everything was going to be different in all the wrong ways when we got back, and I had no idea how to fix that. It's not like I could up and run away to another country.

Luckily our flight put us back in Denver later in the evening and we could just crash for the night. In the morning, Hayes went to practice, or at least to see what the trainers wanted him to do, and I went back to work at the coffee shop.

The memories of our adventures, the intimate moments, and the reality of our very different lives, played on a loop in my mind, making it hard to focus on any tasks. Good thing Javier was there to pick up my slack. He was definitely getting a bonus on his next paycheck.

Near the end of the day, my dad showed up to the shop, a hesitant smile on his face.

"Hey, Dad." I grabbed a mug and started making his usual order.

He waved off the coffee. "Were you able to bring that package I asked for?"

I nodded and had him follow me to the office. "Here it is. What kind of costumes did you order?"

He took the box, hefting it in his arms. "I need you to come over after work tonight, Willa. There's something important I need to discuss with you and your brother."

A knot formed in the back of my throat. The last time he'd looked this serious and we'd had a family meeting, it was when Liam told us about his illness. "Is everything okay?"

Dad shook his head, a sad smile on his face. "No, honey. Just... come over tonight, okay?"

Yikes. I messaged Hayes to see if he could come with me, but he said the doctors wanted to send him for a new scan at the hospital and to meet with the UNC again. It's not like I could ask him to skip that to come to my parents' house.

I did a sloppy job closing up the shop that evening and once again missed Liam and George. If Dad was sick or something... No, I wasn't going to think that. I'd just see what he wanted to talk about before I went all doom and gloom.

When I got to my parents' house, Xander's car was

already in the driveway, but Mom's was nowhere to be seen. Huh.

Inside, Dad and Xander were sitting at the kitchen table, an uncomfortable silence hanging between them. I slid into a chair, my nerves on edge. "What's going on, Dad? Where's Mom?"

Dad took a deep breath, his eyes tired and sad. "Your mother has asked for a divorce."

The words hit me like a punch to the gut. Beside me, Xander let out a low curse.

"But," Dad continued, his voice growing stronger, "I'm not giving up on this family. I'm going to fight for us, starting with being a better father to you two."

He stood up, motioning for us to follow him into the backyard. There, spread out on the lawn furniture, were two padded sumo wrestler suits.

Oh my god. These were the costumes from Japan. No wonder the box was so heavy.

"Do you remember," Dad said, a hint of a smile on his face, "when you two used to fight as kids, and I'd put you in those inflatable bumper balls until you worked it out?"

A grudging laugh escaped my lips. "Yeah, but barely."

Xander crossed his arms and shook his head. "We were four, Dad."

And if I remembered right, Mom hated them. She poked holes in them with her cooking shears so they were ruined.

Dad nodded. "It's time we tried that again. But this time, in these."

Xander and I protested, which was the first thing we

agreed on in forever. But Dad was insistent. Somehow, he talked us into squeezing into the ridiculous suits.

We faced off, circling each other warily. Then, with a grunt, Xander charged. And when I say charged, I mean wobbled toward me. So I did the same.

This was ridiculous.

We collided, bouncing off each other and landing on our backs on the ground.

As we struggled to right ourselves, Xander totally lost it and yelled at me.

"Why do you always get to do whatever you want?" Xander yelled and tried to take a swing at me from the ground. "No expectations, no pressure. You have no idea what it's like to have everyone watching your every move, waiting for you to screw up."

What? I managed to get to my feet, and I used my best move of sitting on him, which sent me rolling ass over head into the grass again. "No expectations? The whole fucking world has expectations of me, Xander. I'm supposed to be pretty and thin, be smarter and get good grades, and a good daughter, and a good sister. You think it was easy for me? All I ever did was watch from the sidelines while you became the golden boy. I was never good enough for anyone."

I'd made peace that I wasn't ever going to fit society's expectations of what I should look like, and decided I, me, myself would like what I looked like. That was hard, and my perfect older brother would never get it.

Xander rolled until he bumped into me. "First of all, brat, you are pretty, you're more creative than anyone I know which also means you're smart, and who the fuck cares if you're thin?"

Half a point to Xan for the sincerity in his voice saying I was pretty and smart. But minus a thousand points for not noticing the bias against anyone not the Hollywood standard size and shape.

"The whole goddamn world cares, oh oblivious one. Especially when my brother is the star athlete. Do you even know how I got teased for being the chubby, dumb sister?"

I pulled up the mean girl voice in my head that was a conglomeration of every asshole who'd ever said anything cruel to me. "Guess your brother got all the good genes, huh? Looks like your brother got all the smarts, dumbass. I bet you were supposed to be triplets but you ate the other one in the womb, didn't you? Too bad you weren't a zombie, you could have eaten the brains too."

Xander didn't move. "What the fuck, beanie. Why didn't you tell me?"

"A, if you call me beanie, or Willabean, ever again, I will suffocate you with the naked sumo wrestler ass of this suit." I hit him in the face with my puffy arm just to emphasize that point. "And B, what would you have done if I told you? People are mean and judgy. That's the reality of the world."

He tried to sit up, but at this point, that was an impossibility for either of us. "I would have beat the daylights out of anyone who said shit like that to you."

He didn't know. He really didn't know. "You were going to beat up half your teammates? All the cheerleaders? Our math teacher? Mom?"

"Jesus, bean... Willa." He was quiet for a minute, and yeah, I wasn't going to help him by saying it was all okay. Because it wasn't. I just let my reality sink in for a minute. He laid his head back in the grass. "I... I'm sorry all that happened to you. No wonder you got the hell out of here the second you could."

I sighed and rolled on to my back to stare up at the blue Colorado sky. Because that would explain why my eyes were getting wet. "I ran away because I couldn't stand feeling like a disappointment all the time."

Xan said something so quiet I almost didn't hear. "I always felt like a disappointment to you."

I rolled to my side, and we stared at each other, chests heaving.

"Why would you think that?" I always supported him.

"You never cared about anything I did. Even at my games, which I know Mom forced you to go to, your nose was always stuck in a book."

Well, shit. I didn't hide that I wasn't the biggest fan of football. I honestly didn't think that affected Xander in the slightest. Maybe I needed to rethink how I'd acted too.

"I'm sorry," I said, my voice rough. "I never meant to make you feel that way."

"I just... I wanted you to be proud of me too." He emphasized that you. "It's why it felt like a fucking slap in the face when you started dating Hayes. He's the only one better than me. I saw you at the Sharks game. You were having fun cheering him on."

"I am proud of you, Xan. I always have been. But dating Hayes doesn't have anything to do with... you. He's sweet, and sexy, and he loves me, faults and all."

"Of course he fucking does. Everyone loves you, Willa. Or if they don't, they're fucking missing out."

Dad came over from the sidelines where he'd been watching, letting us fight this out, his eyes misty. "I'm so sorry, kids. I'm sorry that all these expectations you thought you had to live up to hurt you so much. I'm insanely proud of the adults you've become despite the bullshit you both endured."

Xan and I glanced at each other. I'm not sure either of us had ever heard Dad talk like this.

"And I'm very sorry you couldn't come to me with your struggles. That ends today. I am here for you no matter what."

Xander glanced at me, twin telepathy style, and put his arm up, reaching toward our father. I did the same. "I think what we're struggling with now, Dad, is getting up off the ground."

My dad shook his head and let out a chuckle, and I saw the gratitude in his eyes for this lifeline from us. Xan and I laughed too, the tension of the past few months finally breaking.

"Hey," Liam's voice floated into the backyard. "What are you guys laughing about? Is it because you're so happy we're home?"

Oh my god. Liam and George were home.

WE'RE NOT IN KANSAS ANYMORE

HAYES

I walked out of the doctor's office, a grin stretching across my face. Finally, after weeks of resting, rehab, and endless tests, I'd been cleared to practice. Real practice, not just stretching and running. The playoffs were in a few weeks, and I was more than ready to get back on the field.

We were going to the fucking bowl and winning that ring.

I couldn't wait to share the good news with Willa. She'd been my rock through this whole ordeal, and I knew she'd be just as thrilled for me. Maybe taking her to a couple of new cities would scratch that wanderlust bug just a little bit until the off-season. Then I'd take her anywhere in the world she wanted to go.

It wasn't enough, I knew it. But it could be a start to figuring out how to keep her in my life.

I pulled out my phone to call her, and I noticed a string of missed messages from Willa. My heart dropped as I read through them, her words jumbled and frantic.

Liam and George are back.

They cut their trip short.

They'll be taking back the shop.

I don't know what to do.

I need you.

Shit. Shitty shit shitstorm. This wasn't supposed to happen yet. We were supposed to have more time, more time to figure out our future, to find a way to make this work. More time to be together.

I called her back immediately, my mind racing. "Willa? Baby—"

Her voice was strained, on the verge of tears. "They just showed up, Hayes. Out of nowhere. And I'm so happy to see them. I missed them so much, and I just had a sumo wrestling fight with Xander, and my mom has asked for a divorce, and I thought... I thought we had more time."

"I know, I know." I didn't know. Sumo wrestling with Xan? A divorce? Her world imploded while I was getting my brain scanned. "Listen, don't panic, okay? I'm on my way. We'll figure this out. Together."

But even as I said the words, I felt a sinking feeling in my gut. What were we going to do? Willa couldn't stay in

Denver. Not even my ties, my love, could bind her. I wouldn't even try to do that to her.

We needed help.

An idea began to form, a crazy idea that a few months ago wouldn't have even occurred to me. Because I did not know how to make this work all on my own. "Sweetheart, we need help, okay? I'm going to make some calls, get our families together. We need to talk this out, all of us."

"We're just going to... lay it all out there? Tell them everything?" she asked softly. "They're going to think I'm crazy and selfish."

They might. "But they love you, almost as much as I do, and I'll make them understand this isn't just a compromise you have to make for me, and they'll get on board. Trust me."

"Okay." She sighed. "I'm... going to ask Xander to come. We understand each other better now. I may also make you two put on some sumo wrestling suits at some point."

"I definitely don't understand, but if you want him there, then I want him there too." I really fucking hoped I didn't regret that later.

I spent the next few minutes on the phone, trying to coordinate, but the moment Jules was in the loop, it all came together. Everyone, including Willa's dad, brother, and her uncles were all meeting at the coffee shop at seven.

By the time evening rolled around, everyone gathered in the shop, faces etched with concern and curiosity.

"Thank you all for coming," I said, my voice steady

despite the nerves churning in my stomach. "Willa and I need your help."

I laid it all out—our love, our fears, the impossible choice we faced. Willa's need for adventure, my ties to Denver. The room was silent, everyone processing the weight of our dilemma.

"Why doesn't Willa just stay in Denver?" Mr. Rosemount suggested, his brow furrowed. "And you two can travel wherever you want in the off-season, right?"

I shook my head, my jaw tight. "No. I won't ask Willa to compromise her dreams, her needs. That's not fair to her."

"Then what about you, Hayes?" my dad asked, his eyes soft with understanding. "Are you willing to give up football, your career, for love?"

A roll of murmurs whipped through the room. No one expected my dad to suggest that. But it was bullshit that they would think I wouldn't.

I looked at Willa, at the tears shining in her eyes, the love and fear warring on her face. I took her hand, my decision crystallizing with perfect clarity.

"Yes," I said simply. "I would. I love football, but I love Willa more. I'd give it all up in a heartbeat if it meant we could be together."

Willa's breath hitched, her fingers tightening around mine. "Nope. Absolutely not, Hayes, no. I can't and won't ask you to do that. You've worked your whole life to achieve this goal, and there is no way I'd ask you to give it up. There has to be another way."

The room erupted into a flurry of voices, everyone

offering opinions, solutions. But through the chaos, one voice rang out, clear and calm.

"What if," Liam said, his eyes twinkling with a hint of mischief, "George and I just gave you the shop, Willa?"

George took Liam's hand and kissed it. "If Willa and Hayes aren't willing to compromise on their dreams, I can't let you either. You love this shop."

"I know. But spending the last couple of months with you meant more to me than anything else ever has. I love the shop because I love you." Liam motioned his hand around the room. "And it's not like it would be going anywhere. Obviously Willa is better at running it than I ever was."

George looked at the two of us and winked. "Yes, she is. I saw the bank account. She's actually gotten the place profitable."

Liam gave George a playful smack, but George smiled and looked back at us. "What do you say, sweet wild child? Can we make this a wedding present?"

The room exploded again. Lots of 'whoa-whoa-whoas' and 'when did this happens' and one 'yes, my first sister-in-law.' We waited until they calmed down. Willa explained, "No one is getting married. Yet. So, thank you Uncle George, but no. While I appreciate the offer more than you know, and I've had fun basically turning your shop into a cat café, I was never really interested in the coffee shop business. I hope that doesn't hurt your feelings."

"Of course not. We just want to see you happy," Liam said.

Back to square one.

Chris looked over at Trixie, gave her a quick kiss and wrapped his arm around her before focusing his attention back on me and Willa. "Look, bro. Someone is going to have to make a sacrifice here. You guys choose stability, and career now, set yourselves up for the future, and then you can go flitting around the globe all you want in a few years. It's being handed to you on a silver platter. You play football, Willa runs the coffee shop, you can even travel in the off season like the rest of us do. It won't kill you to do the responsible thing for a little while."

It won't kill you.

It won't fucking kill you?

"Won't it?" They didn't fucking understand and the tightness building in my chest exploded. "Do you not see how dead I already was? I was a god damned robot. Family, football, school. That was it, that was my entire life, and I'm telling you right the fuck now, that's not living."

Willa stared up at me, shocked, but also with an intrinsic understanding in her eyes.

"So when you want Willa to sacrifice who she is, for me, which is exactly what the hell you're asking, you're taking, depriving us all of the joy, the color, the excitement, the part of life that makes it actually worth living, not just existing."

Everyone should fucking know it.

And if they didn't understand? They could all go shove their responsibilities up their asses.

Chris stood up so fast that the screech of his chair just about broke the sound barrier. He marched up to me and I clenched my fists. I was going to have to punch my older brother. But if kicking his ass was the only way to make him understand, that's what I'd have to do.

Even as he charged toward me, I was going to make him understand. "I'm not going back to an existence without the technicolor that Willa brought to my black and white life. I'm not ever going back to Kansas, when Willa is my Oz. Even if the rest of the world thinks that's the responsible thing to do. She's my yellow brick road, and I'm fucking lost without her."

But instead of wanting a fight, Chris grabbed me into a hard bear hug. "Fuck, man. I'm sorry. Sorry I didn't see any of that."

He glanced over at Willa and clapped her on the arm. "Sorry for being a judgy ass."

"Don't worry," Trixie called. "I'll punish him for that later."

Chris let go of me and faced the rest of our families, then gave one big clap. "Put your heads together, people. We've got a problem to solve."

As he returned to his table with Trixie, I caught my dad's eye. He gave me a slow nod and that atta-boy shake of his fist. I got the feeling he'd been waiting for me to show up to life like this.

Declan and Kelsey were sitting at one of the tables with Everett on one side and Penelope on the other. Kelsey sat up in her chair and tilted her head just like Seven did when he thought he smelled catnip. "Oh. I think I have an idea."

She waved Penelope over, and Jules. Everett joined them too, and the five of them put their heads together, whispering and gesturing. I wished they'd do this brainstorming out loud. Willa leaned over and whispered to me. "This must be one hella idea. I can't even imagine what Kelsey thinks would work. It's not like I can go on *The Choicest Voice,* win it, and become an international pop star. I can barely carry a tune."

Kelsey spoke up, her voice gentle but excited. "Willa, I think I've got it. See what you think."

Declan nodded, and I took Willa's hands, feeling an overwhelm of anticipation.

"I'm releasing a new album in the spring. Keep that quiet, it's not common knowledge yet and you know how the Besties like it when I drop hints. Anyway, I'll be doing an international stadium tour to promote it."

Willa squeezed my hand. Did she already see where Kelsey was going with this? Because I didn't. Did Kelsey want to take Willa with her on tour? Doing what?

"I need someone on my team, someone I trust, to scout the locations we're going to for hotels, to make sure they're appropriate for me and the whole-ass entourage, especially for security measures. Would you be interested in doing that for me?"

Willa's eyes widened, surprise and uncertainty flickering across her face. "I... I don't know, Kelsey. That's an incredible offer, but am I really qualified for something like that? I don't know anything about the music industry."

"You'd get to travel, see the world, talk to and charm new people, and I'm sure there will be crazy weird problems to solve." It was perfect except for the part where I didn't get to go with her. "It's everything you're good at, babe."

"But I'd be away from you the whole time. It's no different than if I just got another teaching job abroad. We need a way for us to be together. Maybe I should just—" She shrugged, hesitant, torn.

Everett stood up and pointed at the two of us. "Okay, you two, listen up. There will never be a perfect solution. There is no such thing as perfect. Relationships are all about compromise, and you two are the worst at compromising I've ever seen. You'll compromise to make the other person happy, but not yourselves? What the hell?"

He paced the room, his voice rising with each word. "You're already defying expectations by refusing to allow the other to give up their dreams for you. Everyone would expect Willa to give up her life to be with Hayes because it's always the women who follow the players in football. They give up everything for us. But you two have already said that's not what you're going to do."

Everett marched right up to me and Willa, his eyes blazing. "I've been trying to tell all of you lovesick fools that you need to be true to yourselves. Stop trying to fulfill everyone else's expectations of what they think you should be or how your relationship should look. All of you need to get your heads out of your asses and go after what you actually want the most."

With a final huff and a glance at the table with Declan, Kelsey, and Penelope, Everett stomped out of the room, leaving a stunned silence in his wake. Pen, eyes wide, hurried after him, murmuring something about calming him down. Declan and Kelsey shared a meaningful look. I didn't know what was going on there. Everett had never yelled at any of us like that in his life.

Willa looked up at me. "Is my head up my ass?"

I tipped my head to the side and glanced at her fine ass, then shrugged. I turned around and showed her my tight end, giving it a little wiggle. "Is mine?"

Xander answered for us both. "Yes."

Willa gave him a very polite middle finger. "But we'd never get to see each other if I'm traveling all the time. That's not the point of all of this. How does that work?"

"Duh," Xander threw scraps of his paper cup that had been torn to shreds at us. "Hayes travels almost every week too. And even if the Mustangs do go to the bowl, the off-season is only like a month away. So you take your trips when he does. It's not like Miss Superstar over there needs you to scout the entire world every week." Xander looked at Kelsey and blushed. "Sorry, Ms. Best, I didn't mean to speak for you. I'm kind of a dick sometimes."

When had he figured that out?

Kelsey laughed and waved him off. "You're not wrong. I don't even start the tour until April. Declan and I were looking forward to a little downtime too. I think you'd probably be gone a couple of times a month, depending on how far in advance of the tour you are and how the prospects for the hotels seem. Pen has all those details. You'd work closely with her."

Declan pushed Kelsey's hair out of her eyes and looked at her like I imagined I looked at Willa. "The two of us are on crazy travel schedules too. But we make it work. Kels comes to games when she can, I go to concerts when I can. We have a lot of phone sex."

Jules held her hands out like blocking the sight of them would help her not hear that tidbit. "Ugh. Can you not be all gross and talk about your sex lives in front of me? I'm a minor."

Declan gave her his patented grumpy look. "A minor pain in my ass."

God, could this work? It wasn't perfect, but was it close enough? "You'd still be... tied to Denver. Can you live with that? I'll see if I can get traded if the answer is no."

Willa started to protest my offer, but Xander stood up and walked over to us. "I know the reason you don't want to be stuck in Denver is because of me. And Mom. But when I get drafted next year, it'll probably be somewhere else in the country. I'm leaving. You can stay."

She blinked a few times and then punched her brother in the arm. Hard. "Great, Xan. You're going to leave just when I don't want you to? You are a dick sometimes."

"I know." Xan gave her a cocky grin. "I have been for a while. But I have one redeeming quality, I promise."

I wasn't so sure about that.

Xan gave me the bro-code chin jerk of approval. "What your jackass boyfriend here figured out, about how you're the joy in the world? I knew that. I've seen you be that our whole lives. And anyone who can't understand that, doesn't deserve you. So stay. Nobody says you have to even talk to Mom again if you don't want to. I'll run interference for you. It's my turn."

Willa pressed her lips together, but they were trembling. "It is your turn. For like the next twenty years."

Wait. Did that mean...?

Willa looked up at me and the tears she'd been blinking back pooled on the edges of her lashes. But they weren't sad tears. "No expectations. Just exploring something new together," she said softly, a slow smile spreading across her face.

I grabbed her up in my arms and spun her around. "Hell yeah, baby. We'd better up the minutes on our international calling plan. Because I am so looking forward to phone sex with you."

FOREVER MY HOME

WILLA

The bell above the door to Cool Beans chimed, but this time, it was because I stepped into the familiar warmth of the coffee shop that was no longer my responsibility. The rich aroma of freshly brewed coffees and teas and the soft murmur of conversation enveloped me like a comforting hug. It was strange to think that just a few short months ago, I'd been a mess trying to run this place, and now it was thriving.

I'd done that, and it was something to be proud of.

I watched Liam move behind the counter with the ease of a happy man, and I felt a mixture of nostalgia and excitement. He caught my eye and waved me over, a broad grin on his face.

"Willa, my favorite customer, come, sit. I want to hear all about your plans for this new adventure with Kelsey freaking Best. How is this even real life? We're friends with the biggest pop star in the world. I know her dog."

I slid onto a stool, returning his smile. "I know right? I'm meeting Penelope here to get the list of venues they've already booked so I can plan out the first leg of the scouting trip."

Liam's eyes softened, and he reached across the counter to squeeze my hand. "I'm so proud of you, Willa. You've always had such an adventurous spirit, and it's wonderful to see you finding a path that's right for you."

I felt a lump form in my throat, touched by his unwavering support. "I sincerely wouldn't even have this opportunity, or, I mean, really this whole new life if it hadn't been for you and George. I'm so grateful you're in my life, and if I haven't told you enough, I love you two so much."

He patted my cheek and swallowed a few times. "You were always a little bit mine and George's, since the day you were born. We love you right back, kiddo."

A few blinks to suck those tears back up into my eyeballs, and I was ready to go again. "Okay, enough mushy gushy. I had an idea for the coffee shop that I was working on before you got back. Do you want to hear it?"

His eyebrows raised, curiosity piqued. "Oh? Do tell."

I leaned forward, excitement bubbling up inside me. "What if we converted the shop into a full-time cat café? We've already got a good partner with the cat shelter, and we're the busiest when we host adoption events. But what if it was more? We could really create a cozy space for people to interact with the cats."

Liam's face lit up, his eyes sparkling with enthusiasm.

"Willa, that's a fantastic idea. I love it. George and I tried to do some brainstorming on our cruise to make the shop more unique, and honestly, more profitable. This is perfect. We already have your themed drinks and pastries. Maybe we can add some cat-themed merchandise too."

We spent the next hour huddled together, scribbling notes and sketching out ideas. It was like old times, the two of us lost in our creative flow, bouncing ideas off each other. I'd missed this, missed the way it was so easy to be myself with the Guncles. I only got this at home.

This was my home, and the universe had provided a way for me to actually be comfortable here. I owed some deposits into the karma bank for sure.

While we chatted about the conversion plans, my phone buzzed with an incoming call from Trixie. I answered, putting her on speaker so Liam could hear.

"Willa, I'm so excited," Trixie gushed, her enthusiasm for everything was palpable even through the phone. "I'm starting a body-positive romance novel book club as part of the Take Up Space network. And I'm hoping, hoping, hoping, you'll host it with me."

I did love a good book club. The spicy romance group had only met twice so far, but the third meeting might prove to be the biggest one yet. I was doing my best to make sure my new travel schedule would allow time for my second greatest love, romance novels.

"I'm always down for anything books. But what's the Take Up Space network?"

"What? You mean Marie Manniway hasn't already recruited you? Score one point for me. It's a group of plus-size movers and shakers in all sorts of industries who support each other and do outreach programs to help women from all walks of life embrace and love who they are, no matter their size, shape, or what the scale says."

I felt my jaw drop, stunned and honored by the offer. Liam's eyes widened, and he gave me a thumbs up, mouthing "do it" emphatically.

"Trixie, that's incredible. I would be thrilled to help you host an event like that. Thank you so much for thinking of me."

We chatted for a few more minutes, ironing out the details. As I hung up, I couldn't stop grinning. It seemed like every aspect of my life was falling into place, each piece of the puzzle finding its perfect fit.

Liam looked at me, his expression soft with pride. "Look at you, Willa. You're unstoppable."

I laughed, feeling a blush creep into my cheeks. "I don't know about unstoppable, but I definitely feel like I'm finally on the right track. Speaking of which, there's Penelope. Wish me luck."

Liam came around the counter, pulling me into a tight hug. "You don't need luck, sweetheart. You've got talent, passion, and a heart of gold. Knock 'em dead."

Penelope sat down at one of the tables and waved me over, a warm smile on her face.

"Willa, hi, it's so good to see you. I've been dying to hear about that trip to Tokyo. How was it?"

I slid into the seat across from her, returning her smile. "It was amazing, Pen. The city, the culture, the food, oh the food. But the best part was Hayes and the way everything was flabbergasting to him. Seeing him embrace the adventure, for me, when I knew it was totally weird and uncomfortable for him to be all spontaneous like that, it made me fall in love with him even more."

Penelope's eyes softened, and she stared down at the table. "You two are so perfect together. It's clear how much you love and support each other. I hope I find that someday too."

"Aww, Pen, I'm sure you will."

We spent the next hour poring over maps and travel guides, marking potential locations for Kelsey's tour. Penelope had a keen eye for detail and a knack for anticipating potential logistic issues. She was hella smart. I found myself getting swept up in her enthusiasm, my own excitement growing with each new idea we discussed.

As we were wrapping up, Penelope fixed me with a thoughtful look. "You know, Willa, you're really good at this. You might consider starting your own business, scouting locations not just for Kelsey, but for other celebrities too."

I blinked, taken aback by the suggestion. "I hadn't really thought about it, but that's an intriguing idea. Do you think there's a market for that kind of service?"

Penelope nodded emphatically. "Absolutely. With your talent for finding unique, off-the-beaten-path locations and your skills at navigating different cultures and languages, you'd be a hot commodity. Plus, you've got the Kelsey Best seal of approval now. That's no small thing in this industry."

I felt a flutter of excitement in my chest, the seed of an idea taking root. My own business, my own clients. It was a daunting prospect, but also an exhilarating one.

"I'll definitely consider it, Pen. Thank you for the vote of confidence."

We parted ways with a hug and a promise to meet up again soon. It seemed like everywhere I turned, new doors were opening, new opportunities presenting themselves.

My head was already ten steps ahead, thinking about who and where this business might lead me to. I didn't notice Hayes until I practically ran into him. He caught me by the shoulders, steadying me with a laugh.

"Whoa there, flower. What's got you lost in thought?"

I grinned up at him, rising up on my toes to press a quick kiss to his lips. "I just had the most amazing meeting with Penelope. She had some great ideas for Kelsey's tour locations, and she even suggested I start my own business as a celebrity location scout."

Hayes's eyes widened, a slow smile spreading across his face. "Willa, that's badass. You'd be amazing at that."

Seven meowed like he agreed. Wait, why had he brought Seven to the coffee shop?

He led me hand-in-hand over to the comfy cat-corner, and I was surprised to find Liam and George huddled there together, whispering excitedly.

They looked up as we approached, identical grins on their faces. George rushed over, pulling me into a bone-crushing hug. Weird. I always enjoyed his hugs, but what in the world was that one for?

Hayes cleared his throat, drawing my attention back to him. He looked adorably nervous, fidgeting with something in his pocket.

"So, Willa," he said, his voice slightly unsteady. "There's something I wanted to ask you."

George let out a little squeal, clutching at Liam's arm. I shot them a curious look before turning back to Hayes, my heart suddenly racing.

He took a deep breath, his blue eyes locking with mine. "Willa, these past few months with you have been the best of my life. You've shown me what it means to love, to take risks, to chase my dreams. And I know, without a doubt, that I want to keep chasing those dreams with you by my side."

My breath caught in my throat as he lowered himself to one knee. George let out a gasp, his hands flying to his mouth.

But Hayes pulled a treat out of his pocket to get Seven to come to him. Then he picked up my cat, who had something hanging from the collar around his neck. Hayes held Seven out to me, and indicated to the small, velvet bag hanging there. "Open it."

I pulled the string tied to Seven's collar while he squirmed, not enjoying his role in this show, except for the treats, of course. With more than a little trepidation, I turned the bag upside down to reveal a shining silver... key.

"Willa Rosemount, will you move in with me, officially?"

I felt a laugh bubble up in my throat, relief and joy and love all mingling together. Behind me, I heard George deflate slightly and Liam chuckle.

I took his face in my hands and gave him a big kiss. Seven stuck his nose right between us, purring. "Hayes

Kingman, I would love nothing more than to officially move in with you."

His face split into a grin, and he set Seven down on the nearest cat-safe surface and then surged forward, capturing my lips in a kiss that made my toes curl. We stayed like that for a long moment, lost in each other, until Liam pointedly cleared his throat.

We broke apart, laughing. George rushed over, hugging us both.

"We're so happy for you two," he gushed, his eyes misty. "But you had me going there, Hayes. Just to be clear, this isn't a proposal, right? You're not getting married yet?"

I shook my head, smiling softly. "No, Uncle George. We're not quite ready for that step. But we're committed to building a life together."

Liam nodded, his expression understanding. "That's all anyone can ask for. Love, commitment, and the courage to face the future together."

Everett walked into the shop, and I thought, at first, he was in on this move-in proposal too. But he made a beeline for the counter, barely acknowledging us as he passed.

"I need the strongest coffee you've got," he muttered to Javi at the counter, rubbing his temples and looking uncharacteristically disheveled. "And maybe a shot of whiskey to go with it."

Javier raised an eyebrow but set about preparing Everett's order. I exchanged a concerned glance with Hayes before approaching Everett.

"Hey, bro. You doing okay there, man?"

Everett sighed, his shoulders slumping. "Oh, fine, just fucking fine. Long night. And an even longer morning."

Hayes clapped him on the back, his expression sympathetic. "Juggling too many women?"

Everett snorted, shaking his head. "Nope. Just one who is driving me absolutely crazy."

Hayes clapped his brother on the back. "Oh ho, sounds like the Kingman love guru needs to take some of his own advice. You'd better figure it out before the bowl game. Everyone knows Kingmans play better..." he glanced over at me, and my insides went all flippy floppy like I was a lovesick teenager, "when we're in love."

Everett stared into his coffee cup, his brow furrowed, as if searching for answers in the swirling depths. "The saying goes that we play better when we're getting laid. That part I can do. I don't know about the love part."

Everett had been the rock for all of his brothers, the one they turned to for love advice and guidance. But when it came to his own heart, he seemed lost.

But a few months ago, I had been too. Until I met the one person in the universe who saw me and loved me for me, the most authentic me.

I had found my place in the world, not just geographically, but emotionally, spiritually. And it was all thanks to the incredible man beside me, who had shown me what it meant to love fearlessly, to chase my dreams with abandon, and who showed me how real love meant support, not expectations.

I leaned into Hayes, my heart so full it felt ready to burst. I couldn't wait for a lifetime of adventures with the one man who would always be my home.

EPILOGUE: AMONG THE STARS

HAYES

The sun was high in the sky, the warm breeze carrying the scent of saltwater and sunscreen as Willa and I lounged by the pool. It was the first day of our Star Trek themed cruise, a gift from Liam and George to thank Willa for taking such good care of the coffee shop while they were away.

I still couldn't believe we were actually here, surrounded by fellow Trekkies and a lot of the stars themselves. We were both like little kids in a Star Trek themed playground.

Willa looked over at me, her eyes sparkling with excitement behind her sunglasses. "I cannot believe we get to meet LeVar Burton tomorrow morning. I'm gonna wear my *Butterfly in the Sky* t-shirt. You don't think he'll mind it's not Star Trek I'm fangirling him over, do you?"

I grinned, feeling my own inner fanboy stirring. "Not

even a little bit, babe. Did you see that Jonathan Frakes is doing a panel on directing? We can't miss that."

We spent the next few hours geeking out over the schedule of events, planning our days around the panels, autograph sessions, and themed parties. It was a nerd's paradise, and we were loving every minute of it.

As we made our way to the first panel of the cruise, I couldn't help but notice the glances and whispers from the other cruisers. At first, I thought they were just excited to see the Star Trek celebrities, but then I heard my own name being murmured.

"Is that Hayes Kingman?"

"Oh my god, it is. Do you think he'd take a picture with me?"

Willa nudged me, a smirk playing at her lips. "Looks like you've got some fans of your own, Mr. MVP."

I ducked my head, feeling a blush creep up my neck. "I'm just here to geek out like everyone else. I don't want to take the attention away from the real reason we're all here."

But as the days went on, I found myself being approached more and more. People wanted autographs, photos, and even just to shake my hand and congratulate me on the season. It was surreal, being recognized and admired in a setting so far removed from the football field.

Even some of the Star Trek stars seemed to know who I was. After a very rambunctious karaoke with some of the cast of Star Trek Enterprise, Connor Trinneer clapped me on the shoulder, a wide grin on his face.

"Hayes Kingman! Man, I loved watching you play this

season. That last-minute touchdown against the Dawgs? Incredible."

I felt my jaw drop, starstruck in the presence of my personal favorite starship engineer himself. "Thanks. That means a lot coming from you, sir."

He laughed, shaking his head. "Please, call me Connor. And I should be thanking you. You made me a lot of money in my fantasy league this year. Just keep that head of yours safe."

Willa and I spent the rest of the day in a happy daze, attending panels, getting autographs, and even participating in a trivia contest, which we totally won, thanks to Willa's encyclopedic knowledge of all things Star Trek.

Every evening we dressed up in our cosplay for the theme of the night, which took an entire extra suitcase to contain. On the evening designated for the most illustrious evil bad guys in the mirror universe, Willa emerged from the bathroom, and my breath caught in my throat. She was dressed in a stunning recreation of Captain Killy, her hair straightened and dyed red, and her uniform form fitting in all the right places.

"Wow," I managed, my eyes drinking her in. "You look incredible. I'd let you Killy me."

She did a little twirl, grinning. "Why thank you, Mr. Spock. Or should I say, High Chancellor of the Terran Empire?"

I'd signed up to get Vulcan ears and eyebrows done by one of the professional makeup artists and had even had them do the evil version of Spock's crazy goatee. Willa said it was very sexy when I'd gotten back from the appointment, and her enthusiasm for the beard almost made us late for dinner.

I was definitely growing one of my own this year.

The party was in full swing when we arrived, the band playing, people dancing, and we both gawked at the amazing outfits people had put together. There was one guy who could have been Captain Picard's twin, a whole host of Klingons, and one girl in a wheelchair who very cleverly dressed as space and wore a hat that was an amazing replica of the Deep Space Nine station. We mingled and danced, sipping colorful cocktails with names like "Romulan Ale" and "Borg Sphere."

As the night wore on, our cruise director took the stage.

"Good evening, everyone. I hope you're all having a wonderful time."

The crowd cheered, raising their glasses in a toast.

"I have a couple of reminders for our upcoming port days and programming. We'll get into port bright and early at seven, and you've got the whole day to explore the island. But be back by four, because we will leave your asses here if you don't. Then, on Wednesday, while we're at sea, we have a unique opportunity for any couples out there who might be feeling a little extra love in the air."

He paused for dramatic effect, his eyes twinkling with mischief.

"One of our cast members, I'm going to let you guess who until the day of, is an ordained minister. He will be available to perform a wedding ceremony or a vow renewal for all you love birds. If you're thinking you might want to tie the knot among the stars, we will see you there."

I glanced at Willa, my heart suddenly racing.

She met my gaze, her expression unreadable. "Hayes..."

I took her hands in mine, my throat tight with emotion. "I know we haven't talked about it, not really. And I know it's crazy, and impulsive, and maybe a little bit insane."

She let out a shaky laugh, her eyes shining. "A little bit?"

I grinned, pulling her closer. "Okay, a lotta bit. But, Willa, when I think about the future, about all the adventures I want to have and the memories I want to make, there's only one thing I know for sure. I want you by my side through all of it."

One beautiful tear streamed down her face, but she was smiling, her grip on my hands tight. "Hayes Kingman, are you asking me to marry you? Right here, right now, on a Star Trek cruise?"

I nodded, my own vision blurring with tears. "I am. I don't want to waste another minute. I love you, Willa. More than anything in this universe or any other. Will you be my wife, my partner, my Imzadi?"

She let out a watery laugh, throwing her arms around my neck. "Yes. Yes, a thousand times yes."

The crowd around us erupted into cheers as we kissed, lost in our own little world. I knew one thing for certain.

This was only the beginning of our greatest adventure yet.

NOT READY FOR our adventure with Willa and Hayes to be over?

Grab their bonus chapter when you join my Swoon Zone email newsletter!

READY FOR MORE KINGMANS? Read The Next Book in the Cocky Kingman series now.

A NOTE FROM THE AUTHOR

Okay, cuddle up, it's Fun Times with Amy, where you get to hear how and why I wrote this book.

I was worried about telling you this story, specifically Willa's story.

Why?

I always pull from my own life to write my books. It makes them more authentic. But Willa? She's A LOT me.

I'm the one who taught English as a Foreign Language in Vietnam (and Poland, and the Czech Republic). I'm the one who ran away from home. Although, not because my family was horrible. They're actually pretty lovely. I'm also the one who feel stuck living in Denver, and am DYING to get back out into the world, but can't figure out how to make that work.

Why was I worried to tell you all of that?

Because I don't know if the world understands people like me and Willa. We NEED new and different in a world that doesn't like change. In a world filled with expectations that I don't feel like I ever fulfill.

But I decided to write Willa just the way she is, because I bet if I feel like I have to be something different trying to make other people happy, trying to fulfill the world's expectations (especially when it comes to being a fat person living in an Ozempic world), then I bet a lot of other people do too.

And I was reminded recently, by the beautiful, amazing writing life coach, Becca Syme, that I'm meant to bring joy into the world, and that's a really important thing. (Oops. I'm crying now.)

But we fear rejection, because... we are so often rejected.

Our society doesn't always value the artists, the creatives, the #7 enneagrams, the positivity and joy bringers. The one who help have things in life that are Ozian Technicolor. The things we LIVE for.

Hard work, responsibility, and GOALS! are the expectation and pressure of today's hectic world.

I hate goals.

I shiver at the word.

I actively DON'T MAKE GOALS.

I. Bring. Joy.

And I get judged for it, a lot.

But it's my calling (along with making sure that curvy, chubby, large, thick, plus size women see that they're worthy of love via writing romance novels specifically for them). Which is why I write fluffy rom coms with walking green flag heroes and no third act breakups. Because it brings me joy, and I hope it does you too.

I'm not saying if you're a goal setter, a goal digger, a goals goddess that you can't also bring joy into the world.

Of course you DO! Just in a different way than I do. And there are a lot of times I envy the way you do it. I surround myself with goal setting, beautiful souls in my real life. It's part of how I get anything done.

I also wrote our lovely, sweet summer Hayes the way that I did because we all need a partner who will see us for who we truly are and will defend us, and even sacrifice, for our dreams.

One of my all time favorite sitcoms was Dharma and Greg. It's the ultimate opposites attract. And I would LURRRVE to find myself a Greg. I watched a lot of D+G reruns while writing this book. Which I had dig for. NO streaming services had it, and I found a lovely person who uploaded them all on YouTube.

There are a couple of other inspirations for this book. The absolute number one being my cat Uno. That's him on the cover - I actually sent my cover artist picture (from his catstagram) so she could draw him. I'm definitely a cat lady for Uno, and trust me, Uno knows he's the love of my life.

My other cat Hades The Terrible Snuggler is in here a little bit too. He's the one who thinks he's every kittens' daddy. When Uno and his brothers and sisters were born, Hades, who is definitely fixed, helped their mama by licking their little butts. When they were weaning and first learning how to eat food, Hades always made sure all the kittens ate before he would even take a bite.

Did you know, I actually go on The Star Trek Cruise every year? One of my BFFs dragged me on the first one, and now I'm the one who insists we go back year after year. The Trekkies are the friendliest, most welcoming people in the world, and next year I'm going to try my darndest to figure out how to dress up as Captain Killy (the Star Trek universe's nod to plus-size women, played by Mary Wiseman).

If you happen to be a Trekkie you should come! And if you do, be sure to find me! I'll be the one with a crush on Connor Trinneer.

One of the things that brings me joy when I write books, are the inside jokes that are between me and... me. Hahahahaha. Things that I think are hilarious, but I never know if anyone else gets them. But if you get a giggle out of anything, especially the renaming of football teams, places in Colorado, Trekkie stuff, and punny pet names, we should probably be BFFs.

Okay, I know you're dying to find out who the next book is about, and I'm not saying it's Everett... but... who else would it be?

A LOT of readers have been shipping Everett and Penelope.

Umm, it was not my intention to make Pen a main character.

One of the first romances I ever read with a plus-size heroine was Romancing Mr. Bridgerton by Julia Quinn, and I named my character after hers.

As I was finishing this book, season three of Bridgerton just aired the first four episodes on Netflix. Nichola Coughlan is such a gorgeous Penelope. I'm so glad that Shondaland didn't make her lose weight for this season. I was nervous about that.

Watching Colin 'coach' Penelope to help her find a

husband has been very fun. You know, I am a fan of the dating coach trope. Also the sex coach trope.

Maybe Everett, the love guru should…

Ahem.

Just in case you were wondering, the wolf-shifters-who-play-college-football romance series that Willa recommends to the other girls is real. It's called *Big Wolf on Campus* by Aidy Award and Piper Fox (which is also me, co-writing writing paranormal romance.)

And when Willa asks Hayes if he's been reading *Fate of the Wolf Guard*, that one is real too! I figured if my girl Willa was going to be a book girlie, I might as well give her some of my favorite books to read. ;)

If you like paranormal romance with shifters who fall for curvy girls, have I got a whole binge read for you.

Finally, you should know that a portion of the proceeds of this book will go to Cat Care Society who are a private cat shelter founded in 1981 to improve the quality of life for cats in need. Their unique approach views all cats as worthy, regardless of their age or abilities in my home town.

Once upon a time, my cat Uno got bitten by another animal, and I cried and cried, because I was poor at the time, and didn't think I would be able to afford the vet bills. But the Cat Care Society took care of the love of my life and I want to thank them.

Together, we're gonna save kitties just like how Willa and Cool Beans helps them find forever homes!

Extra Hugs from me to you,

—Amy

ACKNOWLEDGMENTS

This book was kind of hard to write and it took my longer than I expected. Plus I got a late start because I was really ill earlier in the year. I had to take a deep retreat into the writing cave and that usually means I ignore everything else in the world. So I want to thank and acknowledge my family for understanding when I can't come out and play. And for when they make me anyway.

I so appreciate the author talks and days away from the computer at rando coffee shops around the Denver metro area with M. Guida, Holly Roberds, Parker Finch, and Nikki Hall. Y'all are my tribe.

Special thanks to Stephanie Harrell for giving this manuscript and early read and telling me everything was going to work out fine even when I wasn't sure. I really appreciate the brainstorming help and advice from a fellow curvy girl author.

Extra hugs to my curvy girl author friends, Molly O'Hare, Kelsie Stelting Hoss, Mary Warren, and Kayla Grosse. We're changing the world one fat-bottomed woman at a time, and I'm so grateful you're here fighting the good fight with me. I will ALWAYS continue to rec your books when anyone asks for romance with plus-size heroines, because I KNOW readers can trust their hearts with your positive fat rep!

When I was all done with this book, I admitted to Becca Syme that I was worried people wouldn't understand my heroine, and wouldn't like the book because of her. But that also, the parts I was most afraid they wouldn't like were the parts that were most authentically me. Becca told me to go all in and write my hero defending and standing up to the world for Willa, and for me.

I cry and Becca always understands. My books, my career, and my life are better because of her and her insights.

I'm so grateful you're there for me and all the other authors who need help to be our most authentic selves. Extra hugs for you.

I am ever grateful to my editor Chrisandra who somehow still loves me and my stories, even though I still suck at commas and deadlines.

Thank you to Ellie at Love Notes PR for for quite literally helping me make my dreams come true. I can't wait to continue to SLAY with you for a long time to come.

Huge thanks to Leni Kaufmann for giving us another amazing cover. She makes us all feel beautiful with the way she draws plus size women (and the men who are soooo into them!) Thank you for helping me change the world one book cover at a time.

So many hugs to my friends and PAs Michelle Ziegler and Sean Gilmartin. My author life would be such a tangled mess with out. I appreciate you more than you know.

And to my Patreon Book Dragons - you are the reason

I write books. I hope I continue to entertain you and make you proud. Your continual support means so incredibly much to me. You make me smile and happy cry when I read your comments on the chapters.

For my Swoonies, Hayes and Willa's box with some fun swag is coming your way!

- Allie H.
- Amy H.
- Anna R.
- Becky B.
- Belinda M.
- Cara-Lee D.
- Dana R.
- Dominique R.
- Irehne A.
- Janna G.
- Johnna A.
- Judy R.
- Katarzyna R.
- Kathryn B.
- Kaylee B.
- Maria B.
- McKaylee E.
- Montse A.
- Nicole C.
- Paige P.
- Rebecca C.
- Sami M.
- Sophie H.
- Stacey M.

- Tiffany L.

For my VIP Fans, signed books are coming your way!

- Allison M.
- Amanda T.
- Amie N.
- Angelique A.
- Angie K
- Ashley B.
- Barb T.
- Hana K.
- Ilona T.
- Kerrie M.
- Kristin A.
- Lisa W.
- Melissa E.
- Rachael C.
- RaeAnna F.
- Sara W.
- Tracy L.

For my Biggest Fans Ever, book boxes with so much hilarious kitty and football stuff and signed book are on their way. Thank you so much for believing in me.

- Alida H.
- Ashley P.
- Cherie S.
- Corinne A.
- Danielle T.

- Daphine G.
- Elisha B.
- Kari S.
- Katherine M.
- Mari G.
- Marilyn C.
- Melissa L.
- Orma M.
- Sandra B.
- Shannon B.
- Stephanie H.
- Stephanie F.

ALSO BY AMY AWARD

The C*ck Down The Block

The Wiener Across the Way

ABOUT THE AUTHOR

Amy Award is a curvy girl who has a thing for football players, fuzzy-butt pets, and spicy romance novels. She believes that all bodies are beautiful and deserve their own love stories with Happy Ever Afters. Find her at AuthorAmyAward.com

Amy also writes curvy girl paranormal romances with dragons, wolves, demons, and vampires, as Aidy Award. If that's your jam, check those books out at AidyAward.com

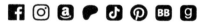

Printed in Great Britain
by Amazon

46217969R00209